THE BUTTERFLY FIELD

The public-spirited ladies of Swanbridge village, led by Lady Janey Utox-Smythe, have been busy fund-raising to buy the butterfly field. As far as Janey is concerned, the village's community centre is as good as built, until she hears the news that the nouveau-riche Carpenters have been granted permission to build houses there. Then the field's owners have second thoughts about selling and finally, the redoubtable Janey is hit by a family scandal just when she needs her wits about her. As rumour and counter-rumour spread through the village, everyone wonders whether Swanbridge will ever be the same again ....

THE BUTTERFLY FIELD

The Butterfly Field

by

Rose Boucheron

Magna Large Print Books
Long Preston, North Yorkshire,
England.

British Library Cataloguing in Publication Data.

Boucheron, Rose
   The butterfly field.

   A catalogue record for this book is
   available from the British Library

   ISBN 0-7505-1359-4

First published in Great Britain by Judy Piatkus (Publishers) Ltd., 1998

Published in Large Print 1999 by arrangement with Piatkus Books Ltd.

Magna Large Print is an imprint of
Library Magna Books Ltd.
Printed and bound in Great Britain by
T.J. International Ltd., Cornwall, PL28 8RW.

Chapter One

Swansbridge was a pretty Surrey village, sitting as it did in green-belt country and within commuter distance from London. As the name implied, it certainly had a little bridge over the fast-disappearing river, and rumour had it that there used to be swans on the pond in the village, but nowadays there were only ducks, and how long it would remain in green-belt country was in question as the urban sprawl of London gradually eroded the countryside.

It was highly desirable as a residential area because of its proximity to London. This kept house prices high, together with the fact that the residents liked a certain air of exclusivity. Although it had a row of small shops and cottages which served the local residents and the elderly, young wives went to the nearest town or took the train from Cobbets Green to London.

There had been a very small development of new houses after the war, nice desirable residences, neo-Georgian or Tudor which had been very fashionable then, and some of the older houses, Victorian or Edwardian, already falling into decay, had been taken over by trendy young couples who had in the beginning Laura Ashleyed them, or nowadays called in interior designers. It rather depended on the state of their finances. Otherwise, dotted around the countryside were several charming cottages which had been extended and enlarged, and now boasted a pool or very swish cars in the drive, one of which would of necessity be a Land or a Range Rover, for young wives seemed to like these as a means of transport and drove them around the country lanes with children and dogs on board as if they were dodgem cars. Also, if it was a very narrow lane and the other motorist was in a Mini, they behaved with a certain respect.

It was a very friendly area and wives got together in each other's houses to discuss village affairs and schools. What they lacked above all was a focal point for meetings, and it was popularly believed that acquiring the Butterfly Field was the best way to answer the problem.

The words 'community centre' were rarely used, although that was exactly what it was to be. As it was, the project was always referred to at committee meetings rather grandly as 'Swansbridge Hall'.

The drawing room at Clyde Lodge was large and impressive, which was why Janey so often used it for committee meetings.

Janey—otherwise Lady Jane Utox-Smythe—was holding forth at this moment on the Butterfly Field, so called because of its plenitude of wild flowers which attracted butterflies in their thousands in summer.

Janey was under the impression that she had the full attention of her committee, which was not strictly true, since ladies' thoughts are inclined to wander off at a tangent unless the talk is riveting—which this was not. Interesting, important in its way, but hardly riveting.

The committee had been set up for the sole purpose of fundraising for the proposed new hall and leisure centre which hopefully would be built on the Butterfly Field after the residents of Swansbridge had purchased it. As yet, it was still owned by a farmer, whose family had held it for generations, but since he had no children to inherit and his wife had recently died, the matter had come to a head.

'So,' Janey declared in her loud, clear voice, 'things are looking quite exciting, and hopefully we shall be in a position before long to find the money to buy the field.' And she beamed as she looked around her, expecting to see delight on their faces.

They had heard all this, had gone over it a hundred times, and knew that if

Janey could call a committee meeting on some pretext or another, she would do so.

She had a magnificent presence, had Jane, wife of Sir John, which was why she was in so much demand for social and charity work. She gave unstintingly of her time for every cause you could name, and it was recognised that anything she had anything to do with was a success.

She was tall, a handsome woman, largely built and closely corseted, and she dressed beautifully. Her skin was smooth as silk as is so often the case in ladies who are overweight, and her hands were small and pretty, and her ankles finely turned. Only the rest of her was large. Sally Sheffield was constantly reminded of Joyce Grenfell's 'Stately as a Galleon', and idly wondered where Janey bought her shoes, which were small and dainty with high heels. They looked like a size four. Valerie Richards meanwhile wondered if Janey still—um—and what it was like to be made love to by a Sir, but since she was always wondering what it would be like to be made love to by someone else, this was nothing unusual.

Only Becky Newman was concentrating on every word, and that was because whatever she did, she gave it her whole-hearted attention.

Janey shuffled her papers and looked around.

'Anything else?' she asked pleasantly.

Sally got to her feet.

'I wonder, Janey, if you would remind everyone about the hat sale at my house next Friday? Christmas Cottage,' she added, just in case no one knew.

Janey beamed. 'My dear, of course, how could we forget it? It will be a wonderful day and I am sure we shall make a lot of money.' She looked around her indulgently. 'Now, girls, turn out your best bonnets, be brave and give them to Sally. It's all for a good cause.'

'Thank you.' And Sally sat down again.

'What time?' Valerie asked.

'Ten-thirty—I expect it will go on until lunchtime,' Sally explained, 'and I shall want all the help I can get to set it up, although I think Jenny and Pam and Greta are coming over. Tell you what,' she said, talking to Valerie, 'I've had one good idea. A huge flowerpot with long sticks, all wrapped in pretty paper, and a hat on each stick—'

'Good', Janey said, interrupting. 'By the way, Sally, I meant to ask you. I believe that The Mount has been sold. Have you heard?'

A Georgian villa, The Mount was quite the grandest house in the village, and could be seen at the end of a long drive entered by massive iron gates. It had been empty for some time.

'Yes, apparently the new owners will move in in the next few days—or so the milkman told me,' Sally said, with an embarrassed smile.

The Mount backed on to the Butterfly Field. 'Well,' Janey smiled reassuringly, 'I don't suppose we shall have much of a problem there. After all, you can't see the field from The Mount's garden, and the entrance to the field is on the other side of the lane ...'

She stood up.

Sally was itching to go. She had to pick up William from the station. He had been up to town for a job interview.

'Well, I think that's all,' Janey said. 'Thank you for coming, ladies. I shall see you tomorrow at the children's union, Sally.'

'Yes,' she said, picking up her cup and saucer.

'Oh, don't bother with that—Mrs Nelson will do it later.'

I bet she will, thought Sally. She couldn't imagine Janey soiling her pretty hands.

'Cheerio then, girls, must fly.'

Left on her own, Janey sat for a few moments collecting herself. Really, it was all going very well. Her dream of a centre for the village of Swansbridge was on the verge of coming true. They had achieved quite a lot in the last five years, money made had been invested wisely and was growing thanks to John's advice, and if they kept it up, at this rate it should soon be possible to buy the field and start building the centre. They might get someone important to open it (a royal?), but nothing too elaborate at first. Just a simple hall, where so many things could take place, and they would add to it over the years. She had an understanding with the council that they wouldn't be too difficult over giving planning permission if the committee managed to buy the field.

Singing to herself quietly—Janey had a nice voice, soft and musical—she collected her papers and put them neatly in a folder, walking along as light as a feather to the study which was her own private domain, and putting the folder in the filing cabinet. People would have been amazed to see the contents of those drawers. Every conceivable charity, in all of which Janey had been involved at some time or other, had its own folder. It gave her enormous pleasure to do this, aside from her work as a magistrate and councillor.

People wondered how she found the time, but Janey knew it was possible to do anything if you had a mind. It came naturally to people like her. She glanced at her watch. John would not be home until late, he often worked long hours in the city where he sat on several boards, and since he had retired, seemed to be busier than ever. All that consultancy work, but he *would* do it.

She locked her filing cabinet—she was nothing if not meticulously careful—and went into the bedroom to change. At the back of her mind all day had been thoughts of Graham, her son, whom she had to admit was a permanent worry to her. Not that she allowed that to deter her from her own life, but the thought of him was there just the same. She was hoping this latest marriage was going to work, unlike the others.

Graham and his wife Julie were calling in to see her this evening. She wished John could be here. And why were they coming, if not to dinner? Also, and here she frowned, it meant that she herself would have to clear away the tea things from the drawing room. What a nuisance! She went to the kitchen and found two trays and stacked the tea things, leaving them on the kitchen table for Mrs Nelson in the morning.

Back in the bedroom, she slipped off her shoes and put shoe trees in them, standing them on the rack inside the vast wardrobe.

She changed into more comfortable shoes, flat soft leather ones, took off her suit and, shaking it, hung it in the next wardrobe. Then she slipped into a housecoat and lay on the chaise-longue looking out over the garden and the fields which disappeared into the distance. Oh, wouldn't it be wonderful when the Butterfly Field was built on, with their own hall and tennis court? Of course, she wouldn't see it from here, but it would be splendid nevertheless. Her thoughts ranged far and wide, taking in the past as well as the promise of the future.

They had come down from London, she and John, when Graham was four years old and Minnie a baby, to give them fresh air and a country background. They bought a fairly new house, they were only the second owners, sitting in a large garden. The views from the back were impressive. They had bought The Lodge quite cheaply, for it was possible do that in those days, and had set about to making it as attractive as possible. It was an airy house, and the rooms were large, and one of the first things Janey had done was to enlarge the drawing room even further, extending it by another twelve feet. Home making was not her particular forte, but one could always find someone to advise and help out, and John was a keen gardener.

Really, she had spent her life in the service of others; it was difficult to see how she could have made such a mistake with Graham ... He had had the best of educations: had gone to boarding school at eight, to public school at thirteen. He had not gone to university, but instead chose to go into property dealing with some help from his father, and at first had been moderately successful. The trouble had surely started with Alice. Such a little hussy she had been—and then to blame it all on Graham. Wicked little hussy!

Of course, Janey thought proudly, he was a handsome boy. Girls everywhere fell over themselves to catch him. He was able to pick and choose, so that there was no one more shocked than she and John when he said he wanted to marry Alice. Still, the girl was pregnant, and after all, one had one's head to hold up in the village. Alice was a local girl ...

The little boy was a dear—not that Janey ever saw him, for the young couple lived in London, and when he was a year old Alice fled, taking the boy with her. There followed a divorce and second marriage to Fiona. Janey had quite liked Fiona, a London girl, well-connected and at least with more brains than Alice ever had. Graham, married her immediately after the divorce, and they set up home in

France—doing what, Janey never quite knew. They had a daughter, Florence. Janey had only seen her once, and then—another divorce.

She sighed. Then Julie ... Now, Julie was a brainbox, highly intelligent—and Janey had hoped with all her heart that it would work this time. Julie held down her own comfortable job, and there was no way Graham, was going to run rings round her like he had the others. She did ask herself why someone as intelligent as Julie had married him, but of course when sex rears its ugly head ... She smiled despite herself. Oh, he was a gorgeous hunk of young manhood. But even so ...

Graham had come by on Sunday to see her on his way home from an important business deal—or so he said. John was out playing golf. Janey didn't think too deeply as to why her son was on his way home on a Sunday morning.

'Will you be in on Friday evening?' he had asked.

'Friday? Yes, I think so, dear, although I don't suppose your father will be here—he usually works late on a Friday.'

'Well, then.' And Graham had smiled that smile that caused many a young girl's heart to flutter wildly. 'We'll call in on Friday. Don't worry about a meal, we'll have eaten.'

Now Janey got up and went downstairs. Things were bad enough with Minnie, her daughter, trawling round Katmandu or some such unlikely place, but she wouldn't think about that now. Come to think of it, she wasn't even quite sure where it was ... was it Thailand or India? And she must remember to cheek the date of the visit to the infants' primary school in Cobbets Green ...

Mrs Nelson had left Janey's supper in the fridge. A place was laid in the dining room, with wine glass ready—Janey liked a glass of red wine with her meal—and the day's paper laid at the side. Oh, she was a treasure, Mrs Nelson. What would Janey do without her?

She had changed into a dress by the time Graham and Julie arrived, her daughter-in-law looking as delectable as ever in her thigh-length skirt and matching jacket. She wore black opaque tights and fashionable clompy heels, and her legs still managed to look sensational. She wore almost no make-up but her lashes were heavily mascaraed. In fact, try as she might, Janey could never fathom whether they were Julie's own or false. Her straight blonde hair hung over her eyes, shrouding her expression. Behind her stood Graham, tall and handsome as ever but, Janey thought, looking a bit sheepish.

'Come on in—it's lovely to see you.' Janey and Julie kissed, a peck on either cheek, and she led the way into the drawing room.

'Well, this is a pleasant surprise,' she said. 'How nice. What will you have? A drink? Coffee?'

'Coffee, please. I'll make it, if you like?' Julie said.

'I already had it prepared, I knew you'd want some.' And the two women disappeared into the kitchen and returned with a tray of coffee and chocolate mints.

'Sugar ... oh, no, of course you don't.'

'Where's Dad?' Graham asked, unpeeling the silver wrapper from a mint.

'Some meeting or other. He often stays in town on Friday after a busy day—I think he goes for a drink with the boys,' she said, with what for Janey might be classed as a wink.

'Well, it is nice to see you,' she said again, sitting back, but she couldn't help noticing they were both a bit edgy. 'How's work going, Julie?'

'Very well,' she said, sipping her coffee. 'And how are you? Busy with one of your projects, I suppose. I know you're always involved with so many different things. I expect you'd have liked an early night?'

'No, not at all, dear,' Janey smiled at her. She had a sudden feeling of foreboding. They were going to tell her something bad, she felt it in her bones.

Graham, put down his cup with a clatter.

'Mum, I don't know how to tell you this but there's no point in beating around the bush—'

Janey's heart sank. 'What is it?'

'The truth is, Julie and I are going to split up. I mean, we thought you should be the first to know rather than hearing it from someone else.'

It was the last thing she'd expected.

'Graham! You can't be serious?'

'But I am, Mother. It's by mutual consent. We just don't get on, do we, Julie?'

He looked at his wife quite pleasantly.

'No,' she said shortly. 'We don't. We'll still be friends, but we can't stay married.'

Inside Janey felt like weeping, which was unlike her. Three wives! How could he? How would she explain that—everyone would talk. Oh, how could he!

'You've only been married a year.'

'Yes, but it's long enough to know it's not going to work,' Julie said shortly. 'I'm sorry,' she said, looking down sheepishly. She was genuinely fond of her mother-in-law.

20

Janey breathed heavily. 'I don't know what to say. Here was I, hoping you were happy together, and settling down, and perhaps a baby on the way ...'

'Oh, no!' Julie sounded quite horrified at the idea.

'Oh, well,' said Janey, genuinely at a loss for words for once.

'We've talked it over,' Graham said reasonably, 'and there's nothing else we can do. As you say, it's not as if we had kids.'

'God, no!' Julie repeated with a little shudder.

'So, a nice clean amicable break.' He looked quite pleased with himself, Janey thought. What was wrong with them? With him? He was still under thirty.

'You don't think—perhaps some counselling, dear? They are very good, some of these people. I can recommend—'

'Oh, no!' they said in unison.

The decision was obviously irrevocable.

'You'll explain to Dad?' Graham said.

Janey nodded. Trust him to let her do the dirty work! Not that she was afraid of John's reaction, but still.

'We wanted to tell you together,' Graham said. 'So you'd know we hadn't fallen out or anything.'

'Fallen out!' Janey exploded. 'I don't know how you can sit there and look at each other so agreeably, know that ...?'

'We like to think we're being adult about it,' Graham said. 'No point in making a fuss, eh, Julie?'

'Not at all,' she said, looking relieved. 'I am sorry, really, Janey. But as Graham said, there's no point in going on with it.'

'No, quite,' Janey said weakly. 'Well ... more coffee?'

After she had closed the door on them, she felt like weeping, with exasperation mostly, but knew she wouldn't. There was nothing to be gained from giving in. Best be resolute and face the facts. Head held high, she walked down the hall, and back into the kitchen.

'Well, that's that,' Graham said, hoisting the seat belt over his shoulder and starting up the car.

'You are a swine,' Julie said amicably.

'Me? It was your decision, not mine.'

'How could I do otherwise? If you think I'm going to stay married to you while you chase every woman in London—'

'Me? Chase women?' He laughed. 'That's a good one!'

She reluctantly agreed. It was quite true that women couldn't leave him alone. She gave him a sidelong glance. Funny how she had never noticed that weakness in his face before. Like the others she had been overwhelmed by his charm—and she'd thought she was intelligent and knew all the answers!

Well, she had grown an extra skin while being married to Graham. She had learned the lesson of a lifetime.

'You know,' she said slowly, 'you can blame your mother for a lot of it.'

'Mum? What do you mean?'

'Well, she bloody spoilt you—gave you everything. You never had to want for anything. It was all too easy, she thought you were the golden boy.'

He grinned. 'Well, I am.'

'You're a rotter, Graham, and one of these days you'll get your comeuppance—I hope! She should have given you a good hiding every now and again,' said his wife grimly, and he laughed out loud.

'I should have listened to Mummy,' Julie went on. 'She had you summed up from the word go.'

He smiled. 'Yes, I always thought she fancied me.'

'Oh, shut up.' And she sank into her corner, biting her lip. 'Will you drop me off first?'

'Sure,' he said pleasantly.

He let her off at the door to her flat, and she unlocked it. No problem there. She had bought this flat in the first place.

After the divorce she would be back to square one, a sadder and wiser woman. No, not sadder, she had had a lucky escape. Still, she did feel a bit sorry for Janey—but basically she was to blame. All that charity work and never much time for her own children.

Funny, really, Julie had never even met Graham's sister Minnie.

She yawned. Time for bed.

She switched on the light in the kitchen and saw her pretty tabby cat get out of his basket and stretch all four legs before coming over to her and rubbing himself round her ankles.

She smoothed his fur, then picked him up and hugged him, unaccountably bursting into tears as she did so.

She hated failure of any sort. Blast that man!

By the time Julie had reached home, Janey had filed the news of the break-up of her son's marriage into the part of her meticulous brain that served as a personal filing cabinet, and prepared herself for bed.

Brushing her teeth in the bathroom, her thoughts centred on the Butterfly Field. It was becoming rather urgent. Surely it was time to contact that farmer about the field? He lived some miles away apparently, a member of an old local family. She would have to get her solicitor on to it. No sense in wasting any more time.

Without waiting for John, she got ready for bed and was soon peacefully asleep.

Chapter Two

In between preparing the house for the hat sale, Sally Sheffield took time off to hurry to the side window where she could see clearly the removal vans in front of The Mount. Although it could be said she lived next door, The Mount was so far away, surrounded as it was by sloping lawns, which led down to Christmas Cottage, that it was difficult to see what was going on. Enormous vans, pantechnicons more like, two of them, stood on the wide drive, while hordes of busy figures could be seen taking loads in and out. Curiosity got the better of her, and she went upstairs to the bedroom under the eaves and knelt down. No one could see her from here and, yes, all right, she was being nosy, but she could see much better. One of the vans had TIR on its side—were they from somewhere abroad? Bored with the fact that she could not really see anything, she rose to her feet, brushed down her trousers and went downstairs.

Not long now, another couple of days, and she was almost ready. The other helpers had been so good with their assistance, and the hats, dozens of them, more than she had anticipated, had been handed in and now sat in the spare room, on the bed, on chairs—some of them really nice. Of course there were some oddities, but if they didn't get sold, they would be given to the next jumble sale.

What she was most pleased with was the new cloakroom. It was quite the prettiest room in the house. Large and spacious, for it had previously been a downstairs bathroom, it had a low ceiling with beams and its original bowl, white festooned with blue flowers. She had bought blue and white Dutch tiles to make a surround, taken out the bath and installed a Victorian dressing table, completing the decor to match. Sally was proud of this room, keen to show it to visitors, and there being a large mirror over the dressing table, she planned that prospective purchasers of hats would come in here and try them on, though the main presentation would be in the drawing room. She thought she might have a standing mirror in there as well. Perhaps bring the cheval mirror down from their bedroom if Tom would give her a hand.

He would carry in the large flower pots for her on the morning for they were heavy, having been filled with earth to take the long sticks bound round with fancy paper. There were a dozen sticks in each pot, tied with pink and blue paper bows, and apart from that, hats would be hung on hat stands. It would depend how many more she received.

Hearing the sound of an engine, she went again to the side window and was in time to see one large van driving away from next door as she went into the kitchen to make herself a cup of coffee.

She sat drinking this and thinking. Moving day! What a drama it always was. Still, they wouldn't be hard up for space as she and Tom had been when they moved into Christmas Cottage. Before it had been extended it had been really tiny. Now boasting four bedrooms, a sitting room, dining room and conservatory, it had become a delightful home, but she had really wanted it for the garden which was a joy. A real cottage garden, full of pinks and roses and lupins and box trees, so well looked after by the previous owner, a Mr Percival, who had lived on well into his nineties. She hoped he would have approved of the way she looked after it.

She loved her home and felt no envy of the house next door, which was palatial even by her standards—Sally had been born with a silver spoon in her mouth.

The only daughter of wealthy parents, she had been brought up to have everything she wanted until she was eleven years old. Then, losses on the Stock Exchange and unwise investments had brought disaster and sorrow to both her parents. Her father, an inveterate gambler—or likeable rogue as the more charitable said—had not only gambled away his own money, but the little her mother had also, which meant that for the first time in her life, Sally's world was turned upside down.

The amazing thing, as everyone said afterwards, was that she remained resilient throughout this traumatic time, even being forced to leave her boarding school for young ladies and being sent to a state school. They moved to a small house in Malvern where her mother eked out a living by sewing and mending, earning wherever she could. Sally's father fled abroad, unable to face the consequences of his actions, and later died, a victim of circumstances. It was generally agreed that Sally took after her mother, who was nothing if not a worker and kindness itself. There was nothing she would not do for anyone and Sally was like her.

When Tom came along, sensible, kind Tom, Sally knew without a shadow of a doubt that this was the husband she wanted. Reliable, a little dull perhaps in others' estimation, but after the flamboyance of her father she wanted some kind of stability. So they had married, and Tom, a moderately successful architect, had bought a small house, thinking to stay there for some years. But out walking one day they had come across Christmas Cottage and fallen in love with it, vowing that if ever it came on to the market they would try to buy it. It came much sooner than they had expected, when their first-born, Tessa, was eighteen months old, but they knew they would stretch themselves to the utmost to buy it. This they had done, and set about furnishing it, somewhat meagrely at first. Now, after more than twenty years, it was at last looking as they had pictured it. Mellow, charming, and a joy to them both, as well as to Tessa and their son William, now eighteen.

Sally had been delighted to find herself pregnant again after three years; she had so looked forward to another baby, and was overjoyed when she gave birth to a son.

Her mother, Emily, had married again, a vicar who had lost his first wife in the second year of their marriage. He was very mission-oriented, and promptly whisked Emily off to darkest Africa and India, where it seemed that they were as

29

happy as the days were long.

Only this morning, Sally had received a letter from her. Ernest, her stepfather, had died the previous year, and her mother hoped that they would come and see her in the pretty Somerset town where she had retired. She had been allowed to stay on in the delightful Abbey Close, where they had been lucky enough to secure the lease of a sort of grace-and-favour residence, mainly due to Ernest's hard work and family connections.

What extremes her mother had known, Sally thought. Married first to a wealthy man, having everything she wanted, and then to a vicar as poor as a church mouse, but there was no doubt as to whom had made her the happiest.

She read the letter again while she was having a spot of lunch. She looked forward to seeing her mother again. Emily had lived for so long abroad, and when they came back to England they had immersed themselves in the life of a cathedral city quite happily until Ernest's death the previous year, but now Sally found herself wondering often about her mother as she grew older. The distance between them was quite considerable, much to her regret, for she dearly loved and admired Emily.

Glancing up, she saw that the second pantechnicon was moving slowly down the

30

drive, and there were several large boxes out on the forecourt. Well, give it a few days and she would be calling on them, and doing her duty as a good neighbour. It was quite exciting to have new people next door. The previous family had kept very much to themselves and saw hardly anyone, and after them the house had been empty for over a year.

Hearing a car pull up outside, she got up to see who it was. It stopped outside the front door. Perhaps someone with more hats.

And then she recognised Jessica Handley —Jessica Handley whom she hadn't seen in ages—and what was more, she was carrying a hat box!

Sally had opened the front door before Jessica had time to ring the bell.

'Jessica! How lovely to see you!'

They embraced, and Sally led her into the hall.

'Come and sit down and I'll make us some tea. What are you doing in this part of the world?'

Jessica sat down and peeled off her gloves. She hadn't changed, Sally thought. Wearing a cloak of voluminous proportions —not just any old cloak, but a magnificent flowing cloak—which she removed to reveal an exquisitely cut mannish-looking suit. Her black hair was pulled back off her face, which was small with regular features, and she wore outrageously large glasses, pebble-lensed, for Sally knew her eyesight was really poor.

She was at once the most striking and most remarkable friend Sally had ever had. She had met her at one of Tom's architectural dinners and they had taken to each other at once, oddly enough, even though Jessica was an exalted blue stocking and Sally a hare-brained idiot—or so she styled herself. Not only had Jessica a commanding presence, but she was a brilliant conversationalist and an excellent wit, unusual in a woman. A scholar of no mean achievement, she had started out as the headmistress of a large modern comprehensive, and during the time that she was there, achieved miraculous results with apparently hopeless boys and girls. It was not to be wondered at that she should then be asked to join a most exclusive but excellent girls' school where she exceeded even the governing body's expectations. Recently, at the end of five years, she herself was made a governor of the school and Sally sometimes wondered how she had ever acquired such a friend, for she told herself they had nothing in common except a strong liking and respect for each other. Attraction of opposites, it was clear.

'Someone told me you were having a hat sale,' Jessica said, touching her very small nose with a tiny handkerchief. 'Something to do with a community centre?'

'Yes, who told you?'

'Can't remember, dear, but I've brought along the hat. You remember—I wore it to the pomp and ceremony when I was installed as governor?'

She began to remove the lid of the hat box. 'I like to think I rose to the occasion. I spent all day—all *day*, my dear—in Harrods before selecting this, and of course I cannot wear it again so I thought you might like it.'

From reams of tissue paper Jessica extracted the hat, and Sally stifled a gasp.

It was magnificent. It was also surely a hat that only Jessica could have worn.

'What do you think?' she said, elbow on the table, balancing it to display the splendid creation.

There was no easy answer. 'Don't laugh, girl,' Jessica cried. 'What do you think? Admit, who on earth but me would wear it?'

'Jessica! It is fabulous! Wonderful!'

It was made of finest Italian silk velvet, a Renaissance-looking affair, rich cerise in colour—not quite crimson, not quite puce—and was more of a festoon than a hat. It hugged the head, then fell in folds

33

to the shoulders. Perhaps Edith Sitwell ... Sally's thoughts strayed. No, only Jessica could wear such a hat.

'It was a wonderful success on the day. Everyone came up and admired it.'

'I am sure they did,' Sally murmured, trying it on and whisking it off again, knowing she looked ridiculous.

'Of course,' Jessica said doubtfully, 'you could cut it up and make a little cushion or a lampshade.'

Obviously Jessica didn't care what was done with it, having decided to part with it.

'Oh, no,' Sally cried, shocked. 'It's too—wonderful. Thank you, Jessica, it's lovely. It will be the *pièce de résistance* of my hat sale.'

Jessica glowed. 'I'm so glad.'

'Tea?' Sally asked.

'Coffee, if you have it,' Jessica answered. 'And how is everyone? What are you doing with yourself—short of selling hats?'

'Oh, lots of things.'

'And you appear to have new people next door, or are they moving out?'

'Moving in,' Sally said, 'How is Freddie? And—Clytie?' as an afterthought.

It was difficult to get used to the *ménage à trois* that existed in the beautifully appointed small Georgian home that was Jessica's.

Jessica, who adored her husband—'little Freddie', as Tom called him—had long ago taken Clytemnestra into her home—Clytie, who had been assistant headmistress at her comprehensive school. No one queried this, knowing Jessica, nor enquired further into the domestic arrangements. That the three of them got on well together was patently obvious whenever you met them.

'I have just purchased a harpsichord,' Jessica announced accepting the coffee from Sally. 'Black, thank you. My latest fad is Turkish coffee, thick and black—you must try it.'

'I will,' Sally said, anxious to please.

'And you must come and hear us play: Freddie on the violin, Clytie on the oboe and myself on the harpsichord.'

'Wonderful,' Sally said. After all, it was impressive.

'Now tell me what this is for—this hat sale? What an extraordinary idea! Is it a Red Cross do?'

'No, it's in aid of funds for the Butterfly Field, the piece of land backing on to The Mount. You remember when we first came here, there was some talk of a community centre?'

'Ah, yes, vaguely.'

'Well, we hope to purchase it and build a hall there.'

'Excellent,' said Jessica who was all for

35

the good of the community at large. 'Well done. Nice to think you are getting your teeth into community work.'

'Well, we try,' Sally murmured.

'And how are Tessa and young William?' Jessica was Tessa's godmother.

'Tessa's doing well at MacBane's.'

'I am glad. I thought of contacting her when looking for the harpsichord—you cannot imagine the trouble I had trying to find the genuine article—but then, she is mainly into textiles and pictures, that sort of thing, isn't she?'

Sally nodded.

'Anyway, I found it eventually, after a long search, I did so want the authentic thing. You must come and hear us play.'

'Love to,' Sally said again.

'And William?' Jessica asked.

'Well, you know William—happy as a sandboy, but academically ...'

'You're not taking enough trouble with him,' Jessica reproved her. 'You should have sent him to a state school as I advised you. Paying out exorbitant fees for a third-class education—'

'Oh, surely not?' Sally cried. 'It's a good school.'

'Pure snobbery,' her friend said. 'You would have found he would have done so much better at a—'

'Well,' Sally interrupted,' Tom wanted

him to go to this school—he went there himself.' Knowing that would finish the argument.

'I know,' Jessica said, implying that Tom was no advertisement for any sort of education.

'Anyhow, what are you doing with yourself—I mean apart from playing the harpsichord?' Sally changed the subject.

'Off to Poland for a visit, I'm looking forward to that—Clytie is coming with me—and then, of course, it's one long round of conferences and so on.'

By the time the door had closed on her, Sally felt quite exhausted. Going back into the kitchen, she picked up the hat once more and bit her lip at the sight of the brilliant cerise confection. She wanted to laugh, except that it looked so—impressive. Well, it had been, and how the ladies helping would laugh! It would be great fun. She would have it as the centrepiece. It would be interesting to see who would buy it.

By the time Tom and Tessa arrived home, the removal vans and all signs of moving house and new occupants at The Mount had gone, but there were lights on all over.

'Nice to see the house lit up again. It always looked sad without occupants,' Tom said.

'My God!' Tessa cried, before she had even got her coat off. 'What's that?' She stared at it, mouth open.

'It's a hat, generously donated by Jessica to the hat sale,' her mother said.

'Jessica? Has she been? Oh, I missed her! It's beautiful,' Tessa said in awe. 'Not as a hat but as a concoction—oh, I must try it on!'

She ran into the cloakroom, but returned with the hat in her hand.

'Yes, well, not me,' she decided, putting it back in its tissue. 'Are the new people in? Have you seen them?' The vans had been there when she left that morning.

'No, but they're safely in and the front door closed,' Sally said. Strange how homely it felt to have someone living there again.

When William appeared, Tessa looked up, concern on her face. She was very fond of her younger brother.

'How did you get on?' she asked.

'They're going to let me know.' He shrugged but seemed in no way concerned, and gave a wonderful smile. He had the nicest nature, one to be envied, but if they were hoping for any academic achievement from young William, there had certainly been no sign of it up to now. Any inherited brains seemed to have passed him by, going straight to Tessa.

'Never mind, you never know,' she said. 'You might be surprised.'

He doesn't really seem to be bothered, she thought, with a worried frown. Just what does he want to do? He's clever with his hands, but these days life can be so difficult without a degree—or even with, she thought dryly.

'Like some tea?' Sally asked. William was always ravenously hungry.

'Please,' he said. 'I'm starving. I only had a pizza for lunch.'

'Yuk!' Tessa said. 'By the way,' she added to Sally, 'I'm going out this evening, and you'll never guess—I'm off to Spain next week.'

'Oh, Tessa, that's nice. When did you hear that.'

'This afternoon, just as I was leaving, Alistair called me in and told me. I'm going with Hugo—he's to see some paintings and I am looking at some early textiles. Some Spanish aristocrat is selling up.' She hugged herself. 'Gosh, I'm really pleased—I could do with a break.'

And a trip with Hugo, thought Sally, but said nothing. For some months now, since Hugo had joined the prestigious fine arts auctioneering firm of MacBane's, Tessa had had difficulty hiding the fact that she was smitten with him. Much to the disgust of Alistair MacBane, who had taken charge of the company when his father died, and unless Sally was mistaken, was himself very keen on her daughter. Oh, the problems of youth, she thought. Still, it was a wonderful job. Tessa had shown a natural talent for art, and after finishing a history of art degree, had secured a job with MacBane's in the field of ancient textiles and ceramics.

No wonder her eyes were shining at this chance to extend her expertise.

'Where are you going this evening?' Sally asked idly, not wishing to pry but wondering if Hugo had asked her out at last.

'I'm meeting Sarah—we're going over to see Kathie. You remember Kathie—she's expecting her first baby soon.'

'Goodness,' Sally murmured. Already. Still, at least Kathie was married, and she was twenty-one—they had all been at school together.

She fell to thinking about this Hugo, who was a new addition to the firm of MacBane's, being an expert on pictures, painting and fine arts restoration. Whenever she mentioned him, Tessa's eyes held a special gleam. At first Sally had imagined he would be middle-aged to elderly, having such a position, but it seemed he was only thirty-five. She supposed he must be able to have got so far in MacBane's. She did hope it would not turn out to be a case of unrequited love, for this was the first time she had seen Tessa impressed by anyone. Except for that boy when she was sixteen, she thought with a grin. He had been a real tearaway, but this one was something different, and judging by the way her daughter always referred to the highly eligible Alistair MacBane, she had no time for him.

'What's he like, your boss Alistair?' Sally had asked one day.

'Bossy,' Tessa answered in a word.

'Well, I suppose he should be, in a way.'

'Oh, don't you start standing up for him. He can do that quite well for himself!'

He had asked Tessa out soon after she joined the company, and she had taken much pleasure in refusing.

'Do him good,' she said. 'He thinks he's the cat's whiskers.'

'Perhaps he is?' suggested Sally.

'He's the only one who thinks so!'

Tessa got so mad about Alistair, causing her cheeks to flush, as she did about Hugo—in a different way. Oh, the problems of youth, Sally thought again, still young enough herself to remember what they were like.

'So, the hat sale is on Friday?' Tessa asked. 'I'd like to be a fly on the wall.' She grinned.

41

Sally had chosen Friday because it was the day her home help Mrs Halliday came, and she would help to serve coffee and clear up afterwards.

On the day there were hats everywhere, for some had thought it was a bring and buy sale, hats of every description. Large and expensive, once-worn wedding hats, wintry fake fur hats, flowered toques, nonsense hats, straws, oddities, atrocities ...

All eyes were immediately drawn to the centre of the drawing room where Jessica's hat sat at the top of a 'tree'. Sally having cut off a branch, stripped off its leaves and sprayed the twigs with gold paint.

She stood and watched with Valerie and Becky, wondering at the hat's drawing power.

It was fascinating to say the least. Everyone, but every woman, tried on that hat. As they tried it on, they turned laughing, puzzled or questioning faces, annoyed to find that it didn't suit them.

The remarks were well-intentioned. 'No, I don't think it's you ...' 'We—ll, no, dear.' 'I picture a classical face—not that yours isn't, my dear, but you know what I mean ...'

Ladies with round faces and long faces tried it on, young mums and middle-aged matrons. One lady, with a low forehead, freckles and sandy hair, kept it on the longest. It was as if she couldn't take it off. She was really waiting for someone to say, 'Oh, you look wonderful in it,' but no one did. They passed by the green tulle, the red rose hat, the pink straw. As each visitor came in they made a bee line for that hat. 'How gorgeous!' 'Did you ever?' Rushing off to the privacy of the cloakroom: 'I must have it!' But none of them did, it was as if no one had the courage.

When almost all the other hats had gone, still it sat in the centre of the room, and, catching Valerie's eye, Sally made a face.

Then Treena Martin walked in with her very pretty daughter, Suzie, who was sixteen. Suzie wore a long black satin skirt embroidered with lilies, a beaded jacket and black feather boa. Her dark hair was piled on top of her head and casually secured with a Spanish comb. Long strands of it fell about her face.

'Mummy!' she shrieked, running over to the hat, and plonked it on her head in one movement where it sat as though made for her. She looked like a creature from another world.

'How much is it?' asked Treena, delving into her handbag.

'Five pounds,' Sally said without batting an eyelid, and while her mother paid, the girl stuffed it into a Waitrose carrier bag. 'That it, then? Anything you'd like, Mummy?'

'No, I think that's everything,' Treena said, and they made their exit.

'Oh!' Valerie cried, laughing fit to burst. 'We must have another hat sale!'

'But where will we find another hat like that?' Sally said, and collapsing into a chair, glanced around the room, which looked as if a bomb had hit it. There were precious few hats left, though.

Chapter Three

'A hundred and forty pounds!' Valerie cried. 'That's fantastic—just for a hat sale.'

Sally looked pleased. 'Well, it was worth the effort,' she said. 'Thanks for all your help, Valerie.'

'I enjoyed it, I don't know when I've laughed so much—just to see their faces!'

'I know. Janey will be pleased.'

'I thought she might come?'

'Where would she find the time?' Sally asked, and they both laughed.

'She is incredible, though, isn't she? What she packs into a day?' Valerie said.

Becky came into the room, face flushed, armed with waste paper baskets full of old tickets and wrappings.

'Well, I think that's it. Your Mrs Halliday can carry on from here.'

'Thanks awfully, Becky. I can manage now.'

'Then I'll be off. Don't forget next Monday's meeting at my house.'

'I won't.'

'I'll come with you,' Valerie said.

Sally watched them both go down the path and get into their cars. They were such a nice couple, and Valerie so helpful when somehow you didn't expect it of her.

Most wives were wary of Valerie because she looked like the most sexy woman in Swansbridge, but really there was nothing more to it, Sally felt, than a desire to look attractive. Sally was secretly sure that if someone took Valerie up on it, she would run a mile. She wore the most outrageous clothes, and her make up was out of this world, but she adored her husband, and if he didn't mind, why should anyone else?

Valerie was as thin as a rod, and as brown as a berry. She spent every spare moment in the sun when it was out, or failing that, under a sun lamp. Her skin was lined and she looked far older than her years where she had wrinkled from the sun, but that never put her off. She had deep-set dark eyes and long, long lashes, which she encrusted thickly with mascara. Her hair was bleached and worn carelessly long, and she wore tight pants or short skirts and a cleavage down to her naval—not that it made much difference for she was built like a youth with no bosom at all to speak of.

But Valerie was Valerie, and Sally was fond of her. And she liked Becky too: sweet, quiet and docile Becky. Always ready to give a hand where she could.

Unlike Sally, Becky had not been born into a life of luxury. A product of the East End, she had been born to a hard-working tailor and his wife whose joy at the birth of her daughter was shared by the rest of the closely knit family.

At nineteen she met Lewis Newman, the junior at a local estate agents. Her Aunt Goldie, who had looked after her since she was orphaned at eleven, had died and left her house to Becky and her own daughter, Sadie, and between them they decided to sell: Sadie because she was getting married and moving away, and Becky because she wanted to move to a flat nearer town where she worked.

Lew was nothing if not anxious to help. He was fired with such a burning ambition that at times it was almost unbearable. He had almost decided to kick over the traces and move to New York where he had cousins when Becky came along, and like many other people he was bowled over by her quiet charm, her gentleness, the sheer ladylike quality of her. What he wouldn't do to have a wife like that!

Becky in turn liked him enormously, admired his enthusiasm, his desire to get on in the world, above all his confidence which rubbed off on her a little. When he passed his first examination he was transferred to a larger branch, and they married when she was twenty-one, moving to a shiny new terraced house in Ilford.

Lew looked around him in disgust.

'This place is piddle, Becky!' he said. 'I tell you, we won't be here long.'

But she loved it. 'It's our very own, and it's brand new and lovely. Just look at the kitchen.' For the kitchen did indeed have a white sink and there was also a modern bathroom.

Lew loved her more than he'd thought it possible to love anyone. Would have done anything for her. She was the light of his life.

By the time their son was born, he could already see that the grass was greener on the other side, and moved to a semi-detached house in Edgware, and by the time their second son was born, he had risen to chief negotiator in a more prestigious firm. They had moved to a detached house in Pinner. But he was far-seeing and had plans, for apart from anything else he was a brilliant estate agent, the perfect salesman—as his employers swiftly realised whenever he moved on.

So they ended up in Swansbridge, with two sons and a daughter, in a lovely detached house, and Lew was now sole proprietor of his own agency in Cobbets Green.

Oh, yes, he knew where he was going. Some day he would open a branch office which Becky would run. For now she brought up her family, running her home efficiently and helping others whenever she could. Unobtrusively, she was always there to lend a helping hand. It was she who did the clearing up after such an event as the hat sale. It was Becky who lent a hand with children left alone while mothers went to work, and started a crèche in the village. Becky who helped with the elderly, while still finding time for her own husband and family.

That evening, when they sat in the garden, it was still warm and little clusters of insects hung in the still air. The scent of roses was all about them. Becky sat still, at peace with the world. Lew stole a glance at her from time to time. He envied that wonderful still quality she had; the way she could sit quietly, not moving. He always had an urgent desire to get up and do something. But Becky was restful. She gave his life meaning.

'We had a meeting today at Janey's,' she said at last. 'About the field—the Butterfly Field.'

'Yes?' he asked. 'What happened?'

'Well, Janey said it was time we began to ask what the owner would sell it for—so we can apply for planning permission to build the centre.'

Lewis jeered. Trust women to think it was as easy as that, especially that Janey woman ... too big for her boots by far!

'He won't sell, Becky.'

She looked quite shocked. 'What do you mean—won't sell?'

'Well, my dear, that land is valuable. No one today is going to sell it cheaply.'

'I don't think we mean to buy it cheaply, we just want to buy the land at the proper price—'

'But it *is* green-belt,' he explained. 'No one can build on green-belt land.'

'Janey says you can—if you know the right way to go about it. And it is for a good cause, not like development of houses or anything.'

Lew's mind was busily ticking over

and he wondered what the possibilities might be ...

Was it true it could be for sale? He might be interested himself ... Then he saw his wife's expression.

If it was one of her pet projects then he wouldn't interfere, and he was anxious not to have any shoddy developments in his prime neck of the woods.

Janey Utox-Smythe was thinking about the same subject. This evening she really would get down to it and ask John what the procedure would be in the event of their procuring the land.

Sir John had left the City at around four o'clock and caught the early train. He was a big man in every way: tall, well-built, with a good head of hair, and carried himself well. Passengers who disembarked at Cobbets Green station were in no doubt as to who he was. Even the porter acknowledged him as Sir John passed by and made his way to the car park. Although entitled to a chauffeur, he chose to drive himself—on certain occasions.

He glanced at his reflection in the driving mirror, and was pleased with what he saw, before pulling out towards the car park exit. But instead of taking the road up the hill to Swansbridge, he turned left and smoothly made his way to a row of exclusive shops, where he drove round the back entrance and parked his car in an empty garage whose door had been left open for him. Walking up the slope, he made his way round to the front of the shops, where stood an expensive car showroom, next door to a pharmacy, then a dress shop. There was a side door to the dress shop which led upstairs to the flat above, and if anyone observed him entering such a place, he was unconcerned. He was strong and sure enough of himself to be impervious to what other people thought.

He did this weekly, but never twice on the same day running.

Now he pressed the entry phone and the door silently opened. He closed it behind him, leaving his silver-topped umbrella in the hall stand below.

Upstairs, in a cosy flat furnished with exquisite taste, Melissa Wilding stood waiting for him.

He put his arms around her and they stood still for several moments, just savouring each other's presence, the scent of her filling his nostrils as he clasped her to him, her arms around his neck. They kissed before reluctantly letting each other go.

No words were spoken until he had found his favourite chair, a soft comfortable one that enveloped his large frame, into

51

which he sank gratefully.

No need to ask what he wanted. Melissa had gone over to the drinks cabinet to pour him a glass of the finest malt whisky which he drank without water or soda.

She took it over to him and returned to pour herself a glass of wine, then sat down opposite him.

It was this quality of repose he loved most about her. She never intruded, never overwhelmed him with conversation. They were so attuned there was often no need for words.

Melissa was small and dainty, fair-haired and very pretty, now in her thirties. She had been his mistress, the only one he had ever had, since she had come to work for him as his secretary in her twenties. Three years had gone by before they faced the fact that the magnetism between them was so great that they had to be together. Melissa knew that he would not leave his wife, that it was important for him in his position to be seen to be toeing the line, and so gladly settled for what she had.

When she had told him she would like a dress shop, he had bought her the small gown shop in Cobbets Green. 'Tanya' it was called, and if the neighbours thought it odd that she had nothing but a small dog to walk and her business to run, they got used to it. She was a widow, they understood, and if they were aware that a handsome well-built man called on her from time to time, they kept quiet about it. No one wanted trouble. It was too nice an area for scandal.

Melissa was as happy as the day was long. She loved the shop, had never wanted children, and it seemed to her that she had the best of both worlds. Of course, if they could have been married it would have been wonderful, but she was no more anxious to go through the messy business of a public divorce than Sir John was, and had no trouble finding things to do with her life.

The best times were when he stayed overnight, but that didn't happen very often. Very occasionally on trips abroad she went with him, but that usually involved difficulties with the shop where she must ask someone to stand in for her. It was a very exclusive shop, the sort of place where one garment in the window, and a display of flowers, was enough to keep the wealthy clientele happy. She knew them, and their measurements, intimately—but they did not know very much about her or her private life.

'How did you get on today?' she asked, for she was always interested in financial affairs having worked as John's secretary and knowing the business world inside out. If she sometimes thought she could have been quite a success in the City, she quickly abandoned the idea, knowing that without him there would be no happiness for her.

John filled her in on news of the commercial world before coming to the topic which was occupying his mind.

'And how is Janey?' Melissa was always polite enough to ask after his wife, whom she admired but did not particularly like.

'Up to her eyes as usual,' he said. 'But we have another problem—Graham.'

'Oh.' There was no need to say more.

'He is leaving young Julie.'

Melissa looked incredulous.

'No! Not again!'

'Yes. I can't think what's the matter with the man—three wives, two children, no sense of responsibility.'

Melissa thought she knew what the trouble was—he had been hopelessly spoilt. Had never had to do anything for himself. Chauffeur-driven to his nursery school, then away at boarding school at eight years old—and his mother had always had more time for charitable works than she had for him.

She put out a hand to cover his. 'Oh, John, I'm sorry. You can well do without any more worries.'

Indeed, things had not been going too

well in the world of finance. Life in the City was never easy, and the politicians didn't help. Scandals all the time, one after another.

'Have you seen him?' she asked. 'Graham?'

'He came down with Julie last Friday evening—I'm not sure if he knew I wouldn't be there but I expect he didn't want to face me. Anyway, he knows I'd give him short shrift. Fortunately he seems to be doing well in the business field—London property is perking up again, although I don't think we'll ever see a return to the figures of the seventies and eighties. Still, he's not a liability as far as I'm concerned—not yet at any rate.'

Graham would pick himself up, he always did, she thought. There would always be girls in his life, women went mad about him, yet he couldn't hold a candle to his father for looks. There was a weakness in that face of his. But although she had never met the first two wives, she had seen pictures of him with Julie and had thought that this time perhaps he might make a go of it.

It was not to be apparently. Fortunately, Janey was always able to throw herself into her charity work; she was not the sort of woman to stay home and brood over a thing like that.

'Well, it's a pity,' said Melissa succinctly, getting to her feet, anxious to change the subject. 'I have salmon for dinner—fresh salmon with cucumber sauce. I'll just check the oven, if you'd like to open the wine?'

John was so much at home here. If only it could be like this all the time. But that was impossible. He took his duties seriously, at least as far as he was able, and the fewer people who were hurt by his personal life the better. He was lucky to have retained the love of a woman like Melissa—she was everything to him. But if there were times when he thought of throwing in the towel and fleeing abroad and making a life for himself there with her, he quickly put the idea to the back of his mind. That way madness lies, he thought, and they must make the most of what they had. No point in hurting more people. What the eye didn't see ... Time was precious as one grew older.

He drew the cork on the chilled wine, and stood it in the ice bucket.

'Janey is working on the Butterfly Field project,' he said as Melissa came back into the room. 'Do you remember I told you about the possibility of buying it for a community centre? It's a great idea, but whether or not the farmer chap will sell, I don't know.'

'Is that the only available piece of

land—in the event of his not wanting to sell?'

'Well, it is the most convenient, nearest to the village, and as far as I know, he just tethers horses there. And, of course, it's green-belt.'

'Oh, well, there's no way then, is there?'

'Oh, it can be done—has been done in our lifetime. You know how it is these days. Rules were made to be broken and nothing is sacrosanct.'

She came and sat on a stool by his side and picked up her glass of wine.

'Aren't we lucky, John, to have this? Is it enough for you? I know it's hard.'

'On both of us,' he said quickly. 'You are the one who is losing out. When you think, you could have a good husband, live a normal life ...'

'This is as normal a life as I want,' she reassured him. 'I wish it would go on forever.'

He kissed her cheek. 'By the way,' he said. 'Next Wednesday—I'll check my diary—we'll go out for a meal and stay somewhere overnight.'

Her eyes lit up. 'Oh John, really?'

'I expect you thought I'd forgotten your birthday?' he teased her. 'You choose—somewhere nice, wherever you say.'

She knew exactly where she wanted to

go: a small hotel in the Cotswolds. They had been there once before.

'Will you make a reservation for us?'

'Once you confirm the date,' she said. 'Of course I will.'

She got up once more. 'Take your time, I'll call you when it's ready.'

John stretched out his feet on the stool in front of him. He was becoming more relaxed minute by minute.

When it was time to go home, he went reluctantly, as always. It was quite dark when he left, just before midnight knowing that Janey would be sound asleep when he arrived back at Clyde Lodge. She never waited up for him—never had.

Chapter Four

Sally closed the front door of Christmas Cottage and made her way slowly down the drive towards The Mount to pay her neighbourly respects, past the frontage of fir trees through which she could glimpse occasional vistas of the house itself before finally turning in at the wide iron gates which were the entrance to the prestigious residence. She went up the drive, flanked by low rhododendron bushes and, glancing back, saw how tiny Christmas Cottage looked from here. Then the ground flattened out, giving way to lawns and rockeries, and finally the wide deep terrace of York stone.

She had not visited the house since the last owners moved in, some three or four years ago, and knew that they had done a lot to the place before moving on. Now she was curious to see what the new owners would be like. Neighbours made such a difference.

There were two steps leading up to the front door, and wistaria climbed over the house, now almost in bloom, the long narrow racemes even at this stage giving out a heavenly scent. She pressed the large brass doorbell, and waited. Had they perhaps a maid or a housekeeper—but the door was being opened, and judging by her clothes, here stood Sally's new neighbour.

She hadn't known what to expect, certainly not this tall beautiful creature dressed totally in white silk. Sally took it all in at a glance: white skirt and shirt, white shoes, and immaculately dressed black hair—Imelda Marcos sprang to mind, for she was tall and well-built. Junoesque, even.

'I'm Sally Sheffield from next door—Christmas Cottage,' she said, holding out her hand and feeling very mundane and countrified in her tweed skirt and sweater beside this vision of elegance.

The woman smiled, showing lovely teeth, and took her hand, holding on to it. 'Come in, love, we're in a bit of a muddle.' Her accent was purest Cockney.

Stepping inside the huge hall, Sally could see no signs of a mess. The place smelled of polish and disinfectant and fresh air.

'Come in, I'm Pauline Carpenter, but call me Pauly—everyone does.'

Another voice came from the kitchen. ''Oo is it, darlin'?' An elderly voice, a woman's.

'All right, Mum,' Pauline called. 'It's the lady from next door—what did you say your name was?'

'Sally Sheffield.'

'Mrs Sheffield, Mum, from next door—you know, that little house we said you would like. We thought it was the gardener's lodge when we first come.' Pauline leaned forward confidentially, but there was no unkindness in her remark.

'Well, it is small compared to this.' Sally smiled. 'I just came to welcome you to Swansbridge.'

'Oh, that's reely nice,' Pauline said.

'And if there's anything I can do, or that you want to know, just ask.'

'Would you like some coffee?' Pauline

offered. 'I've just made some.'

'No, thank you—I won't stay. I'm sure you must have lots to do, but if there is anything you need, please call me.'

Pauline reached for a notepad on the elaborate hall table, ebony encrusted with brass.

'Give me your number.'

Sally told her, noticing the beautifully manicured nails, the black straight hair like silk, brushed back and falling to either side of her face, the exquisite fair skin and dark brown eyes, slightly almond-shaped.

'Perhaps you would like to come in for coffee to meet the neighbours? I'll ring you,' Sally said.

'Now that *would* be nice. That's reely kind of you.'

'I hope you will be happy here. It's a nice area to live.'

'I'm sure. I've been wondering a bit about Sandra—she's my daughter. She goes up to town every day on the train from Cobbets Green. There's not much for her to do here.'

'How old is she?' Sally asked, not wishing to implicate Tessa just yet.

'Nineteen,' Pauline said. 'She's a lovely girl, so pretty and a bit shy—you know how you are at that age?'

'Well, we shall have to do something about that.' Sally smiled, without knowing quite what she meant to do. 'Anyway, you have my number and I'll ring you about the get together. Are you free most mornings?'

'Well, I have me hair done twice a week, and of course I never know when Ron will want me. We do a lot of entertaining and that. Anyway, you let me know.'

Sally walked down the steps and the door closed, only to be opened again.

'Thank you for coming,' Pauline called after her.

Sally smiled to herself How lovely her new neighbour was. She herself was always impressed by beauty. What would Pauline's husband be like? And the shy pretty daughter? She couldn't quite see them in Swansbridge—but here they were. It took all sorts, as Sally well knew. Perhaps the place could do with a bit of interest. She wondered what Tessa would say to the idea of having a contemporary living next door. And Mum—there was Mum too—did she live with them?

Well, time would tell. But how interesting. They obviously had a great deal of money to buy such a lovely house. She had heard figures quoted of nearly half a million, and it could be that Pauline would be a great asset when it came to working for charities and raising money.

Two days after this, a Rolls appeared on

the drive, and a huge man got out of the driver's seat and made his way into the house. The husband, Ron?

I wish I was noble like Mother, Sally thought, and not so nosy, but I can't help it. I'm just curious, that's all. It's just healthy curiosity.

'I drove up behind a Rolls on the way home from the station and it pulled in next door,' Tom said when he arrived home that evening. 'Navy blue. Is that the one?'

'Yes, did you see him?'

'No, not altogether. Big chap, quite young.'

'And there's a daughter,' Sally said.

'By the way, when is *our* daughter due home?' Tom asked. He always liked his children to be safely under his roof.

'I'm not sure. She'll ring when she gets to the airport. Friday, I think.'

That evening she had a telephone call from Janey who sounded quite excited.

'Listen, Sally, I've finally got round to finding out who actually owns the Butterfly Field, and it turns out to be a man called Mathieson. He farms over Hassington way and it's true, as we heard, that he recently lost his wife and has no children, so I imagine—'

'That's a step in the right direction, Janey.'

'Yes. So I have instructed my solicitor to write to him—on our behalf, of course. I have said I represent the local committee, the ladies' section, and we would be interested to know if he would be prepared to sell the Butterfly Field. I said no more at this juncture.'

'No. Well, that's a start, Janey,' Sally said. 'Good for you.'

'Well, my dear, let's keep our fingers crossed. I'm sure he will agree once he knows what it is for. My solicitor knows of him, says he is an awfully nice man, a member of a very old local family—goes back generations.'

'So perhaps he might not be agreeable to letting the land go,' Sally said doubtfully. 'If it's family land.'

'Well, let's be optimistic.'

'Yes, of course, Janey. While I'm on to you, there is something else ...'

'Yes?' By her voice, Sally guessed Janey was glancing at her watch.

'Look, I've met our new neighbours—the Carpenters.'

That caught Janey's attention.

'From The Mount? Oh, you have. What are they like?'

'Very interesting ... a very good-looking woman.'

'Yes, but what like? A possible member of our little circle?'

'Could be,' Sally said carefully.

'What does he do?' Janey asked.

'I've no idea,' Sally said honestly. 'But I said I would invite her over for coffee and she said she would be pleased to come, so what do you think? Could we fix a date? You know how difficult it is to get everyone together.'

'Let me see.' Janey was referring to her diary. 'Not this week or next week—I only have Tuesday free. Oh, wait, I have a cancellation here. Is this Friday morning too soon, do you think?'

'It's all right for me. I'll phone the others and ring you back.'

Well, whether they were free or not, Sally knew they would manage to come somehow in order to meet the new neighbours. The Mount was Swansbridge's most prestigious residence and curiosity would get the better of most women.

'That's great,' Pauline said, when Sally telephoned her. 'I have me hair done Friday mornings, but I'll change it to the afternoon. Do you mind if I bring Mum—my mother?'

'Of course not,' Sally said without a moment's hesitation.

'Oh, thanks, she'd love that. I don't want to leave her on her own.'

They all arrived at eleven, in rather nice casual clothes as befitted a London

65

dormitory town, countryish but smart. Pauline was the last to arrive, in white again, this time a white dress and jacket which showed off her fine skin, white beads and shoes, and a long scarlet scarf. Mum turned out to be small and eager-faced, happy as a sandboy to be taken out.

'We walked round, it was such a nice day. It seemed a shame to get the car out,' Pauline said. 'Oh, isn't this nice? A dear little house. I told you you'd like it, Mum.'

'Pauline Carpenter, our new neighbour, and her mother,' Sally introduced them.

'Call her Beattie,' Pauline said.

'And this is Janey—Lady Utox-Smythe, Becky Newman, and Valerie Saunders.'

'Pleased to meet you, I'm sure,' Beattie said, shaking everyone vigorously by the hand. Her small blue eyes glowed with sheer pleasure.

'Sit down and make yourselves comfortable—I'll get the coffee,' Sally said, going into the kitchen to speak to Mrs Halliday. It was fortuitous that Janey had chosen Friday, for Mrs Halliday was here to make the coffee and had sorted the biscuits on to plates. The trolley was laden and Sally pushed it in.

'I told you you'd like it and make friends quickly, darlin',' Beattie said. 'My daughter was anxious about coming to a noo place, but I said to her, I said, "You've lived so long abroad, you've forgotten what it's like, duck." Thank you,' she said, taking her coffee. 'English people don't change much.' And she bit into a biscuit with relish.

'Oh, have you lived abroad a lot—er—Pauline?' Janey asked, little finger poised outwards, her pretty legs and feet projecting from her large expensively suited body.

'Yes, quite a bit, on and off,' Pauline said.

'Sally says you have a daughter?' Becky said. 'Does she live at home?'

'Oh, yes!' Pauline said, shocked by the alternative. 'My Sandra wouldn't leave home to live on her own, would she, Mum?'

Valerie appeared fascinated by her: the lovely face, the black hair.

''Course, she's gonna 'ave her 'ands full, I tell 'er, 'cos I'll be living with her as well,' Beattie said.

'Now, Mum, we always said—'

'I know, darlin'. Still, she's a lovely girl, my daughter.' And Beattie dunked her biscuit and looked around her triumphantly.

'What made you—er—choose to come to Swansbridge?' Janey asked. Alone of all of them, she felt a slight hostility towards

Pauline Carpenter.

Pauline turned her bright, open face to Janey, her brown eyes looking alert and a little wary.

'Well, we was trying to find somewhere in England—you know, near to London, having been abroad a lot—and someone suggested Swansbridge. And once we see—saw—The Mount, well, that was it. Of course, we've a lot to do to it before it's ready to live in.'

'I believe the last people quite restored it?' Janey said.

'Oh, well, it depends what you mean by restored.' And Pauline laughed out loud. 'It's ever so old-fashioned, a terrible kitchen.' She turned to Beattie. 'Isn't it, Mum?'

And Beattie nodded. 'Oh, yes, don't suit my daughter at all—she likes everything nice, and she's all for the latest—bless 'er.'

'So the builders will move in sometime in July, and we'll move out and leave them to it.'

'Where will you go?' Valerie asked, suddenly finding her voice.

'Oh, Spain, I expect.'

'Lovely,' murmured Janey.

'And then we'll really settle in, get me a good housekeeper and that, and plenty of help. Lovely coffee, Sally.'

'Another cup?'

'Yes, please.'

Pauline turned bright inquisitive eyes to them all, as though she had come to terms with them. 'And what do you ladies all do?'

'Well,' Janey began, 'we have a Swansbridge Women's Club, which we hope,' and she smiled, turning to the others, 'works for the good of the community. We meet once a week and discuss local matters.'

'Oh, that's nice,' Pauline said.

'Yes, very nice,' Beattie agreed, taking another biscuit. 'You can do with that. I know, living on my own all those years.'

'Where was that?' Janey asked.

'Shepherd's Bush,' Beattie said. 'I was born there. It's like home to me, but when you're getting on, you know—'

'Well, you won't have any worries now, Mum,' Pauline said, reaching over and patting her mother's little workmanlike hand.

'Oh, she's ever such a good girl,' Beattie cooed.

'Well, I hope you will be very happy here. Is there a chance you might be able to lend us a hand with village affairs, charities, that sort of thing?' Janey pressed on.

'She don't get a lot of time, do you,

duck?' Beattie answered, but Pauline's dark eyes bade her be quiet.

'Oh, yes, I'd like to do my bit—I'd like to become part of village life,' she said, and Sally thought how sharp Janey could be if she didn't approve of someone. Pauline was a poppet, anyone could see that.

'Well, what we are engaged in at the moment is buying the Butterfly Field on behalf of the community.'

'And where is that?' Pauline asked.

'It's in the village. The land actually marches with yours, but it dips where you are, and of course you have so much of your own you'd hardly be likely to see it.' Janey smiled. 'It would be for a community centre, probably a tennis court, the hall to be used for all sorts of things: children's activities, social events—'

'And have you planning permission for that?' Pauline asked, taking a biscuit, leading Sally to think she was more than just a pretty face.

'Oh, no, not yet, but I don't think we will have any problem there.' Janey sounded very sure of herself.

'So you don't own the land?'

'No, but we're negotiating the purchase at the present time.'

'Well, that's good,' Pauline said, giving her beautiful smile to everyone. 'And Mrs

Newman—Becky, is it? Where do you live?'

'I live at April Cottage, just down Harcourt Lane.'

'And you, Valerie?'

'Down in the village, actually in the High Street. It's an old house, nineteenth-century.'

'Sounds nice ... and do you all have children?' Pauline asked. 'I'm a bit worried about my Sandra—'

'Lovely girl,' Beattie said. She seemed sleepy after her coffee and biscuits.

'What age is she?' asked Janey.

'Nineteen.'

'Oh, there's lots to do in Cobbets Green, and of course we're not that far from the West End on the train. But that's the whole point of the social centre. It will be for young adults: a tennis court, a hall, for drama festivals, a swimming pool ...'

Janey got quite carried away.

'Oh, no problem, there, we'll build our own swimming pool,' Pauline said. 'I can't imagine life without one.' And she raised calm brown eyes to meet Janey's blue ones.

'Oh, well then. Does your husband work in the City?'

'Oh, no, he's in property. Well, I mean, 'e has an office in the City, but ...

well, we go everywhere. Developing, you know.'

'So you've lived—?'

'All over the world,' Pauline said. 'You name it: Florida, Hong Kong, South Africa. Mind you, when we was first married we lived in Kent for fifteen years, so we're not movers in that sense. When we move it's to stay, so you'll be seeing a lot of us.'

'She was married at sixteen,' Beattie said proudly.

'Ron was eighteen,' Pauline said fondly.

'Goodness,' murmured Janey.

'We've only been living abroad for the last ten years.'

'But I am pleased to 'ave her 'ome,' Beattie said.

'And I'm pleased to be home,' Pauline said, 'especially amongst a lot of lovely ladies like yourselves. You must all come for a swim and to play tennis. I love tennis.'

'You'll build a tennis court?' Sally asked.

'Oh, yes,' Pauline said comfortably. 'Still, it all takes time and I mustn't bore you with all my ideas—I'm a great one for ideas—and interior decorating and that.'

'I'm sure,' Becky said gently.

'Would you think me awfully rude—er—Pauline, if I told everyone about the latest developments on the Butterfly Field?' Janey enquired.

'No, you go ahead.' Pauline smiled.

'As we are all together—and hopeful of course, that you will join us in our little project?'

Pauline smiled. 'Of course. Glad to.'

'Well, ladies, I have written to the owner of the field, a Mr Leopold Mathieson. It appears that he farms in Hassington. Anyhow, his wife has died in the last year, and he has no children, so I have written to ask if he would be prepared to sell the land, which I understand is a very small part of his estate. It really wouldn't make a lot of difference to him—just another field.'

'Oh, that's wonderful, Janey!' Becky cried.

'Well done,' Valerie said. 'So now we're just waiting for his reply?'

'Once he gives us his assent, then of course we shall set the wheels in motion.'

'Well, I wish you luck,' Pauline commented.

'Would you like me to post you details of further meetings, that sort of thing?'

'Yes, I should like to help where I can.'

And Janey looked very pleased. More power to her elbow, she thought.

'But now we must be going,' Pauline

said, 'if you'll excuse us? Come on, Mum.'

Beattie looked reluctant to go, but stood up.

Pauline held out her hand to each of them in turn,

'Thank you ever so much for having us,' she said. 'Come on, Mum. Thank you, Sally,' she said again, taking her mother's hand, and walking gracefully down the drive from Christmas Cottage towards The Mount.

'Well!' Janey said when the door closed after her. 'Would you believe it?'

'She's awfully nice,' Sally said defensively.

'Yes, but not quite—well—what you'd expect.'

'Takes all sorts,' Becky said mildly.

'Cor!' Valerie said. 'Did you see that jacket? Armani, I'd say, and those shoes—pure Blahnik.' Not that Valerie could ever afford those things herself, but she did know what was what. 'And wasn't Mum a sweetie.'

Janey's face was a study.

'It's just amazing to me, how people like that can buy something as lovely and classical as The Mount and then turn it into a modern monstrosity.'

'We don't know that she will,' Sally remonstrated.

'My dear, you *bet* she will. Probably got

all the money in the world to do it, too.'
Janey shuddered delicately.

'Well, it's good news about the field,
isn't it?'

'Super,' Valerie said.

When they had all gone, Sally took the
trolley back into the kitchen, where
Mrs Halliday was waiting to stack the
dishwasher. She had known her cleaner
long enough to be on very friendly terms
with her.

'Well, now they have met our new
neighbour, so that's broken the ice,' Sally
commented, moving the cups and saucers
off the trolley. She stood for a moment,
arms folded, staring across at The Mount,
which she could just see from the kitchen
window.

'I wonder what she will do with it—to
it,' she said.

Surprised at Mrs Halliday's silence, she
turned round.

'Everything all right?' she asked. Mrs
Halliday was usually a mine of gossip,
always singing or smiling. Today her rather
nice olive-skinned face and dark brown
eyes looked a little woebegone. She was
a handsome woman, dark as a gypsy.

She sighed deeply. 'Oh, I dunno.
Sometimes it's nothing but trouble. My
young sister—you've heard me talk of her,

75

Mandy, lives just outside Yeovil—well, her husband's ordered her out of the house, and her with a little girl, a bit younger than my boys.'

'Oh, I'm sorry,' Sally said.

'He was a downright bad lot, always has been. And I'm close to Mandy, we always got on. When Mum died, we were so close. Well, she phoned me last night, and I could tell something was wrong.' She bit her lip.

'I don't know what she'll do. I said to her, "Good riddance to bad rubbish." He's always knocked her about. I said to her more than once, "You should leave him," but she never would. More fool her. And now he's brought his fancy woman to live in the house—can you believe it?'

'Oh, dear,' Sally said. 'How awful. But can't she ...'

'They rent the house, it's not theirs, and what can she do? he says she's got to leave.'

'But he can't turn her out just like that, can he? With the little girl and all. Where would she go?'

'You wouldn't think a man could be so cruel, would you? Oh, I'd kill him if I got my hands on him! She was a beautiful girl—still is—but my husband can't stand her. Never could. Isn't that funny? Never liked her even before we were married.

Still, as I say, she's my own flesh and blood. The least I can do is to take her in for a few days till she gets settled.'

'Oh, but you couldn't—'

'What?' Mrs Halliday stood and faced Sally, the light of battle in her eyes.

'Well, it wouldn't be fair on your husband, would it? If he dislikes her so much. Even for a short time.'

'Well, she's got to go somewhere, and my heart bleeds for her.'

'There are places, aren't there? The Citizens' Advice Bureau would tell her where.'

But Mrs Halliday snorted. 'They're no good! Try and find her somewhere to live? I should say so! They always blame the woman.'

'Social Services?' Sally suggested, wishing she could do something to help. People had such awful problems.

'Well, you mustn't worry too much,' she said. She liked Mrs Halliday, who had been a good friend to them: babysitting when the children were small, helping out on odd occasions, to say nothing of the one morning a week she had free from her other jobs.

'Where is your sister now?'

'That's what I'm wondering. She rang me last night because he'd just brought this woman home, and she slept in the

77

little girl's room but he ordered her out—I can't believe it! If I could get my hands on him! You see, she's not like me. I'd stay put, but not Mandy. She's as weak as dishwater, that's why she put up with him all this time. She'll be out on the streets tonight, you see if she isn't. And that little girl—young Kylie.'

'There's always the police station—perhaps they will tell her where to go? Then the Salvation Army, battered wives, that sort of thing.'

'She wouldn't think of that—she's as soft as they come. Wouldn't say boo to a goose, that's why she's in this mess ... and I couldn't give her a home, even if I wanted to, it wouldn't be right. But just for a while, I thought ... Only Eric, well, he wouldn't. More trouble, he said. Nothing but trouble. And we've got enough of our own.'

'Oh, it's very hard,' Sally said, genuinely upset to see Mrs Halliday in this situation.

What did young women do in cases like this? Forced out of their homes, prey to physical violence ... She shuddered. Some people had really bad luck, and often through no fault of their own.

She so looked forward to Tessa's homecoming this evening and hearing about something light and interesting as an antidote to Mandy's problems.

Chapter Five

Tessa boarded the plane from Madrid. Putting her hand luggage overhead on the rack, she settled herself into the window seat. Fastening her seat belt, she saw Hugo boarding with the other passengers, his height and handsome head setting him apart from other men, his sheer good looks drawing a sigh from deep down inside her as he smiled and took his seat.

She saw the stewardesses give him a second glance. As well they might, she thought morosely.

'Everything all right?' he asked her solicitously.

'Yes. Fine, thanks,' she answered, from time to time giving a sideways glance in his direction. So much for her trip with him to Madrid! she thought.

They sat, each deep in their own thoughts, as the plane waited for take off. They had discussed their visit pretty thoroughly back in the hotel. Now there seemed nothing left to say.

The revving of the engines was a momentary disruption from their thoughts. Soon they were being lifted off the ground and into the clouds, and presently into the blue clear skies above them.

When the moment came to relax and take off their seat belts, Hugo sat back and closed his eyes. Tessa stared out of the window, unseeing. She could hardly believe it was over, the trip she had so looked forward to. It was difficult now to relive the excitement she had felt at the outset of the journey, but then how could she have known it would turn out as it had?

It had proved to her once and for all that Hugo knew his job. He had told her on the journey out of his training and the prestigious museums he had worked for, the foreign travel, his stints in Italy, France and New York. Paintings were his life and he made no effort to conceal his excitement at the projected trip in the hope of finding a masterpiece. Perhaps that was it, she had thought, there is nothing else in his life but art ...

It was a morning flight out, and they had been asked to contact the Contessa Maria Teresa Perez on their arrival at the hotel, when she would advise them what time to come to her house which was tucked away in the old part of Madrid. Once settled in the beautifully appointed hotel, Hugo telephoned the Contessa who suggested they take a taxi and call as soon as was convenient to them, perhaps before lunch, between twelve and two?

It was not far, and Tessa was soon engrossed in studying the old buildings, which she thought looked to be decorated with stone lacework, the balconies and the church towers which soared up into the sky, the iron grilles in front of every balcony, the strange square windows ...

'What a lovely city!' she exclaimed, entranced.

'You've never been here before?'

'No.'

'Then you have a treat in store.' And Hugo smiled.

The taxi stopped outside a building, hardly differing in its façade from its neighbours except it was obvious that this was still an individual house and had not been divided into flats. The ornate doorway of fancy ironwork had a large doorbell which Hugo pushed, and almost at once a man came out dressed in the black livery of a manservant. He was unsmiling but polite, and opening the gates, led them across a courtyard and into a cool shady interior, which took some time to get used to after the bright sunshine outside. The man telephoned to announce them, then escorted them upstairs to the first floor where the Contessa would be waiting for them.

It was sumptuous. The wonderfully textured window hangings, rich and dark, almost excluded the light. Tessa held her breath in delight. Thick and heavy, the tapestries were as fine as others she had seen in museums, and such colours—vivid vibrant colours! At the top of the stairs a maid was waiting to show them into a salon. She was dark and pretty, dressed in black, and like the man, unsmiling.

Waiting for them inside the salon was a woman whom Tessa thought must be the most beautiful she had ever seen. Tall and statuesque, her mass of jet black hair tied back, she could have been any age—thirty, forty—and such eyes! Great dusky eyes which glowed as she came forward, her hand outstretched.

'I am the Contessa Maria Teresa Perez. Welcome to Madrid.'

Hugo took her hand and inclined his head. 'I am Hugo Blanchard, and this is Miss Tessa Sheffield.'

'How do you do?'

Glancing at Hugo, Tessa saw that he looked more than impressed, and not surprisingly. Not only the Contessa but the room was magnificent. Opulent, even for the Spanish aristocracy, its walls were hung with rugs and carpets, the floor of wonderfully colourful Spanish tiles. Fine oil paintings too hung on the walls, and elegant tables and chairs stood about the room.

'Come and sit down.' The Contessa's voice was low and musical, with the merest trace of an accent. They sank into deep silk-covered chairs. She rang a small bell beside her own chair, and when the maid came ordered coffee, then sat back and considered them.

'You are both younger than I imagined,' she said. 'Are you experts in your fields of work?'

'We like to think so,' Hugo said reassuringly. 'I hope the references which were sent to you have helped overcome any doubts you may have had? It is a very private matter in which hopefully we shall be of some assistance. Your English, if I may say so, Contessa, is remarkable.' He was looking at her with unconcealed admiration.

'I was educated in England,' she said, which seemed to please him even more.

'I hope you approve the paintings. I, of course, am desolate at having to sell them but—'

She looked down, her long lashes fluttering against her cheeks, then looked up and smiled, showing lovely shining teeth. Perhaps she was younger than Tessa had first guessed? Her skin was unlined, fine and pale. The black dress she wore was simple, without any adornment except a fine leather belt which hung loose around her narrow waist.

In her ears, though, she wore long drop earrings of extravagant beauty, antique silver earrings which almost reached her shoulders.

'I thought we should have a little talk before I showed you the paintings. I should explain—' She hesitated while Hugo waited, knowing how important it was to let her take her time.

'I—we—have two Goya paintings as yet unattributed, as I think I explained to you in my telephone conversation? They are to my mind magnificent and came to us by way of my father who, I regret to say, is not well.'

'I'm sorry,' Hugo said.

'But he is old, and I hope I can keep from him the fact that you are here to examine them. If he were to have any idea at all, he would be devastated.'

'You may trust me,' Hugo said.

'That is why I came to MacBane's. It is one of the smaller, more exclusive fine arts dealers—without any of the attendant publicity one finds with some of the others.'

'Exactly,' said Hugo with an understanding smile, designed to put her at ease.

'And you came by the paintings ...?' he prompted her.

'My father—they were in his family. They were given to his great, great—oh, so far back great-grandfather by Carderera, who was a friend of Goya and also of Velasquez.'

'Which period would you say. Early period? Not after he lived in France?'

'Oh, no, long before, when he was younger. I would say between 1782 and 1794—when he was court painter.'

'And the subject matter?' Hugo asked.

'They are portraits, unsigned.' And Tessa could see that Hugo was now having difficulty in hiding his excitement.

The maid brought in the coffee and the Contessa handed it round. It was delicious coffee—why couldn't they get this at home? Tessa wondered. Small iced biscuits were offered on eggshell thin plates.

'Now.' The Contessa set down her cup. 'Before I show you the paintings, we have a little conspiracy to deal with. Oh, have no fear—it is just to save my father any embarrassment. He would be quite shocked—no, horrified is more the word, if he knew what I am about to do.'

'You see,' and she leaned forward and spoke softly, 'we are having to leave this house, after living in it for generations.

My father needs a great deal of expensive medical treatment which we can get in the United States, and although I expect you think we certainly are not—hard up, is that the term?—well, I am having to sell a few things to raise the money.' Here she smiled divinely. 'Possessions we have—money we do not.'

Tessa could see that Hugo was unused to dealing with people who were so frank.

'Let me assure you, Contessa—'

'Oh, if it was for me, but Papa, you understand—he does not know how ill he is, so we will play a little game if you don't mind? If you would kindly co-operate?'

Glancing at Hugo, Tessa could see this was not in his usual run of business, that he did not approve of anything which was not straightforward, but faced with this beauty, he was prepared to go along with it.

'So—later I shall show you the paintings.'

Hugo smiled at her reassuringly. 'I suggest at first I give you some sort of valuation—after all, we are only in the preliminary stages as yet. How would that be? That way you may then decide whether to keep them or—'

'Oh, how nice and understanding you are,' said the Contessa softly. They looked at each other, eyes locked for a second, maybe more, until politeness made her remember that Tessa also was sitting there.

'Miss Sheffield, forgive me. You are interested only in the textiles, tapestries, rugs, that sort of thing? Well, I have some wonderful things. They mean nothing to me, have been in the family for ages—and I don't in the least mind letting them go. The paintings, of course, are something else.'

'I should be pleased to see them and give you an opinion,' she said. There was no doubting whom the Contessa would rather be dealing with—but that was the way of the world, Tessa thought sharply.

The Contessa got up from her sofa and rang a bell again. 'I will ask Juan to bring in my father. He will be pleased to see you. I have told him that you are here to value the rugs and things—he accepts that since we have to leave this house.' And her face took on such an expression of sadness that even Tessa was forced to feel sorry for her.

'Yes, sadly. But I have said, we no longer need this house now—it is expensive to run, and we shall be moving to an apartment a quarter of the size. Once he gets used to it, we shall be happy.'

The wide double doors opened, and the Contessa's father appeared in his wheelchair: a handsome, elderly gentleman probably in his seventies, with a clipped white beard and a fine head of white hair.

The Contessa introduced them.

'Welcome to my house,' the old man said. 'You have come from London?'

Hugo nodded. 'Yes, sir.'

'I know it well. My daughter went to school in England.'

'Well, Maria Teresa, make your guests at home. Would you care for something? A sherry, perhaps something else?'

'A dry sherry would be very welcome,' Hugo said.

'*Señorita?*'

Tessa joined the Contessa in a fruit cup.

'I understand you have come to see the rugs and tapestries. Well, I can tell you, they are rather splendid. My daughter has never appreciated them, but we have some of the finest Moorish work, as well as some Persian rugs. You will perhaps be surprised when you see them.'

He was trembling, Tessa noticed, his fine hands moving all the time—how sad for the old man. She couldn't help but hope that he understood and accepted that he would soon have to move from here.

He nodded to the manservant. 'I have to leave you now but make yourselves comfortable. I am sure my daughter will look after you.'

'Papa, take care. I will see you in a little while.'

The Contessa sighed with relief when he had gone. 'There, you see, that wasn't so bad, was it? I feel guilty, but what can I do? The Goyas are the most valuable things we have, and sadly we shall have to part with them. Well, that is,' and here she smiled at Hugo, 'providing of course that you approve?'

She glanced at her watch.

'May I tempt you to stay to a light lunch, some *tapas* and a typical Spanish *paella?*'

Hugo hesitated but only for a moment. Tessa knew there was nothing he would like better.

'Well, if you are sure?'

'Of course,' the Contessa said. 'We would have time to look at the textiles before lunch.' She smiled at Tessa. 'Would you care to join us, Senorita?'

She rang for the maid to take the coffee things away, and spoke to her in Spanish. 'The *señor* and the *señorita* will be staying for lunch.'

She led the way out of the salon into a cool stone-flagged corridor before unlocking a door which led to a small room, the narrow windows of which were fitted with iron bars. It was absolutely chock-a-block full of rugs and carpets and embroidered objects. Even Hugo was impressed.

'Good Lord!' he said. 'An Aladdin's cave!'

'Yes, it is. Now, would you mind if I left you here while I go to see about lunch?'

Once the door closed behind her, Tessa let out a little squeal. 'Hugo! Did you ever see such treasures! They're magnificent!' And she fingered first one and then another, picking up a rug here, a tapestry there, touching and feeling the swathes of heavy embroidered stuffs hanging from stout iron poles. 'Oh, my goodness, what a find—imagine what they would bring. A fortune on their own.'

'Yes, quite,' Hugo said. 'If these are the textiles, what do you think the Goyas are like? Oh, I can't wait. What a nuisance to have to sit through lunch!'

'Never mind, Hugo. Help me with these.'

She took out her notebook and got to work, while he explored the room. They were twenty minutes solidly working and making notes before the Contessa returned. It would take Tessa ages to catalogue the textiles, she realised.

'Well, what do you think?' their hostess asked, knowing full well what the answer would be.

'They are magnificent,' Tessa said.

'What a collection!'

'Yes, I suppose it is—one gathered over many generations. It is sad to see them go but what would I do with them in an apartment, eh?' She turned sad eyes to Hugo whose own responded instantly.

Tessa stepped in.

'If and when you decide to sell, we should have to come back to catalogue them—quite a lengthy procedure,' she said.

'Naturally,' the Contessa agreed. 'I understand that. Now, lunch is ready.'

On the way to the dining room, they passed several doors.

'Would you like to freshen up?' she asked politely.

Hugo went in one door and Tessa another, later meeting outside at the end of the hall which led to the dining room.

The long table was laid at one end for three, with a selection of *tapas* and *paella* to follow. They dined with the Contessa alone.

'Papa always eats in his room at lunchtime,' she explained, breaking off the sweet-tasting Spanish bread, which was so good Tessa could have made a meal of it alone.

They talked of her time in England. No mention was made as to whether or not she was married, and she wore no rings except on the little finger of her right hand, an antique ring with a yellow stone which shone dully in the light of the hanging lamps.

The lunch was excellent, and after serving more coffee she offered Hugo brandy and a cigar, which he refused, and they spent a little longer sitting and chatting.

Hugo and Tessa felt thoroughly at home, as if they had been there for days instead of a couple of hours, but he was growing more and more eager to see the paintings and glanced at his watch.

Presently the Contessa rose to her feet and smiled at him.

'Well, shall we go?' she said.

She led the way downstairs by dark deep steps to what was obviously the cellar area. The lighting was dim as in most Spanish houses, and she brought forth a large iron key and unlocked the massive doors which led to a much smaller room, heavily padlocked and secured with stout iron bars. The Contessa then walked forward to take off the covering from one painting which stood leaning against the wall. She turned it round slowly, and stood waiting. Tessa heard Hugo's sharp intake of breath and the sibilant hiss as he breathed out.

'My God,' he said softly. Presently he looked up at the Contessa, seeing the brilliant eyes focused on him. She said nothing but took off the cover and did the same thing to the second painting.

He seemed to have lost his voice. After a time he said, 'They are masterpieces ... I can't believe it—undiscovered after all this time. Are you sure of this?'

'Of course, or I would not have sent for you,' she answered.

She turned on more lights overhead, and now the pictures could be seen more clearly. They were truly magnificent: the dark Spanish backgrounds, the faces of the sitters, one a Spanish grandee, the other a beautiful woman. There were the unfathomable eyes seen in so many of Goya's portraits, the passion yet above all the humanity. Even Tessa could see they were special.

'May I?' Hugo took out his glass and peered through it, running a finger gently along the edge, of the canvas before peering at it again. After what seemed ages he stood up, looking almost drained.

'You realise I should have to see them in a better light? Although it is fairly obvious these paintings have never seen the light of day. They are in remarkably good condition.'

'They have never been exposed,' the Contessa agreed.

'So you can understand why I have to be so careful, Contessa? They could prove to be a major find in the art world. They must be brought up and subjected to the most stringent examination. It is all going to take some time. Several visits will be necessary before I can take them back to London, always supposing—'

Her lustrous eyes met his.

'Of course.'

'We should have to make an appointment for you to bring them upstairs and proceed from there.'

Tessa thought she was in wonderland. How incredible! It was like something out of a book.

The Contessa covered the pictures again and stood them as they were before.

'Well, there you are. You are satisfied?'

'So far, Contessa.' And Hugo smiled at her. 'There is one other thing. We would have to know that you are the rightful owner of the paintings. If not you yourself, then your father's permission would have to be obtained.' But she put up one hand.

'Of course, but I can assure you there will be no problem there. The paintings belong to me. They were given to me by deed of gift on my twenty-fifth birthday.'

'Indeed?' Hugo said. 'Well, I cannot recall seeing anything that has given me more pleasure.'

And I can believe that, Tessa thought miserably. What with the paintings *and* the

Contessa. We mustn't forget her ...

He and Maria Teresa walked side by side along the stone-flagged corridor, while Tessa walked behind. We've forgotten to mention the textiles, she thought. Still, they were wonderful. I too shall have to come again to catalogue. Will it be the same time as Hugo, I wonder?

They ate in the hotel that night, and Hugo had only one subject of conversation: the possible shock to the art world when the Goyas were announced, the price they would fetch, the fact that he was the first one to see them, then, finally, the Contessa herself

'Interesting,' he said, 'wasn't she?' And his eyes glowed as Tessa had never seen them glow before.

'She certainly was,' Tessa agreed. 'Quite stunning.'

'Yes.' He smiled smugly. 'I don't know when I've seen a more attractive woman.'

But Tessa was thinking something else. So you *can* meet a woman who moves you, she thought. At least you're human. Still, I wish it were me. Here I am, in love with you. And here you are, besotted with a Spanish Contessa, no less.

What chance do I stand against her?

Still, she thought, I have one advantage. At least I live in England, and she's in Spain.

Chapter Six

On Monday morning Alistair MacBane sat like a caged tiger in his sanctum, anxiously awaiting the outcome of his two representatives' visit to Spain. He had half expected a telephone call to his home from Hugo—perhaps they had gone on a wild goose chase. He was more concerned, he had to admit, if grudgingly, about Tessa Sheffield's reaction to a weekend spent with Hugo Blanchard. If anything had come of it, then it was better he know before making a complete fool of himself. For smitten he was with the girl, even if reluctantly. Couldn't get her out of his mind: the small heart-shaped face, the wide dark eyes. There was a sort of fearlessness about Tessa—she'd stand up to anyone. Even him, he thought grimly. No one knew how hard it had been for him to take over the reins so suddenly when his father died. No one had expected the old man to die for donkey's years, but, well, that was the way of it. A sudden death, and Alistair had had to step in and fill the breach. It had been accepted that he would eventually succeed—it was what he had been trained for—but not quite so soon.

In all fairness, he told himself, if Tessa hadn't been around he would probably have been able to stomach Hugo a bit more easily, but seeing her obvious infatuation with the man, it was as much as Alistair could do to be civil to him. Oh, there was nothing really wrong with the chap, but for a girl like Tessa? Absolutely not. She needed a real man, someone like himself. What was putting her off him? He had tried several times to date her, but to no avail. Not only that, but sometimes she looked as if she positively disliked him.

He tapped his fingers on the desk and glanced at his watch. There really had been no need to get in this early, but there was a certain amount of excitement to it, wondering about the outcome of the trip to Spain and the possible Goyas. Was it true? Could it be? Such a scoop for MacBane's.

There was a tap on the door, early though it was. He called out: 'Come in!' and was surprised when in walked Hugo Blanchard with an almost beatific grin on his face. Alistair froze. Was this due to Tessa? A conquest?

'Morning,' he said with as much warmth as he could muster under the circumstances. 'How did you get on?'

It was impossible to ignore the gleam in

Hugo's eyes—the eyes of a man who has made an important discovery. The Goyas? Or Tessa?

'Sit down,' said Alistair brusquely. Hugo was obviously bursting to impart his news. 'Well?'

'Fantastic!' he said. 'Two of them— portraits, different subjects, one man, one woman. I couldn't believe my eyes ...'

Alistair felt a surge of relief followed by a rush of adrenalin. 'Are you sure?'

'As sure as I can be without the tests,' Hugo said.

'Fill me in.'

And Hugo told him, scarcely dwelling on Tessa and her textiles and ceramics, full of enthusiasm for the Goyas.

'And you really believe they are genuine?' Alistair asked when he had finished. 'As she says? Never before seen in public?'

'Absolutely,' Hugo answered reassuringly. 'Magnificent. Well, I need hardly tell you how a find of this sort will rock the art world?'

Alistair sat thinking. How best to tackle this important coup which had fallen straight into his lap?

'This Contessa, what was she like?'

And at this, Alistair saw a change come over Hugo's face. He looked away, at the floor, at the far corner of the room, before finally meeting Alistair's gaze and answering.

'Quite stunning,' he said. 'A beauty.' And again that faraway look, as if he were reliving his meeting with her. So that was it! The Contessa had captivated him. Well, that sounded a bit more hopeful as far as Alistair was concerned.

'A tragedy for her,' Hugo went on. 'To have to let them go. But the old man, her father, is in a bad way. Otherwise, of course, she wouldn't be selling them.'

'Now—what do you think is the best way to tackle this?' Alistair asked. Paintings and pictures were not his particular forte, his strength was furniture, but he was always willing to learn from the experts.

'Well,' Hugo answered, 'first I shall have to make another visit—several in fact, and as soon as possible. But initially I'll test them thoroughly—get them up out of that cellar and into the light.'

'Can you tackle that on your own, or do you want Cuanello to go with you?'

'No, not initially,' Hugo said, perhaps a little too quickly.

Another chance to see the fabulous Contessa unaccompanied?

There was a tap on the door, and when it opened there stood Tessa. Alistair's heart missed a beat as it did every time he saw her.

'Oh, sorry,' she said. 'I didn't know anyone was here—I'll come back later.' And the door closed behind her.

They discussed the paintings at some length before Hugo left, leaving Alistair to sit back and contemplate this slice of good fortune which had fallen their way.

Some twenty minutes later, the door opened again and Tessa stood there. No smile from her, and the thought passed through Alistair's mind that of course she would be upset at seeing Hugo's reaction to the Spanish beauty.

'Sit down, Tessa,' he said. 'Good journey? Worth the trip?'

'Oh, yes,' she said, 'very much so,' sitting down and opening her notebook.

He decided she was the prettiest thing—he wasn't wrong about her. That lovely little face with its high cheekbones, wide eyes and short dark hair that fell over one cheek when she bent her head. The slim neck like a white swan, the almost arrogant set of her head, the conscientious approach she took to her work ...

He took hold of himself 'Well, it was successful, I understand?'

'Yes, in every way, I expect you've heard about the wonderful Goyas? And as for my side of it, the textiles were better than anything I could have imagined. Some

100

of the ceramics were really ancient too. A collection gathered over many years.'

'And you found the Contessa easy to get on with?'

'Yes, very nice.' And those eyes were carefully bland, the lovely lips firmly closed.

'So you will need to go again shortly, I imagine?'

'Yes. They'll take a lot of cataloguing, and since our next sale is in November, it would be good to get them over by the end of July if possible.'

'By all means,' he said. How to break the ice with this girl?

He looked at his watch—for no reason at all.

'Um—how about lunch today? Perhaps we could discuss the visit then and arrange things?'

It was on the tip of her tongue to refuse, but she hesitated.

'Well, I—'

'Oh, do. I should like to hear about it all—it's ages since I went to Madrid.'

What harm would it do? Tessa thought. For sure, Hugo wasn't going to ask her to lunch.

'Yes, my lunch today is around one.'

'See you then,' Alistair said, and positively beamed as the door closed behind her.

He had made the first move.

Tessa drove up from the station with her father; they often travelled home together and caught the same train.

'So you're off to Spain again?' he said, folding his newspaper preparatory to getting off at Cobbets Green.

'Yes. I'm taking Carla with me. You know, she's the American junior—the experience will be good for her.' Tessa could afford to be magnanimous now she had reached her present position.

When they reached the house, they found William walking up the drive, gardening boots in one hand, his jacket and jeans only too clearly showing how he had spent his day.

While her father parked the car, Tessa walked back down to meet him.

'How's it going, Will?'

'Fine. Just bedded out Mrs Thing's petunias and begonias. I don't think I could face another box of bedding plants.'

'You're getting quite a tan, being outside all the time.'

'Am I?' He looked pleased. 'I'm not keen on the finicky work. I'd rather be doing digging and clearing, that sort of thing. Still, it's all experience.'

She linked her arm in his. 'Is that what you'd really like to be doing?' she asked him. She adored her young brother.

'If the old man would go along with it. I'd be bored to tears in an office, and I'm sure I could make a go of market gardening or garden design.'

There was evidence enough to prove that, Tessa thought, in the rows of beans and peas, and lines of carrots and onions, that now graced the vegetable plot beyond the formal garden. They had lived off Will's frozen produce in the winter months for the first time since he had left school and showed his interest in gardening.

While William went up to shower, Tessa stood watching her mother. 'What's for dinner?'

'I thought after your Spanish trip you'd probably like some English food, so I've done lamb chops in the oven with tomatoes.'

'Lovely,' said Tessa. 'I'm starving.'

'Well, how did you get on? I can't wait to hear about it.'

'Let me go up and change, and I'll come down and tell you all about it. I bought Dad a couple of bottles of Spanish wine, which they say has improved more than somewhat in the last few years.'

'Oh good,' Sally said slicing the cooked potatoes and placing them on top of the vegetables and lamb in the casserole then dusting them with chopped oregano before placing them back in the oven.

Tessa looked so fresh when she came down in a light cotton dress, her dark hair shining, eyes contemplating the labels on the bottles of wine.

She's not going to say anything unless I ask her, Sally thought, drying her hands. 'Now tell me, how was it?'

'The trip? Oh, wonderful. I loved Madrid. Did you and Daddy ever go?'

'No, we never did.'

'Well, it's lovely, but of course I hardly had time to see much of it and I should love to go back again. Anyway, I will, but on business—Alistair says I shall have to catalogue all the wonderful things belonging to the Contessa.'

Alistair says? Hmm. Sally digested this, and waited. You could never rush Tessa.

'But, the most magnificent things were the two Goyas. Can you imagine—never before seen, in private ownership, passed down from generation to generation. What a scoop for MacBane's!'

'Goodness,' Sally murmured.

'Of course, Hugo was over the moon—he could hardly contain his excitement. And you can't blame him.'

'And this Contessa—what was she like, an elderly lady?'

At this Tessa's expression changed.

'Oh, no. No, indeed. Young—well,

about thirty-five—but absolutely beautiful. Needless to say, Hugo was enchanted with her. Swept off his feet.'

Oh, thought Sally. Poor little Tessa.

'What with her and the two Goyas he had an eventful trip,' Tessa said. 'Still, I have to say, the textiles were wonderful too. Cushions, tapestries ... I shall probably go back early next week, Alistair thinks, if it can be arranged. I had lunch with him today.'

'Oh, did you?' Sally's voice was casual. 'Ah, here comes your father. We could take a glass of wine outside, it's a lovely evening. Can you imagine—Wimbledon starts next week. Oh, and that reminds me—I saw Pauline this morning, Pauline next door—and she says perhaps we would like to go in on Saturday lunchtime for pre-lunch drinks? They will be going off early in July to Spain while the builders move in. Goodness knows how long that will take.'

Tessa frowned.

'You mean big building works?'

''Fraid so, darling. Swimming pool, tennis court ...'

Tessa's face brightened. 'Oh, well, perhaps when it's finished we will be asked over to swim?'

'Can you manage it Saturday, midday? I said I thought you could but I wasn't sure, leaving it open if you decided you didn't want to come.'

'Oh, of course I can.'

They turned as William came back, freshly scrubbed, his handsome young face glowing, hair wet from the shower.

'You are invited too, William,' Sally said 'to the Carpenters for drinks on Saturday.'

'Sorry, Mum,' he said. 'I'm seeing Suzie.'

Suzie of the hat, thought Sally, half smiling. What a pair they were—one as dotty as the other.

On Saturday at midday, Tessa, Tom and Sally walked up the drive towards The Mount, and were greeted at the open door by Pauline.

'Oh, lovely,' she said. 'I'm glad you could come.'

'Hello, Pauline. This is my husband, Tom, and my daughter, Tessa. Tom—Pauline Carpenter.'

Pauline gave him her beautiful smile. 'Pleased to meet you, I'm sure,' she said. 'Look, Ron and them are in the garden —shall we walk round to the back? Isn't it a lovely day? It's a shame to be indoors, and I'm afraid we're all upside down in the house waiting for the builders.'

Sally smiled, and they began to follow

her round the side of the house with its gracious long windows and shrubbery towards the back, where on the terrace sat Ron Carpenter, Pauline's mother, and a young woman.

Ron Carpenter got to his feet immediately, coming towards them while holding out his hand. He was a huge man, well over six feet in height, with a build to match and a booming voice.

'Well, glad to meetcha,' he said, taking Sally's hand in his huge paw then turning to Tessa, half bowing for he was so tall. 'And you're the lovely young daughter. Well, you must meet our Sandra.'

'Coo-ee,' called out Beattie. 'Come and sit over 'ere, duck.'

Then the girl eased herself out of the lounger, a large young lady in a brief dress. She had long blonde hair, and what William would call a pretty moon face.

'Oh, no,' Sally heard Tessa say under her breath, but when she looked at her, her daughter was smiling quite warmly.

'Oh, so you're Tessa,' Sandra said in a little girl voice. 'I've seen you on the train. Look, come and sit down, make yourselves at home.'

There was a drinks trolley outside, a most expensive designer trolley, and several wonderful chairs and umbrellas.

Sally thought wistfully of their own garden furniture, as old as the hills and shabby to boot. The men were talking together agreeably, and every now and again Ron's booming laugh would ring out across the garden, but Sally had to admit Tom seemed to be enjoying himself

'Don't they look lovely together, them girls?' Beattie said. 'One so dark, and the other so fair.' She beamed, wrinkling up her weathered face, blue eyes shining.

Sally smiled. 'Yes, don't they?' she said. 'And have you quite settled in, Beattie?'

'I should say.' She grinned. 'I've got a lovely room all to meself. Looks over the garden and out to the fields, proper country—I can't believe it sometimes.'

'Here you are, Mum, white wine,' Pauline said to her mother. 'Ron's bringing the other drinks.'

She smiled indulgently. 'Look at these two young things—don't they make you feel old?' She glanced at the two girls sitting side by side in their chairs.

All in white again, Sally thought, a stunning-looking woman in her long white dress and simple flat shoes. She obviously knew what suited her.

'So you are off to Spain?' she asked.

'Yes, can't wait—I love the sun,' Pauline said. 'Oh, thank you, dear.' And they each took a drink. Ron certainly knew how to mix a Martini, Sally thought, taking her first sip, while Pauline delved into her Pimms, which was a sight for sore eyes with its greenery and fruit piled high.

'Well, this is nice,' Ron boomed, looking down at them from his great height. 'I think we're going to enjoy it here. Well, we will when it's done,' he said. 'There's a lot to do, Tom,' he added gravely. 'Still,' and his face brightened, eyes twinkling, 'you won't know it when it's finished. The old Mount won't be what it was—and not before time.'

'What do you plan to do?' Tom asked, half fearful, half interested.

'Well, for starters ...'

Pauline turned to Sally. 'Oh, I am glad to 'ave you as a neighbour,' she said. 'You know, it's the luck of the draw—I've had some terrible neighbours in my time—and meeting all them other ladies ... It's nice to get your teeth into something.'

'That's what I always say,' Beattie said, helping herself to peanuts.

'And I must say that—um, what's 'er name—Mrs Lady Smythe—Janey—she's a nut, isn't she? A real worker, though, she knows what she's doing. Has she heard any more about the Butterfly Field?'

'Not as yet, I don't think,' Sally said. 'At least, she hadn't when I last saw her. I expect it will take some time. As far as I know, she has sent off the letter enquiring about it.'

'Oh, that's good,' Pauline said. 'Nibbles? Nuts? There's crisps for you girls over there.'

'Thank you,' Tessa said, and Sally thought how agreeable it was in this lovely garden with the scent of roses all around her, and pleasant neighbours—even if Sandra's high-pitched little voice showed no sign of stopping. What was Tessa making of her?

She bit her lip.

Ron was taking Tom around the garden—or estate more like, she thought, pointing out where the tennis court would go, and the pool.

'You won't recognise it,' Pauline said proudly. 'And you must all come in and have a swim, and the girls can play tennis.'

'Lucky young things,' Beattie said approvingly. 'Is there another one, duck?' lifting her glass to Pauline.

'Of course, Mum,' she said. 'But that's your lot.' And she wagged her finger at her mother.

'And here,' Ron was saying, 'we shall have the changing rooms, screened of

110

course by high walls. We shall have stuff growing over them, some—what's that stuff called, Pauly?'

'What's that, darling?' she called back.

'That fencing stuff, criss-cross ...'

'Oh, trellis,' she said. 'Oh, yes, there'll be lots of trelliswork.'

It occurred afterwards to Sally that no one had mentioned them at all. How long they had lived there, who and what they were, how many in the family—all the talk had been of the Carpenters and their doings.

Well, what did it matter? she thought. Of course they were obsessed with their new home. Still ...

Walking back up the drive afterwards, Tessa turned to her.

'Mummy, you could have knocked me down with a feather!'

'Why, Tessa, did you recognise her?'

'Of course I did! You couldn't forget her, could you? She's an absolute menace. She talks loudly at the top of her voice on the train, everyone gets so embarrassed, and sometimes to people she doesn't even know.'

'Oh, well, I expect she's anxious to make friends—'

'Oh, come on! That little high-pitched voice—it carries so, and she tells everyone all about her boyfriends and what she does—what they do—' Her face was flushed with embarrassment.

'Oh, Tessa, it can't be that bad!'

'It is! Now that I know her, I shall catch another train. I couldn't bear to have to sit and listen to that awful girl—oh, how unlucky can I be to have her living next door? And you can count me out about taking a swim there.'

'Well, they're off to Spain soon.'

'Thank God,' Tessa said fervently.

'You can't see the funny side of it?'

'You must be joking!' she said stormily. 'You don't have to travel up to town with her. And I'm not going to, that's for sure.'

Tom caught up with them.

'What was all that about?' he said, taking Sally's arm.

'The girl, Sandra.'

'Yes, I'm afraid I recognised her too. You'd be surprised for such a little voice how far it carries. Still, they're a nice lot. I thought Beattie was a darling. Not exactly Swansbridge, but then who is these days?'

'I'm beginning to wonder,' Sally said. 'I like Pauline, though. But Ron ...'

'How long will they be away?'

'Two or three months, Pauline said.'

'Two or three months' building work?' Tom said thoughtfully. 'Hmmmmm.'

Chapter Seven

'You're early,' Sally said as Tessa arrived in the kitchen for breakfast at half-past seven on Monday.

'Mummy, could you be a brick and drop me at the station this morning? I'm not leaving with Daddy, I'm catching the seven fifty-five—and I've left it too late to walk.'

Sally looked at her daughter, enlightenment dawning.

'You're not catching the earlier train because of Sandra Carpenter?'

'Afraid so.'

'You mean you'd arrive at the office half an hour early just to avoid her? She can't be that bad.'

'She is,' Tessa said grimly.

'And there's your father catching a later train—the eight fifty-five. What's got into the pair of you?'

'I told you, anything rather than risk sitting next to Sandra Carpenter.'

'But surely your father—'

'She would think nothing of latching on to him on the platform, and after that he'd be sunk. And you know how he likes to read the paper on the train.'

'Good thing then that she's going to Spain.'

'I should say.'

'Where does she work?'

'Somewhere in Covent Garden—a boutique or something, I expect. A temporary sort of job, I think.'

'Oh, well, here's your coffee. Just toast?'

'Please, and then we must fly.'

On the way back from the station, Sally decided it was time she went to see her mother. Time was when Emily Pargeter used to come down to spend a long weekend with them, but those days had gone. Now she was happy to stay in her own home, and wait for them to visit her. Usually they went at a weekend when William was home. He always liked to visit his grandmother, had a soft spot for her. But now that he was older, and Tessa too, times had changed. The outing to their grandmother was no longer the special event it used to be.

Tom and William were already sitting having breakfast when she returned, William about to fly to his gardening job, Tom relaxing before catching the later train.

'I think I'll drive down to see Mother today, Tom,' Sally said. 'I'll give her a ring. Sometimes it's better to do it on impulse, then she can't get het up about my going. I thought we might have lunch out if she feels like it.'

'You don't want to wait until the weekend?'

'No, I'll go on my own. I'd quite enjoy the drive and it looks as if it will be a lovely day—no rain forecast.'

'Give Gran my love,' William said. 'Tell her Suzie and I will be up to see her one day when I've finished this job.'

'Yes, I will.'

Sally glanced at the clock. 'Hadn't you better be going, Tom?'

'No hurry. Actually I'm going to call in at the council offices. Something I need to check.'

He often did this, so it was no surprise.

Later, when they had gone, Sally telephoned her mother and arranged the visit, and the call was followed by one from Janey Utox-Smythe.

'Janey, how are you?'

'I'm fine, dear, just thought I'd let you know that I had a reply from Mr Mathieson.'

'Oh, good.'

'Well, not so good, really—he writes that he has no intention of selling the field and is sorry he cannot be more helpful. Quite a brief letter.'

She sounded very down.

'Oh, I'm sorry, Janey. Well, you tried.'

'Oh, I'm not giving up, dear. He hasn't heard the last of me yet. No, we must press on. Nil desperandum, and all that.'

You had to hand it to her, Sally decided. Janey would get that field eventually, she was sure of it.

'We won't, incidentally, be having Pauline with us for about three months. She's going to Spain while the builders do up the house and so on.'

'Oh, that's a pity When does she go?'

'At the beginning of July, she says.'

'Oh, well, my dear, can't be helped. She looked like being a useful member. Now, children's union—Saturday is the day of Becky's fête, isn't it? I hope to be there. You're doing the cake stall, aren't you?'

'Yes, for my sins. I'm so pleased Becky has given us the garden—it was nice of her.'

'Well, I would have given up Clyde Lodge,' Janey said, 'but you know how it is, we've so much on at the moment—'

Sally couldn't quite imagine her giving up the garden of Clyde Lodge—still, she was so good in other ways.

'I'll see you then, Janey. I'm just off to visit my mother.'

'Oh, remember me to her. She's such a darling.'

'Yes, she is.' Sally smiled, and got herself ready for the trip.

It was all of fifty miles, but she stopped to buy some flowers and chocolates. Nowadays her mother loved sweets and at her age, what did it matter, Sally thought, as long as she enjoyed life?

The countryside was beautiful at this time of year. The blossom trees were just going over, but the elderflowers and may trees were particularly wonderful this year. It was surprising how far you could go in this small island without coming across a large town. Acres and acres of countryside, sheep and cows, and a slight heat haze promising a fine, warm day.

Drawing up in the car park alongside the cathedral she was struck as she always was at the peace of this place. No wonder her mother loved it. England at its best, she thought. The tiny houses, dark outside, with narrow mullioned windows, stood on the green by the churchyard, but far from being depressing the scene was peaceful and tranquil, each little house with its own roses and country flowers, and number six was no exception. Her mother had always been a gardener. Perhaps William got it from her.

'Mummy!' Sally smiled as the door opened before she had rung the bell. Her mother stood there looking surprised. Sally thought these days she seemed smaller every time she saw her. She remembered

Emily as a tall woman, but that was when she herself had been young. Today she was dressed in her favourite Parma violet colour, which suited her silvery hair. Very dark-haired people always went a nice shade of white or silver, Sally decided, and her mother was always careful to choose the colours that suited her most. A straight skirt and matching cardigan worn with a cream blouse, all in purples and palest mauve—the colours most people found difficult to wear. And, of course, the ubiquitous pearls.

Emily's dark eyes shone at the sight of her daughter.

'What a lovely surprise,' she said, kissing her warmly. 'I was so pleased when you rang this morning. Ah, and sweet peas!'

Sally followed her mother into the interior, cool because the walls were so thick. It never got uncomfortable even in very hot weather. But there was central heating for the winter, when it was very cosy. The sitting room was full of small pieces of furniture and bric-a-brac which Sally remembered from a small child. They had been put into store when her mother sailed off to Africa with her second husband. It was all so familiar, she always felt at home here.

While Emily was busy in the kitchen with the coffee, Sally saw that the tray was already laid with pretty china and there were biscuits.

'Lovely,' she said, 'I could do with coffee.'

'Good drive up?' her mother asked.

'Yes, no problems. It's a good time of day to come.'

'You mustn't leave it too late otherwise you'll catch all the traffic going home,' Emily said, as Sally carried the tray back into the small sitting room.

'And what have you been doing with yourself?' she asked.

'The usual things. We have a new man in the Close, a retired bishop—rather a nice man, very shy, believe it or not, and we have all made him most welcome. We have been busy with church activities, raising funds for repairs to the roof—it seems everyone is doing that these days—and of course embroidering hassocks. There's never a dully moment. Tomorrow we're having a bring and buy for the unmarried mothers.'

It was wonderful, Sally thought as she stirred her coffee, to see her mother so occupied. What did people do who were really alone? Her mother was fortunate, blessed with a temperament that never seemed to be gloomy, with a predisposition for helping others.

Of course, her main interest was William,

whom she adored. She was fond of Tessa but he was her favourite.

'Well, he's gardening at the moment,' Sally said in answer to her question.

'Good lad,' Emily said.

'Yes, but Mummy, we had wanted more for him. You know what I mean—he can't make a career out of gardening.'

'Why not?' Emily asked sharply. 'A great many worthwhile people have made a career out of gardening.'

'Well, I didn't mean that, but you know his A levels were not all that good, and he didn't get into university ...'

'Well, perhaps he has no desire to go to university,' Emily said. 'If you want something particularly badly, a degree or something or other, or you long to go ... but he doesn't, does he?'

'No,' Sally sighed. 'That's true.'

'Well, then, he's not an academic, and that's no sin,' she said. 'He's a lovely young man and you should be proud of him.'

Sally sprang to his defence. 'Oh, we are, Mummy, he's such a nice boy—we just want the best for him.'

'Well, things have a way of sorting themselves out.'

'He's got a girlfriend now, Suzie. It was her birthday this week, she's seventeen, and he's taking her out on Saturday.'

'Yes, I know, he wrote and told me.'

'Did he?' Sally was surprised. But who knew what went on between grandparents and grandchildren? Parents lost out sometimes.

'And Tessa?'

And Sally told her about the trip to Spain while Emily listened avidly. She loved hearing about other people and what they were up to.

'By the way, I thought we'd go out to lunch. How do you feel about that?'

'Love to,' Emily said. 'The Green Door?'

'Yes, is it still as good as it used to be?'

'Yes, it doesn't alter much,' Emily said. 'Old-fashioned English food—but that's the way we like it. We're quite laid back here, you know.'

The meal turned out to be the same as always. Roast lamb and mint sauce and a delicious home made apple pie.

Sally thoroughly enjoyed herself, and left soon after taking her mother back home, for she knew Emily rested in the afternoon, and at her age this was enough excitement for one day.

Sally drove home, pleased with her day, thinking about William and Tessa, trying to imagine William writing to her mother and what he'd said. He was far too young to have a proper girlfriend like Suzie, but they had so much in common. Suzie was no brainbox either, but such a nice girl. She wore the strangest clothes which always somehow suited her, a little eccentric perhaps. And what was Suzie going to do with herself now that she had left school?

Well, Sally had enough to worry about with William, and was thankful to see the road leading to Cobbets Green in front of her.

She arrived home just after Tom and Tessa who were standing in the kitchen having a laugh about the way they had missed Sandra Carpenter.

'Oh, you are unkind,' Sally said.

'Not at all—just looking after our own interests,' Tom said. 'And how was Gran?' He was very fond of Emily Pargeter who in some ways had taken the place of the mother who had died when he was a small boy.

'Oh, fine, as usual.' And she began to tell them about her visit before going upstairs to change and come down to prepare the evening meal.

'By the way,' Tom said, 'a couple of things. I went to the council offices today and looked up past applications referring to Swansbridge. I saw that the Carpenters had put in a planning application for The

Mount some three months before they bought the house.'

'Oh, is that unusual?'

'No—but they wanted to make sure they got it before buying. And not only for a pool and tennis court, but a pretty big conservatory too.'

'Really?'

'A huge thing, magnificent on the plans, and on *our* side.'

'Oh, Tom—you mean, we shall be able to see it?'

'Probably. I'm just surprised that the council didn't notify us. It's usual to let neighbours know when pools and tennis courts and that sort of thing are going to be built.'

'Why do you think they didn't? Let us know, I mean?'

'I'm not sure. Anyway, planning permission went through and it's a bit late to fight it now. Not that I'd want to—it's not going to affect us. Still, cheeky of them.'

Tom had such an equable nature, Sally knew that he must feel that in some way the Carpenters had jumped the gun.

'Mind you, Ron must believe the place is worth it. He's not going to spend that kind of money unless he thinks it's in the right location. All the better for us, I suppose.'

'That's true.'

'The other thing is, I bumped into Ken

123

Collins—do you remember him?'

'The name seems familiar.'

'I was at school with him and he used to live in Swansbridge until he left to open up a market garden—well, he's really a botanist, and is opening a place just outside Cobbets Green. He'll specialise in trees and big exotic plants you can dig up and plant just where you want them—sort of designer trees. It's an expensive business, but today people will pay anything to get what they want. A fifty-foot-high oak tree, for instance.'

'Oh, surely not, Tom?'

As an architect he was always receptive to new ideas.

'Well, I'm guessing. What I'm saying is, I was telling him about William, and he was very interested. We ended up with my promising to send young William along to have a word with him.'

Sally's eyes were shining. 'Oh, Tom, if only ...'

'Well, it's something to think about. I'll have a word with him when he comes in.'

There was no doubting William's enthusiasm when he was told of the idea.

'Now, nothing's promised, but it's perhaps a step in the right direction,' his father told him.

'Brilliant!'

'Look, lad, play it by ear. See what comes of the interview, OK?'

'Yes, Dad. And thanks.'

The result of the interview for William was that Ken Collins agreed to take him on for the rest of the summer. 'See how you go, William,' he said. 'If you're any good it might be worth your while to take up gardening seriously.'

'I'd like to think so,' the boy said earnestly.

On Friday morning, Mrs Halliday, most unusually for her, was fifteen minutes late.

'Oh, I'm ever so sorry,' she said breathlessly, taking off her jacket and putting on her apron. 'I've had such a rush, what with one thing and another.'

'Oh, don't worry, Mrs Halliday,' Sally said, knowing that her cleaner would soon give her the reason.

Mrs Halliday rolled up her sleeves and stood at the sink, running the water.

'Well, I know you said it wasn't a good idea—but what could I do? I've had to take my sister Mandy in.'

'Oh, dear.'

'Well, I told you, didn't I?' she said, trying to justify to herself what she had done.

'Poor little devil, there she was, nowhere to go, and little Kylie homeless. Oh, it made my blood boil. So I said to Eric: "Look, I know you don't get on with her, but she's my sister, and just for now ..." Well, he was mad! "What about my feelings?" he said. "You've got a duty to me and the family."

'"Duty!" I said. "I've got a duty to my kith and kin as well. My sister—I can't see her chucked out just like that."'

'"It's not your problem," he said.

'"Now," I said, "how is it going to affect them—her just being round for a few days until she gets herself together? She just wants someone to talk to." Oh, I couldn't see her wanting, Mrs Sheffield. Homeless, indeed!'

'I can understand your feelings,' Sally commiserated with her. 'Where will she sleep?' She knew Mrs Halliday had a small council flat.

'Well, I've got a put-u-up, and it's only temp'ry—she won't be there long, just until she decides what to do for the best. She needs all the help she can get, poor little beggar.'

'It's not going to be easy for you,' Sally sympathised. She felt more sorry for her than for her sister. Trouble with husbands was never a good thing, and she knew Mrs Halliday was only being kind and

126

doing what she thought best in a difficult situation.

The cleaner finished putting the crocks in the dishwasher and began to clean the sink.

'Men!' she said.

Sally could imagine how Eric Halliday must feel, coming home to another woman in his house of whom he didn't approve.

'I mean, just kindness—that's all she needs. And young Kylie, without a dad. "She should have stayed at home and worked out her own problems, not troubled you with them," Eric said. "You've got enough to do looking after me and the boys."

'Well, if I can't do my sister a good turn,' Mrs Halliday grumbled. But all the same, she wasn't looking forward to Eric coming home that evening.

Some people had so many problems. They could seem insoluble at the time, and yet somehow or other in the end were usually resolved.

Upstairs, Sally took down William's curtains. It was time they were washed. Looking around at his posters, she thought, such a boy's room! Rock and pop stars, a giant blow up of a Harley Davidson.

You had to be thankful that they weren't on drugs. Or at least you prayed they weren't.

Chapter Eight

Graham Utox-Smythe, driving back from the Sussex Downs where he had been for a business conference, decided to take a detour and call in on his mother.

It had been a very successful conference, in one of those hotels that had sprung up like mushrooms, where everything was provided for the businessman with no effort on his part.

Sunk deep in every conceivable luxury, Graham had lunched there after the conference. He had noticed this little secretary bird before, assessing her and the possibilities, but this time, somehow or other, when after lunch a couple of them had gone off for a round of golf, Graham found himself in her room at the hotel. He had no need to worry. Her clothes had come off before he had got inside the room, and what followed had surprised even him.

Little minx! He had already decided that this was the life for him. Far better the bachelor life, with constant access to fascinating females, and there were enough of those about to keep him going until such time as he was no longer interested—not that he could visualise such a day. Marriage was for the mugs, he thought. A disaster area: mortgages, kids, difficult wives who wanted it all.

No, this way was far better, only it had taken him the misery of marriage to three wives before realising it.

He felt on top of the world. Could afford to call in on his mother. After all, they wouldn't always be there, these parents of his. Best to take advantage now—one never knew when one would need them.

Singing along to the radio, Graham turned off at the next junction and made his way to Cobbets Green. Glancing at the clock on his dashboard, he saw that it was half-past seven—what had happened to the afternoon? Smiling wickedly to himself, he thought: You know damn' well where it went.

His mother's car was in the drive. No sight of his father's. She would be pleased to see him. Women usually were.

He let himself in with his key and called out. She was probably in her study, she often worked there in the evenings.

'Mother! Mother—it's me, Graham.'

He heard her answer him before she appeared and looked over the banisters, coming swiftly down the stairs, her neatly turned ankles and well-shod little feet

129

tripping down as though there was no weight to carry.

'Hello, dear.' Janey was genuinely pleased to see him and lifted her face for his kiss.

'Well, this is nice. Have you eaten?' she asked.

'Yes, thanks. Well, I had a hefty lunch.'

'What are you doing down here?'

'On my way back from Sussex—thought I'd call in,' he said.

'That's nice of you, dear. Come along, I expect you could do with a drink.'

'Yes, thanks. I'll see to it. One for you?'

'No, thank you, dear. I've just had a glass of wine with my meal.'

'Where's Dad?'

'In Leeds, I think. Just an overnight stay. He rang me earlier to say he couldn't get back, it wasn't worth rushing.'

'No, of course not.' He wondered if she suspected that his father had a mistress—not that Graham himself knew for sure, but surely that contented temperament didn't come from living with his mother? Stood to reason. His father was a healthy, good-looking man—of course he was having a bit on the side. Graham didn't blame him, not at all.

'So what've you been up to?' He hitched

up his trousers and sank into the deepest, most comfortable chair.

'I've just been drafting a letter to Mr Mathieson.'

'Who's he?' Graham asked.

'The owner of the Butterfly Field,' Janey said patiently, as though everyone should know that.

'Oh, yes, I'm with you,' Graham said, although he was not.

His mother was always working on some project or other. He was used to it, had had a lifetime of living with it.

'I had a letter from him last week saying he had no intention of selling the field. But I feel—well, I know I can't give up as easily as that.'

'No, of course not,' Graham said, wondering what she wanted it for. But she'd tell him if he waited long enough.

'You see, it's so convenient—and really it would make no difference to him. He only keeps a couple of horses on it, or lets it out for grazing.'

'And you think you ...' he prompted.

'Well, it is the most convenient spot and the nicest to build the community centre—or rather a social hall for the benefit of the residents of Swansbridge. As a matter of fact, it wouldn't hurt him to donate it to us.'

'I see,' Graham said, although he didn't.

'Well, I wish you luck. You're about to do battle, are you?'

'No, not exactly, dear. Of course I shall use all the tact in the world, but I am determined to get that field, Graham. I shall be assertive, not aggressive.'

He could believe her.

By the time he left, she hadn't asked him one question about Julie or either of his two previous wives. Good, she was getting used to the idea, and now he was on his way home to Georgette—though God knew where she had got that name from. She was a dancer in a West End show, and had no objection to his sharing her flat. 'For as long as it suits me,' she said. 'Any problems and you're out.'

So far, so good. It would be mutual when it came to an end.

Janey thought about Graham, though, after he had gone. She had made up her mind not to ask any questions. That way, she wouldn't receive answers which she found hard to take. He was up to something—he wouldn't be without a woman for long.

She went back to composing her letter to Leopold Mathieson.

It was half-past nine when the telephone rang, and she thought it might just be John although it was unusual for him to ring her when he was away.

'Hello. Janey Utox-Smythe.'

There was rather a lot of noise on the line.

'I'm sorry—what? Could you speak up?'

'Minnie ... it's Minnie, Mummy—I'm at Heathrow.'

'Minnie!' she shrieked. It couldn't be, after all this time! Why hadn't the girl written to say she was coming home or sent John a fax?

'Can you get a taxi?' she shouted to be heard above the din.

'Yes, of course I will.' She sounded so young, such a faraway little voice. 'I just thought I'd better let you know I'm home.'

Janey sat back in her chair, unable to believe Minnie was coming home after all this time. Eighteen months she had been away. Her daughter—Minnie—her youngest. Her eyes almost filled with tears, but not quite.

More worries, more troubles. She hoped her daughter was all right—not pregnant or on drugs—but she had sounded reasonable enough. Just that small voice, like a child's.

She hurried into Minnie's room, where the bed was stripped of its bedclothes, the furniture covered with dust sheets, unused for eighteen months. What a nuisance! She would have to make up the bed, put on the heating in this room, make a bottle for the bed. She began running this way and that, and stopped when she realised that Minnie herself could help make up the bed.

Still, with all the fuss, there was an element of excitement too. Her daughter returning, after all this time. Oh, no, she thought, thank God it's dark. She won't be wearing a sari, will she?

It was half-past ten by the time the taxi arrived and deposited Minnie on the doorstep, along with several bundles—and, Janey noted with dismay, not a single decent travelling case among the lot.

She did, though, bite her lip, when this small, almost fragile figure stepped out of the taxi and called out: 'Mummy—have you any change?'

Back to square one, Janey thought. 'Of course, darling, here.' And went to get her purse.

She felt enormous as she put one arm around Minnie's thin shoulders.

It was difficult to see her daughter's face in the dark, but the small diamond at the side of her nose shone brilliantly in the moonlight.

Once inside, Janey closed the door, and surrounded by various bundles on the hall floor, put her arms around her daughter, genuinely relieved to see her. She was aware of some kind of scent. Incense? she wondered. Cocaine? Drugs of some sort? But she rejected the idea. No, it was just a foreign smell. The girl looked so ordinary—but quite worn out. Well, Janey told herself, she would be, travelling all the way from—wherever it was she had come.

'Where did you fly from?' she asked.

'Delhi,' Minnie said. 'It's only eight hours, but I'm exhausted.' She sounded tired, thought Janey, and so small, swathed in a long black dress and an embroidered waistcoat in bright colours, her black hair tied back with a ribbon. How could this young stranger bear any resemblance to the little girl of yesteryear in her short white dresses and little white sandals ...

'Come along in, darling,' she said. 'What would you like? Are you starving—some coffee?'

'No, thank you, Mummy. Tea, please.'

She was so pretty, Janey thought, seeing her now with her skin several shades darker than when she'd left, the long hair—it had been close-cropped when she'd gone—and those dark eyes, so unlike Graham's, more like John's.

It was almost like having a stranger in the house.

'Well,' she said brightly, putting on the kettle, 'your father will be delighted to see you.' Knowing he would at that. Minnie had always been his favourite. The girl

135

looked ready to drop.

'Sit down, darling,' said Janey. 'We can move all your stuff in the morning, Mrs Nelson will do it.'

'Is she still here?' Minnie asked. 'Where's Daddy?'

'Away, just for the night. He's in Leeds.'

'Oh,' Minnie said, her eyelids drooping.

'You look done in,' Janey said, a rush of motherly feeling coming to the fore. 'You must be absolutely whacked. How would it be if you went into the spare room and I'll bring you up a hot drink? We'll get your room ready tomorrow.'

'Thanks, Mummy,' Minnie said. 'I didn't sleep a wink on the plane.'

'Come on,' Janey said. 'Up you go. Would you like a bath?'

'No, thanks—just bed,' Minnie said, looking lost and bewildered.

Janey led the way upstairs. 'Now in you go, you'll be comfortable in that bed, and I'll bring you up a hot drink.'

'Thanks, Mummy,' her daughter said again, and Janey went back downstairs. She made hot milk instead of tea, and carried it up the stairs, but by the time she had got there, Minnie was stretched out on the bed, still in her clothes, fast asleep. Janey put the quilt over her, and tiptoed out of the room.

How could that be? she thought, going

downstairs. Two hours ago I didn't even know she was back in England, and now, at eleven o'clock, my daughter is home again and sleeping upstairs.

It was a strange feeling. They had never really seen eye to eye. But it was more a lack of understanding than anything else. Minnie had been away at boarding school for most of the time, and apart from holidays, when she and Graham had tended to go and stay in Devon with their grandparents, Janey hardly ever saw her. She was closer to Graham, she felt she understood him. But Minnie ... Christened Araminta, a name Janey had always admired, she had become Minnie a long time ago. John always said Araminta was too flowery.

She had travelled all over Europe when she was nineteen, and after a short spell at home had announced her desire to go to the Far East. India mainly. Of course, John had financed her. 'She's my only daughter,' he had said. 'If that's what she wants—'

But what did she want to do with her life? Janey wondered. Now she was home? It would be strange to have a daughter in the house again. Another woman, for that's what it meant. But she cheered herself up with the thought that one day Minnie would probably get married—or go off to live with someone. Wasn't that what they did these days?

Well, John would be pleased. It was too late to ring him now, but she would ring him first thing in the morning at the office.

She switched off the lights downstairs and locked all the doors. She was used to this. She always did it even when John was home. Passing Minnie's door, she half smiled. It was rather a nice feeling to know that she was safely under the family roof again. Always provided she was not at home too long. Young people needed space of their own. But it would be interesting to hear about her travels. They had received few cards from her, always supposing she had sent any. Sometimes it was months before they heard from her. There had been that time in—Burma, was it? Was it still called that? Whatever, Thailand, perhaps. There had been one occasion when she had grown a little concerned, but that was mainly because John worried about his daughter.

Then she had gone back to India.

Janey was on the phone to John at nine in the morning, having peeped inside the spare room to see Minnie just as she had left her. She closed the door softly after her. John was not in yet so she left a message. Thank goodness she had nothing pressing on this morning, just a council meeting which she would telephone and make her excuses from, something she hated doing. Janey was very conscientious.

A call from Mrs Nelson, apologising for not coming in until the afternoon if Lady Utox-Smythe didn't mind? She had to visit the dentist with her grandson because her daughter was working, as Lady Utox-Smythe well knew.

'No, that's all right,' Janey said. As long as she turned up sometime in the day.

Minnie put in an appearance around ten o'clock which surprised Janey, who'd thought she might sleep all day. She had heard the bath water going, and when Minnie finally appeared, fresh in a white wraparound skirt and flowered top, but minus the diamond in her nose, Janey felt she hardly knew her. For she had changed.

She looked older, Janey thought, as well she might, though it was only eighteen months she'd been gone, or was it twenty? She looked a mature young woman, no longer the girl who had left. She had always been the restless sort, itching to be moving from one thing to another. She would tease her hair and tap her foot, drum her fingers as though she was impatient to get on with things. What things, Janey never knew. But now there was a stillness about her. The lovely dark eyes seemed deeper set, there was a quiet strength about her. All in all, Janey felt she hardly knew her. This was not the girl who had left Swansbridge all those months ago.

'You look lovely, darling,' she said. For Minnie did. Different, but still lovely. Not pretty as a girl might be, but attractive. A young woman. She had become more rounded, had a bust where none had been visible before. She had been a girl, a little thing. Boyish, almost.

Janey poured the tea.

'Well, I'm dying to know all about the trip. Did you take many photographs?'

'Some,' Minnie said, and gave a smile, looking round her. 'It's nice to be home. I'm glad to be back.'

'That's good,' Janey said, gratified for some reason.

'I brought you some things—you'll see when I've unpacked. I didn't bring a lot—so many Indian things you can get here, and I know you're not that keen.'

'And how was India?' Janey asked. 'Are you still as much in love with it as ever?'

'Yes, it's a lifetime love affair I have with India,' Minnie said. 'But, before I go on, I have something to tell you.'

Here it comes, Janey thought, and her

heart sank. She's pregnant. Oh, my God, she hasn't got AIDS? And Minnie saw the colour drain away from her face.

'There's nothing to worry about,' she reassured her mother swiftly. 'Well, that is, unless you—'

'Just tell me,' Janey said through stiff lips.

Minnie took a deep breath. 'I have a baby,' she said. 'Mine. She's six months old.'

Janey sank back in her chair, all the strength kicked out of her.

When she spoke it was in a voice she didn't recognise. 'My God,' she said. 'You don't mean it?'

But Minnie just smiled. 'I do, Mummy. She's a darling and just six months old.'

'But where is she?' Janey asked.

'With her ayah at a hotel near Heathrow,' Minnie said.

'My God ... with an ayah! You mean, she's—'

'No, she is not Indian,' Minnie said. 'The ayah is, but not your grand-daughter.'

I am a grandmother, thought Janey. The shock is enough to kill me.

'I'd better tell you about it. I met him, her father—he's English, a student—I met him on the journey out. We travelled out together, and most of the time afterwards. All through Thailand, and Tibet, and back to India. He only left when he found I was pregnant. He was sorry, he said, but it wasn't in his scheme of things. I didn't tell him it wasn't in mine either, but I've no ill feelings and neither will you when you see your grand-daughter. She was born in a convent run by the Sisters of Mercy in Lahore.'

'Oh, Minnie,' wailed Janey. 'How could you? You're only just twenty-two and already saddled with a baby of six months. What will you do? How will you keep her?'

'I shall work,' Minnie said. 'That's why I've come home. And if you don't like the idea, I'll go off somewhere—I don't want to embarrass you with the neighbours.'

And going through it all on her own, Janey thought. 'The ayah? How can you afford one?'

'An English family loaned her to me—just for a couple of days until I'd told you and got settled in somewhere. They are staying in the hotel until I fetch the baby.'

'We must go at once,' Janey said, getting up and walking to the door.

'No hurry.' Minnie smiled. 'I've got until tomorrow—except that I can't wait to see her again. I'm really sorry to shock you, Mummy. I had no idea it was going to happen and I certainly didn't feel I could write to you and tell you. I thought the best thing would be, when I finally got home, to tell you then.'

Janey stood in the doorway. I suppose I should be glad that she has come home, she thought. We might have lost her, if she had been too scared to come home—and I'll have to worry about the neighbours and Swansbridge later. But what will John say? He'll be horrified, and *I* want to kill the young man, whoever he is.

'What happened to the father?' was all she said.

'He left me in Nepal,' Minnie said reasonably. 'I could see his point, it wasn't all his fault.'

'It certainly wasn't all *yours,'* her mother said tartly.

'No, but I felt I could cope better on my own—rather than be tied to a man who doesn't want to be tied down.'

So she has learned some lessons, Janey thought. My God, how will I explain this?

She sank down abruptly on the nearest chair.

Somehow she didn't care. Suddenly, it didn't matter. It was bad enough having Graham with two babies whom she never saw, and she never would have believed she cared so much about that. But this was her daughter. Little Minnie. The small girl in white at her birthday parties, with her fat

143

tum and little fat legs, smiling all over her pretty face.

'Come on, let's go,' said Janey.

'Where are we going?'

'To Heathrow, to pick up my grand-daughter. In a hotel indeed, with an Indian amah or whatever she is. What would your father say?'

Janey waited in the hotel lounge while Minnie telephoned from reception. She disappeared into the lift and was gone for ten minutes. Then out of the lift she came holding the baby, accompanied by an Indian ayah, and Janey thought her heart would burst out of her chest.

She saw Minnie thank the nurse and say goodbye before the ayah disappeared back into the lift and Minnie walked over to Janey, holding the baby out to her like a present.

'Here you are, Mummy, your grand-daughter,' she said. 'India Utox-Smythe.' And Janey took her, holding her close, looking down into very blue eyes and a tuft of fair hair, and felt an emotion she had never felt with either of her own two children.

'Mummy—' Minnie began.

'What?' Janey turned tear-filled eyes to her daughter.

'You're a late developer,' she said.

144

Chapter Nine

It was a glorious July morning as Sally stepped outside into the garden and felt the warmth of the sun on her back. There was a continuous humming of bees, and the scent of the roses and lavender bushes fringing the path was almost overpowering. But audible over and above everything else was the whine of a machine saw, the occasional clang of heavy hammers and the devastating sound of iron pounding on unrelenting concrete. Sally frowned and wondered how long this would last. At least three months, Pauline Carpenter had said before she left, when she'd called round to say farewell.

'Off now, Sally,' she said. 'And there's no need for you to worry about a thing—if you hear any strange noises and that—because our foreman will be living on site.'

'Really?' Sally said.

'Bert Golding has worked for us before and is very reliable. He'll oversee the workmen and keep an eye on the place, and he'll sleep on the premises so you've nothing to worry about.'

145

She'd looked very pleased with this statement.

'Oh—so there's nothing you'd like me to do? Keep a look out for—'

'Not a thing, love. We're leaving the whole project in Bert's capable hands. And if you want anything doing yourself—'

'Oh, I wouldn't think so,' Sally hastily assured her. 'Still it's nice to know someone will be there.'

'Ron will be back quite a bit, just to see everything is OK.'

'Right,' Sally had said.

'Not me, though. I'm not coming back into it until it's all finished, believe me!'

'Well, have a good time. Er—are you all going?'

'Yes, me and Mum and Sandra. You'll see, when she gets back, she'll be as brown as a berry.'

Sally smiled, and watched the vision in white walking down her drive.

Pauline turned and waved. 'Cheerio, then,' she called out as Sally waved back.

Now, leaving the shrub roses, she walked towards the top of the garden where the ground undulated into a hill, the other side of which led down to the Butterfly Field. She saw William's neat rows of lettuces and carrots, the well-trained runner beans and tomato plants. There was no doubt that this new job filled a long-felt gulf in

146

her son's heart. He loved it, and when he wasn't with Suzie, spent all his time in the garden, hoeing the peas and beans, as happy as a sandboy. Well, if that was what he wanted to do, so be it.

Little could be seen of the Carpenters' land from here, for it was land rather than a garden, but already she noticed that the tall beech tree had gone—and wondered about the oak which served as a barrier between the two houses. It would depend on where they sited the swimming pool, she supposed, and the tennis court, and they were sure to have to get permission to take down the oak.

The noise was louder up here, and she could hear more than one transistor radio blaring away, and worst of all a pneumatic drill breaking up the terrace, she wouldn't wonder for the proposed swimming pool. And there was still the conservatory and tennis court ...

She sighed and silently walked back down the garden. Rather Pauline than her. She couldn't imagine they would get it all done in three months, but Pauline said you could do anything if you greased enough palms and she should know. She'd had lots of experience, apparently.

Sally bent down and picked a couple of weeds from William's immaculate vegetable rows, and taking the secateurs from her pocket, cut a few dead heads from the roses, bending low to absorb the scent of the old Bourbon rose Madame Isaac Perreira which was at its best on a summer evening. She loved these old shrub roses, which were among her favourites, lots of them having such a history. Souvenir de la Malmaison had first been grown in St Petersburg and named after a visit to Malmaison by the Grand Duke of Russia; Old Blush China had been so named after being crossed with the first four original roses brought from China. Oh, yes, there was lots of history in a garden. The pinks, for instance, clumps of scented white ones, were Mrs Sinkins. Who would have thought they were named by the master of the workhouse in Slough after his wife who was the matron?

She picked a small spray from the bush roses, kicking some stones from the lawn on to the border where a busy blackbird was foraging for food. Tom got so cross when stones hit the mower ...

The shrill sound of the telephone disturbed her thoughts and she hurried indoors to answer it.

'Sally Sheffield.'

'Oh, it's me, dear—Janey,' said a familiar voice. 'I just wondered if you were at home this morning? I thought I'd have a word.'

'Yes, of course,' Sally said. 'Come when

you like, I'm not doing anything.'

It was quiet now, although probably not in the village of Cobbets Green where the children would have broken up from school and harassed young mothers would be trying to get used to the idea of the long holidays and making adjustments.

There were no women's club meetings in July and August, most people going away, but there were one or two fêtes, and Sally guessed Janey wanted to talk about those.

After parking on Sally's drive, Janey made her way up to the front door, well-dressed as ever even on a summer's day in navy blue with touches of white. She always had a tailored look. Sally couldn't imagine her in trousers or casual wear.

She looked flushed now, perhaps from the heat, and her eyes were unnaturally bright.

'Come in, do. It's warm, isn't it?' Sally said, closing the front door after her. 'How about a cool drink in the garden?'

'What a lovely idea,' Janey said, a little breathlessly, and Sally realised that she was rather het up—had something on her mind.

She led the way through and out on to the lawn beyond the terrace where dappled shade was provided by the old plum tree.

'Oh, this is lovely!' Janey said, sinking

into a brightly cushioned garden chair and putting her legs up on the stool provided.

'Won't be a moment,' Sally said, and Janey took a deep breath. This was going to be difficult, but it had to be done. There must be no beating about the bush. She smiled as Sally returned with a tray of iced drinks and little sugar biscuits.

'No, nothing to eat, dear,' Janey said, 'but the drink—ah, that's lovely.'

Sally settled herself. 'I hear Minnie's home?' she said. 'She phoned Tessa. You must be pleased, Janey. It's ages since she went away, and don't tell me you didn't have a few anxious moments.'

'Yes, well,' Janey said hurriedly, putting her glass down and looking straight at Sally. 'I've something to tell you about that and there's no easy way of putting it.'

Sally made no answer, guessing Janey wanted to take her time.

The words came out in rush. 'Minnie has brought home a baby—hers. She's six months old.'

'Oh!' And Sally gave herself a moment for the shock to sink in, knowing how much it must have cost Janey to tell her.

'But that's wonderful, Janey,' she said finally. For part of her did think so. The other half wondered how her friend would cope with the situation.

'Well—' Janey began. 'It's the old story.

She met a boy on the way out to India, they travelled around together, God knows where—and once Minnie was pregnant, he didn't want to know and left her. She seems to have accepted that quite philosophically. She made her way back to Lahore and had the baby in a convent run by the Sisters of Mercy there. And, well, that's that.'

She sat back, obviously relieved she had got the worst part over.

'Janey, my dear.' And suddenly Sally's eyes filled with tears. What a shock for a mother with a young daughter, whoever she was, whatever the circumstances—it took a bit of admitting. And Minnie herself, how did she feel?

'Want to talk about it?' she asked gently.

'Yes,' Janey sighed. 'And of course everyone will have to know sooner or later.'

'How did John take it?'

'Strangely enough, considering how fond he is of his daughter, he's livid with her, furious with the boy, can't look at the baby. I must say, I feel he'll need considerable time before he can adapt to the situation. He adores Minnie, you know. I thought he'd be so pleased to see her back home.'

'Isn't it the age-old thing of a father hating to think of his daughter with any other man than himself? In the normal way when a girl meets a man, the father has to accept it. But in this case you have a girl who, as he sees it, was taken advantage of by a bad lot who deserted her.'

'Then you'd think he wouldn't blame her. It's as if he thinks, if she was old enough to go to India on her own, then she should have known how to take care of herself. He doesn't like the carelessness of it, that's my opinion.'

'Poor Minnie.'

'You say that, but honestly she's absolutely delighted by it all. Now that we know, that seems to be that as far as she's concerned.'

'What is she going to do?'

'Says she'll stay with us, if we will have her. Otherwise she will move out and make some arrangements for the baby—but obviously she really doesn't want that. Says she will find something to do if someone can be found to look after the baby. Later on, of course.'

'And you wouldn't see her doing that either, would you?'

'No, of course not. The thing is, Sally, the baby's a joy. Minnie's called her India, isn't that wonderful?' And Janey beamed.

'And appropriate. But, yes, it's a pretty name. Who is she like?'

'Well, not like Minnie. She's very fair,

with blue eyes. A real little darling. And Minnie, would you believe, is the perfect mother. It's as if she has been waiting all this time to find her niche in life, which seems to be motherhood.'

'Well, it happens.' And Sally wondered how Janey really felt about it.

'As for me, I have to say I wish the circumstances had been different but I adore her—I never felt like this with my own two children.'

'I can't wait to see her!'

'My dear, any time you'd like to call round, Minnie will be glad to see you.'

'And won't Tessa be surprised!' Sally said.

'Yes, well, everyone will have to know—you can't keep a baby hidden for long, especially as she's going to live with us, at least for the time being. I'm quite happy with the arrangement. My biggest problem seems to be getting John to accept the situation. I thought I'd call on Becky—she's such a tower of strength where babies and young mothers are concerned, and she might come up with some ideas. After that, the news will have to seep out of its own accord. Oddly enough, after the first shock, I find I can live with it. Just one look at that darling baby and I don't really give a fig for other people's opinions.'

'Good for you,' Sally said. 'After all,

it's your own business—what's it got to do with anyone else?'

'But that's just it. "Other people" can make life difficult. Well, I'm off. It was so nice to talk to you—I knew you'd understand.'

Sally closed the door after her, and going back into the garden, sank into her chair. Well, who would have thought it? Young Minnie Utox-Smythe! But how awful for Janey and John. Yet, all in all, at least she didn't come back ill or on drugs—there was a lot to be thankful for, and they weren't lacking money so it would be no hardship. Minnie would suffer most, but at least today such things were not the disgrace they used to be when Sally was a girl. Times had changed. Was that a good or bad thing? Still, having a baby in such circumstances was certainly not the best way to bring a new life into the world. Bringing it up on her own, the hardship, whatever the background—no, she wouldn't wish it on her own daughter. The loneliness, too, of not having a father to share in the joys as well as the problems.

Then the overpowering whine of a woodsaw hit the air, and hastily Sally collected up the tray and went indoors. What a nuisance this building work was going to be, especially on a fine summer's day! It was such a peaceful quiet area, they were unused to noise except for birdsong and the occasional lopping of trees or whine of a lawn mower.

She wouldn't do any gardening today— far better go into Cobbets Green and do a big shop. Not much point in cleaning the house with Mrs Halliday coming in the morning, and Sally wondered how she was getting on with her visitor—poor Mandy. Last week Mrs Halliday had seemed really down. The little girl had broken up from school, apparently, and although she and Mrs Halliday's boys got on well, it did make extra work. And it seemed that Mandy had quite settled in now, which made it very difficult when Mr Halliday was on nights.

'One week on, one week off,' she'd explained.

'But what will Mandy do?' Sally asked, concerned for Mrs Halliday who was such a hard-working woman.

'Well, I left her to go round to the council offices to see if they could help. I did tell her, Mrs Sheffield, I said to her, "It's only temp'ry, staying with me." 'Course she knows that—still, I couldn't put her out.'

What a problem! Sally already disliked the sound of pretty Mandy. She seemed to Sally the sort of person who would

155

latch on to anyone as kind-hearted as Mrs Halliday.

Well, there would be some news for Tessa this evening, and Sally could visualise her wide-eyed look of surprise.

A baby!

People in Swansbridge lived fairly quiet lives. It was an event when something like an illegitimate baby arrived on the scene.

Poor little thing, Sally thought. I shouldn't think of her like that. She's Minnie's baby, and that's all there is to it.

In the event, when Tessa arrived home it was obvious that she was not in the best of moods.

Her pretty face wore a scowl, and there was something about the belligerent way she entered the kitchen that told Sally there was something wrong.

'Everything all right?' she asked as Tessa flopped into a chair. She looked hot and tired, it had been a warm day, and she kicked off her shoes.

'Phew!'

'Was it hot on the train?' Sally asked. 'Go up and shower and come down for a cool drink. We'll have it in the garden. At least the noise has stopped, I suppose they've clocked off.'

'They were at it before I left this morning,' Tessa grumbled.

156

'Still, it won't worry you too much—it's mostly while you're at work. Anyway—I've something to tell you.'

Tessa's eyebrows were drawn together in a frown.

'What?'

'It can wait.'

But Tessa glowered, staring hard out of the window although it was obvious she wasn't seeing anything.

'You'll never believe it,' she said eventually. 'That bitch of a Contessa has cancelled my sale.'

'Oh, no!' Sally cried, knowing how important this was to Tessa.

'Just like that. Out of the blue. She's no longer interested in selling—has changed her mind.'

'Oh, dear. But what about the Goyas?' Sally asked.

'Oh, they'll be all right, it seems. Hugo went over last weekend and came back on Monday morning like a dog with two tails.'

'Oh, so it's just the textiles and ceramics?'

'Yes.' Tessa was obviously livid. 'I mean, I had done a lot of work on the cataloguing already—I can't think why she told us to start in the first place. I thought she was a bit offhand at the time ... Oh, I'm fed up! I'm fed up with MacBane's too.'

And fed up with Hugo, Sally thought. Poor Tessa. Unrequited love was very hard to deal with.

'Well, go up and shower. And don't be long.'

There was lemonade waiting for her when she came down. She looked cooler now, and more rational.

'Minnie's mother came round this morning.'

'Oh,' Tessa said in a non-committal way.

'Minnie's home.'

'I know—she phoned me.'

'But what you don't know is that she has come home with a baby—hers.'

'What!' Tessa shrieked, collapsing into her chair with shock. 'Good Lord. Whatever did dear Janey say to that?'

'She's taken it pretty well, really.' And Sally told Tessa all she knew.

'Oh, poor Minnie—still, what a surprise. I would have said there was a girl who knew how to look after herself.'

'Well, she didn't, did she? Janey says the baby is lovely: fair-haired, blue-eyes ...'

'Like the father then?' Tessa said mischievously.

'Probably.'

'What will she do?'

'Janey says she can stay there. I have

to say, she seems quite reconciled to the idea—but Minnie's father is taking rather a dim view of it.'

'You can't blame him,' Tessa said. 'Well, what a turn up for the book, as William would say. Could I go round to see her, do you think?'

'Janey said any time. Perhaps you could ring first, though. She's called the baby India.'

'She would!' Tessa said. 'Although I do like the name—sounds romantic.'

'Perhaps you could pop round this evening? Take some flowers from the garden—you can buy something for the baby later.'

'Good idea,' Tessa said, work and Hugo forgotten, going to telephone and coming back quite excited.

'I'm going round to see her after dinner,' she said. 'She sounds marvellous—and happy to be home.'

'That's good then,' Sally said, pleased that Tessa had got the black dog off her back.

After dinner, when Tessa had gone with a posy of sweet-scented flowers from the garden, Sally told Tom about Minnie's baby.

'God, I can't think of anything worse—for your daughter to arrive home with an illegitimate child!'

'We mustn't use that word these days,' Sally remonstrated with him.

'Well, it is, though,' he said. 'Whether you like it or not. Poor old John.'

'He's not best pleased, apparently.'

'Well, neither would I be,' Tom said. 'I mean, get your children off hand, indulge them in a trip to India and they come back with a baby—not exactly in the order of things, is it? While one can only feel sympathy for the girl, it's hard luck on Janey and John.'

'I know.'

'And it will make a big difference to them—after all, they haven't had much luck with the son, have they? What's his name?'

'Graham.'

'Yes. Oh, well, rather them than me— still, poor kid, I feel sorry for her. She had some pluck to come home and face them, that took a bit of doing.'

'Well, I think she knew it was the best thing to do from her point of view. Nothing like loving parents, is there?'

'No. Did the local paper come today?' he asked suddenly.

'Yes, it's over there, I haven't had time to look at it yet.'

Tom sat browsing through the pages for a few minutes until he came to something which obviously caught his attention.

'My God!' he said. 'I say, Sally, look at this!'

She went over and stood behind him, reading over his shoulder.

'Look—in the column under "Planning Applications".' She saw where he was pointing.

There was a long reference number, followed by the words 'P.C. and R.C. Developments, The Mount, Swansbridge. Outline planning application to build six detached houses with garages in Cobbets Lane on land known as the Butterfly Field, part of Mathieson's Farm ...'

Sally read it again, and stood open-mouthed. 'What does it mean, Tom?'

'It means, darling, that our neighbours have applied for planning permission to develop the Butterfly Field,' he said, looking grim.

'But they can't do that, can they?'

'Oh, yes, they can!'

'But they don't own it! It's not theirs.'

'No matter—anyone can put in a planning application for anyone's land. I'm not going to say they would get it, but it's worth a try and will sit on the records. Well, I'll be damned!'

'P.C. and R.C.—Pauline Carpenter and Ronald Carpenter,' Sally said. 'I can't believe it!'

'Well, I knew he was a developer, but

this is going a bit far. Not that he'll get it, but that's not the point.'

'What are you going to do?' Sally asked. It still had not quite sunk in.

'Follow it up,' Tom said grimly.

'But they're away,' Sally said.

'How convenient. Makes no difference,' he said. 'If they think Swansbridge is going to take that lying down, they're very much mistaken.'

'Oh, dear.' Sally bit her lip. She had liked Pauline Carpenter.

'And I am still concerned about the work they're doing next door,' he said thoughtfully. 'I wonder if the fact that it's a listed property has been overlooked ... though it hardly seems likely.'

He was like a dog with a bone, Sally thought. He'd worry away at it until he was satisfied.

Chapter Ten

On this Saturday morning, Tessa was on her way to see Minnie and her baby. The night before, little India had been fast asleep in her cot, and Minnie had suggested that Tessa might like to see her awake.

162

'Come round in the morning,' she said. 'We shall have the place to ourselves then. Mother and Dad are going up to town for the day.'

Tessa had thought it a great idea, calling on her way to buy a little present for baby India. She had no idea what babies wore, was quite out of touch, but looked forward to browsing in the Tiny Tots shop in Cobbets Green. She had never been in there before.

William and Suzie had gone up to see Grandma Pargeter for the day, by train.

'It's time you had some driving lessons,' his father had said, but William had never shown any enthusiasm. He loved his old bicycle, whereas Tessa had pressurised her parents to be allowed to take driving lessons as soon as she was able. Now, in Sally's car, she stopped in the village and shopped for baby India.

She came out of the shop with a pretty little white dress, with lots of embroidery and smocking. It had been quite expensive but Tessa was thrilled with her buy.

By daylight, Minnie looked changed. Older—older perhaps than her years, for she and Tessa were about the same age. But she had softened, Tessa thought. There had been something brittle about the old Minnie, she used to be impatient, always wanting to be on the move, now she was more gentle, quieter.

Tessa found herself liking her more.

'It is lovely to see you Tess,' she said, closing the door. 'We're in the garden. Isn't it a super day?'

'Reminds you of India, this weather, I suppose?' Tessa followed her out into the garden where India lay in her pram in the shade.

'No, not really. For one thing there isn't the humidity, and there's always something fresh about English weather even when it's hot. Sit down—would you rather have a cold drink or coffee?'

'Cold drink, please,' Tessa said. 'May I peep at her?'

'Yes, she's awake. I fed her at ten, and she's lying there looking up into the trees—she's probably never seen anything really green before. She loves to see the leaves moving.'

Tessa tiptoed over to the pram, which was an old-fashioned model, where two firm little legs were kicking away, and little fists were punching the air, and at the sight of Tessa, India broke into a beaming smile.

'Isn't that a tooth coming?' Tessa said to Minnie when she reappeared with the tray.

'Yes, at the bottom, you can just see where it has broken the skin. Aren't you a clever girl?' And Minnie cooed to her baby daughter.

'What a lovely old pram!' Tessa said.

'I know, it was mine.' Minnie laughed. 'Mummy got it out of the attic and Mrs Nelson cleaned it up—isn't it super? I can't wait to push it out but I'll have to hang on a bit.'

'I brought her a pressie,' Tessa said, pleased now that she could see she had bought the right size. She could just imagine the little girl wearing it.

'Oh, Tessa, how lovely!' Minnie cried, taking it out of its flowery wrapping and putting it against the baby. 'Oh, you are sweet, it's her first real present.' And she turned shining dark eyes to Tessa.

Who would have believed it? she thought. Minnie and motherhood.

'So,' she said, 'tell me about India, or is that a closed book?'

'Not at all,' Minnie said, settling herself. 'Well, to Mother and Daddy perhaps.' And they both laughed.

'What was he like? Her father?'

'Tim? Nice,' she said, taking a sip of her drink through a straw. 'Good-looking, fair, tall, archaeology student, so of course he was able to take me to places I might never have seen—all over India and Tibet. You name it, I've done it.'

She was thoughtful for a minute.

'I think most young people tend to pair up mainly because, well, it's more fun that way. Someone else with you while you're a long way from home. And it was great fun. Well, most of the time. There were some bad moments—dangerous moments—and I'd never tell my parents about those. But Tim, well, I suppose we were in love, or thought we were. When I first suspected I might be pregnant, I said nothing, you know, thinking perhaps the different climate, something like that. But really, deep down, I was sure. Anyway, I was almost three months when I told him and, by golly, he almost ran off there and then! To say I was shocked is putting it mildly. He was horrified, said he felt guilty. But I said, well, it's done now. Then, the next day, he said he'd have to go, couldn't face it felt like a dog, but there you were. And so, there I was.'

'Oh, Minnie, how awful! You must have felt suicidal, I should think.'

'No, I was surprised at myself. I somehow accepted it. There seemed to be a certain inevitability about it. There is, you know, in India. You learn to accept. So I packed up my things. I knew there was a convent in Lahore I could go to and I stayed there. I worked for a while in the convent, and when my time came, well, here she is.'

And Minnie bent over and kissed her baby. 'I wouldn't change anything,' she said.

'You're very brave,' Tessa told her. 'I should have died.'

'No, you wouldn't,' Minnie said. 'Not when you knew you had a new little life inside you. It somehow gets to you. Well, it did to me, anyway.'

'And you never saw Tim again?'

'No, I didn't want to. I wondered at first what he would say if he knew he had a baby daughter, but after a week or so that wore off. I was so busy looking after her. The sisters showed me what to do—they were wonderful. I almost wanted to stay there but I couldn't. Besides, I had to get home. The worst thing was having to tell my parents.'

'How long were you in India?'

'Twenty months altogether.'

'Do you suppose you would have wanted to come home if you—'

'If I hadn't got into trouble?' Minnie grinned. 'I don't know. I've often asked myself, but of course there's a limit to how long you can stay in a country like India, unless you marry an Indian, which isn't very likely. Not many girls do. They're even more against mixed marriages there than we are.'

She poured out some fresh orange juice from a jug and topped up Tessa's drink.

'What about you?' she asked, glancing down at Tessa's hand. 'No engagement, nothing like that? You're still living at home. Mummy said you have a fantastic job.'

'Yes, I have. I've been lucky, I suppose, doing what I want to do.'

'Where is it?'

'In town. At MacBane's, the fine arts people,' Tessa told her.

'Oh, very swish,' Minnie said. 'Antiques, that sort of thing?'

'I'm primarily interested in textiles, early artefacts, rugs and carpets.'

'Good Lord! But you always were very artistic. You used to paint, I seem to remember.'

'I dabbled but I wasn't good enough to make a career of it, but I love what I'm doing now, and I get the chance to travel.'

'Well, that's good.' Minnie sat back in her chair, very relaxed. 'But boyfriends—not? Someone special?' And she saw the slight flush which stained Tessa's cheeks.

'Oh, so there is someone?' she teased.

'Not really. I have to admit I have a soft spot for one of the staff there—he's an expert on oil paintings, as a matter of fact.'

Minnie waited.

'I've just been with him to Spain for a couple of days. He was to look at a couple of Goyas.'

'What—real ones?'

'Of course,' Tessa said, 'and I was looking at some textiles. Wonderful stuff, you should have seen the colours. Old tapestries, embroideries, super oil jars and other artefacts. Some of the pottery was a thousand years old.'

'Well, that was interesting,' Minnie said, thinking she had obviously been on a trip with her boyfriend, so there was someone.

'But,' Tessa sighed, 'unfortunately the Contessa ...'

Minnie whistled. 'Contessa, eh? Was she the owner? What was she like?'

'Simply gorgeous,' Tessa said honestly, 'and I think Hugo—that's his name—was bowled over by her. In any event, it doesn't matter now. She's cancelled the sale of all the things I had been looking at.'

'Oh, how disappointing!'

'But the sale of the Goyas will go on. Hugo has gone over again this weekend.'

Minnie felt a pang of sympathy for her friend. It was obvious that she was very fond of this man. Life had its disappointing moments for everybody. She glanced across at the baby and nudged Tessa. 'Look, she's asleep,' she said, and Tessa glanced across at the flushed little face, the golden eyelashes like twin fans, the little rosebud mouth.

'How lucky you are!' she said.

'Yes, I suppose so. Despite all the difficulties, I'm home now and I've made my peace. Mummy has been a brick. Daddy well, he's taken it very badly, which has shaken me a bit. Still, he'll come round.'

'You were always closer to him than your mother, weren't you?' Tessa observed.

'Yes, that's the odd thing, although perhaps that's why. Still, things have a way of sorting themselves out.'

'What will you do—stay here?'

'At the moment it's great. I'm enjoying myself with nothing to do but look after the baby. But I'm well aware that it can't go on like this. I owe them something, and the last thing they really want at their age is a daughter at home with a baby and no father in sight.'

'What about Graham? Has he seen her yet?'

Minnie pulled a face. 'Not yet. Poor Mummy, she hasn't had much luck with her offspring, has she? Do you realise Graham got married and separated again during the time I was away?'

'What would you do if Tim suddenly turned up?' Tessa asked.

'That's not likely,' Minnie laughed.

'Well, he presumably knows where you live—it's possible he may one day turn up and want to see his daughter.'

'Over my dead body,' Minnie said grimly. 'No, that's a closed book now.'

How matter-of-fact she was, so practical —and she had always been a bit of a nut case before, Tessa thought, as she got into the car and drove home. She wished she didn't keep wondering what Hugo was doing. She imagined an intimate candlelit dinner with the Contessa in that beautiful house in Madrid. It was all so romantic, no wonder he had fallen for her. And what of the Contessa herself? Was she married, divorced, had she children? Tessa really knew nothing about her.

She almost wished she had taken Alistair up on his invitation to have dinner with him this evening. She hated weekends when there was nothing doing. Or she could have gone up with William to see Granny Pargeter and taken the car. But she'd so wanted to see Minnie and her baby.

Minnie relaxed with her eyes closed. Poor old Tessa. But why did she feel sorry

171

for her? Her whole life was in front of her. She obviously had a thing about this Hugo chap, who somehow didn't sound quite right for her. Not that Minnie knew anything about it. She opened her eyes and glanced across at the pram where a beautiful butterfly hovered, gently waving it away with her hand.

There had been butterflies in India— huge, colourful things, like small birds. What an amazing country it was, despite the heat and dirt and the poverty and the children, often maimed, who crowded round the buses, begging. The small carts filled to overflowing with people; the trains, where people were so tightly packed you wondered how they could breathe; the peacocks on a lawn, the painted elephants, and the awful sight of the dancing bears, mercifully being stamped out now as people recognised the cruelty of such a thing. The sight of a whole family clinging precariously to a three-wheeled tricycle; lorries filled with workmen who spilled out of every window. And the nights ... those she would never forget. They were indelibly stamped on her memory. Not just the sights but the feel of India, the warmth; when the stars hung so low in the sky you felt you could touch them; when whole little shanty towns came to life, with hundreds of flares and the pungent smell of cooking oil.

She stood up and stretched and began to walk across the lawn which was beautifully cut, for Roddis the gardener had been with the family for some ten years and was very proud of this garden. The shrub roses were out, and borders of delphiniums and lilies—and she thought of the gardens of India where almost everything was grown in pots so that plants could be moved at will. Oh, there was nothing like an English garden.

She turned at a sound, it was probably the side gate, and wondered idly who it might be. She had not been home long enough to realise that in England these days one must be alert to sounds—that it was not impossible for strangers to walk into back gardens, and that there might be danger. Such a thought was the furthest from her mind.

The gate clicked shut, and glancing down the path she saw a tall man, young and well-dressed in sports clothes. He was walking straight towards her, carrying a folded newspaper.

'Hello,' she said, smiling at him. 'Can I help you?'

Close to, she saw that he was dark and handsome but scowling, a lock of hair falling over his eyes, his eyebrows drawn together, dark eyes fixed on hers accusingly.

'Is this the Utox-Smythe residence?' he asked, somewhat pompously.

'Yes, it is,' Minnie began.

'I rang the bell, but there was no reply.'

'No, there wouldn't be,' Minnie said. 'There's no one at home except me.'

'Are you Lady Utox-Smythe?' he asked coldly, glancing towards the baby in its pram.

'No, I am Miss Utox-Smythe. I expect it's my mother you want to see.'

He drew from his inner pocket a long white envelope and extracted a letter from inside.

'Lady Utox-Smythe,' he said. 'She lives here?'

By now, Minnie was getting a bit annoyed with him.

'Yes,' she said patiently, 'when she's at home.'

What an extraordinary young man. He looked at her so furiously.

'Then perhaps you—or she—can explain this?' And he thrust the letter under her nose.

'Excuse me,' Minnie said, coldly, 'but who are you?'

'I am David Mathieson.'

The name meant nothing to Minnie.

'And what right have you to come barging into private property without so much—'

'I think I have every right,' he said. 'As much right as your mother has to ask for permission to build on my—I should say my uncle's—land.'

'And who are you, and who is your uncle?' Minnie asked.

'My uncle is Leopold Mathieson, who farms at Hassington.'

'Who?'

'He is the owner of the Butterfly Field, and I think you will understand from this letter sent by your mother to him about selling it for, she says here,' and his lip curled, "a local community centre", and I quote.'

Minnie took the letter from him, and scanned it before handing it back.

'What's your problem?' she asked, the light of battle in her eyes.

'My problem—*our* problem, Miss Utox-Smythe—is the recent application for development of the Butterfly Field as a housing project.'

'And what's that to do with us?' Minnie said, her curiosity roused.

He said nothing but opened the news-paper and pointed to the list of planning applications.

She read it through, then folded it and

handed it back to him quite brusquely.

'There you are then,' she said. 'This has nothing to do with us. If you read the name you will see that it says P.C. and R.C. Developments of The Mount, which is—'

'I know where it is, I have already been there,' he said coldly. 'The only people present were builders, and I daresay developers. The house is empty, the owners away. The people who are doing the work of course know nothing about the request to build on Butterfly Field—but I daresay your mother does,' he finished angrily.

Minnie stared back at him and folded her arms.

'You really are a very rude young man,' she said looking at him with dislike. 'How dare you come here and—'

'And how dare you and your family apply to develop my uncle's field? It's disgusting—nothing whatever to do with you.'

Minnie could make neither head nor tail of anything he said, but she was prepared to stand her ground.

'I suggest you get off our property. You are trespassing,' she said coolly.

'Perhaps you will tell your mother I called? I shall certainly be coming back. Will she be home this evening?'

'I have no idea,' Minnie said coldly, 'but

I can assure you she will not welcome a visit from you on a Saturday evening—nor at any time, I shouldn't wonder,' she added quietly.

They stared at each other for what seemed like ages.

'I can tell you, we are disgusted as a family,' he said, fine nostrils flaring and eyes blazing. 'And of course, it will not rest here.' He raised his voice, causing little India to stir in her sleep and open her eyes, dropping her lip and starting to cry.

'Now see what you've done!' Minnie cried. 'Go away!'

She picked up the baby and hugged her, and India turned bright blue eyes to the visitor and stopped crying.

'Is that yours?' he asked.

'"That" is my daughter,' she said coldly.

'I see,' he said coolly. 'Goodbye, Miss Utox-Smythe,' stressing the 'Miss'. And he walked briskly towards the gate. 'I shall be back, never fear.'

Minnie followed him and banged the side gate shut.

'Oh!' she cried with controlled fury. 'Oh, India, my darling, wasn't he horrid?'

But India beamed back at her. She loved the click of the garden gate.

What had her mother done now? thought Minnie.

Chapter Eleven

Minnie was in bed long before her parents arrived home, and was already up and feeding India before Janey came down to breakfast the next day, John having gone off for an early-morning game of golf.

'You were late last night,' said Minnie almost accusingly, for she had been troubled by dreams of an angry young man who shouted at her, while baby India suddenly had dark curly hair which fell over her blue eyes.

Janey was putting the coffee on.

'Oh, darling, did you mind? We went to a show, as we were in town and Daddy had a couple of tickets. It was excellent, a new play by—'

Minnie felt mean.

'Oh, Mummy, I didn't mean to sound cross, but—'

'Everything all right?' Janey asked anxiously. 'Is it India?'

Minnie smiled. 'She's fine. It's just that a young man called David Mathieson called by.'

Janey turned to her with shining eyes.

'Oh, really, did he? Young, you say? But—'

'Apparently he's the nephew of the man you wrote to about the Butterfly Field.'

'How kind of him to call!' Her mother beamed. 'What did he say?' She could hardly curb her impatience.

'Well, he was very angry.'

'Angry? Why?'

'Well, apparently ...' And Minnie told her mother the story of the application for development of the Butterfly Field.

Janey's frown drew deeper by the second. 'I don't understand what you mean. I wrote asking to buy the land for a community centre.'

'Yes, Mummy, but someone has put in an application for a housing development on that field.'

'A what?' Janey sat down abruptly. 'How can they do that? It belongs to the Mathiesons.'

Minnie shrugged. 'I've no idea, but there it was in black and white. Don't you get the local paper?'

'We do, but I don't suppose we still have it. It came out on Tuesday.'

'I should have thought you of all people would have looked at the planning applications.'

'Well, we usually know what's going on. Still, let me see if it's in the cupboard.'

179

She disappeared and came back with the local newspaper, turning the pages hurriedly until she came to the right one, when her face flushed angrily.

'I don't believe it!' she cried. 'There must be some mistake.'

'Well, he didn't seem to think so.' Minnie came over and made the coffee. 'Such a disagreeable young man, David Mathieson, nephew of—'

'Leopold Mathieson.' Her mother was thoughtful. 'It says here. "P.C and R.C. Developments, The Mount". But that's where the—'

'He'd been there, apparently, and found the house empty except for the builders.'

'My God! P.C. and R.C. Developments —Pauline and Ron Carpenter.' And Janey hurried out of the room to the telephone in the hall. 'I must ring Sally.'

Minnie followed her out, going into the garden to see little India in her pram. She lay there awake, looking up at the trees, giving a toothless grin at her mother and kicking even more vigorously at the sight of her.

'Oh, poppet, beautiful darling,' Minnie cooed. It was lovely to get back to the peace of her own little world. She just wished she could get that young man out of her mind. What a cheek! Who did he think he was?

Presently Janey followed her out into the garden and subsided into a cane chair. She was breathing heavily, and Minnie could see she was upset.

'Mummy, nothing is that important,' she said, trying to console her.

'You have no idea,' Janey said grimly. 'You cannot believe people would do such a thing.' And she sat quietly until she recovered her composure.

'Who lives in The Mount then?' Minnie asked curiously. 'Was it sold?'

'Indeed it was,' Janey said. 'To a very wealthy couple. Not exactly ... well, I don't wish to be unkind, but who turned out to be property developers. And I must say, I am not surprised! She looked exactly the sort of person who—'

'Who's she?' Minnie asked, becoming interested against her will and better judgement.

'Pauline Carpenter. She and her husband Ron, or should I say Ronald, recently moved in and the builders are doing the most enormous conversion of The Mount: swimming pool, tennis court, conservatory. Poor Sally is having to put up with all the noise and dust.'

'But why would they want to develop land that runs alongside theirs?'

'Thereby hangs a tale, I daresay,' her mother said. 'Oh, people like that know what they're doing. I just cannot believe it! The cheek of it ... someone else's property.'

'So what did Mrs Sheffield say?'

'They knew about it, had seen it in the paper, and Tom is taking it up with the council and trying to find out more about it. Sally will let me know. In the meantime—'

'Well, he's going to call back, your David Mathieson.'

'Oh, dear.'

'And not best pleased to do so. He seemed to think it was all your fault.'

'I hope you told him it was nothing to do with me?' her mother said severely.

'I tried, Mummy, I did try,' Minnie sighed. 'But really he didn't want to listen.' She couldn't help wondering how her mother would deal with the irate young man.

'Well, I don't suppose he would come round today, it being Sunday,' Janey said, relieved.

'I wouldn't put it past him.' And Minnie grinned.

Later in the morning she began to help her mother with the vegetables, for they always had lunch on Sunday rather than an evening meal, peeling the stored Bramleys for a pie before going to see to little India. She had had her sleep, and was ready for a cool drink and a nappy change.

Having seen her daughter freshly changed and put back in her pram, Minnie went into the kitchen where her mother was still making comments on the disgusting behaviour of the Carpenters. 'Traitors,' she muttered to no one in particular.

'Blessed nuisance,' Minnie grumbled. 'I've run out of disposables, and on a Sunday too.'

'That's a problem we never had,' Janey said smugly. 'Always a neat snowy white pile of nappies and muslins.'

'Not that pleasurable when it came to washing them, though,' Minnie commented.

'That's true. I say, Patel's in the village opens until one on a Sunday.'

'Really? Opening on Sunday? Are you sure?'

'Sure as sure,' her mother said. 'I've often popped down for things I've forgotten, although to tell the truth it makes one more careless when one knows one can always rely on Sunday opening. Take my car, darling. I'll watch India. Have you some money?'

'Well ...'

'Put them on my account, you can pay me back later.' Knowing that she would never ask Minnie to.

Back in the driving seat after a long

absence, Minnie thought: It's like swimming or riding a bike, you never forget how. It was lovely to be driving along the narrow lanes and out into the main road towards the village. The Patels were recent arrivals in the village. When Minnie had left it was still an old-fashioned store with the Harrisons in residence. When the Patels had bought it they had scoured it from top to bottom, got decorators and put in new windows, all without disturbing, they hoped, their precious customers.

Once inside, Minnie was surprised at how efficiently they had taken over. When she saw Mrs Patel at the counter she automatically placed her hands together, so long had she been used to greeting people that way. The beautiful Mrs Patel, with her large liquid brown eyes and black shiny hair, smiled widely, showing excellent teeth.

'Oh!' Minnie cried. 'How nice it all looks. I haven't seen it before, you've done wonders with it.'

'Thank you,' Mrs Patel said, while her son, sixteen-year-old Trishna, stood idly by the doorway leading to the back of the shop.

Mrs Patel clicked her slim fingers. 'Get on with it,' she said sharply. 'I need a box of butter for the fridge.'

She shook her head from side to side.

'Young people today—they don't want to work. What can I get for you?'

Minnie walked over to the toiletry shelves. 'Two packets of these will do for now,' she said.

'You have a baby?'

'Yes, she is six months old. I've called her India since she was born there.'

Mrs Patel's lovely eyes shone.

'You have been to India?'

'Yes, I've only been back a week or so,' said Minnie. 'It's nice to be home, but I loved India.'

'I have never been,' Mrs Patel said gravely.

'Oh,' Minnie said, and they both laughed.

The boy returned and stacked the butter in the refrigerated shelves as his mother and Minnie talked, his long-lashed eyes glancing over towards them from time to time.

'I suppose he has left school?' Minnie asked.

His mother nodded. 'Yes, and he is bright, wants to work on a newspaper—but he is a born accountant.' She looked at him reprovingly and shook her head. 'Now, that will be ...'

'Would you put it on my mother's account? Lady Utox-Smythe. Is that all right?'

'Yes, of course,' Mrs Patel said. 'So you are her daughter. I should have known, you look like her.'

'Do I?' Minnie wasn't sure whether to take that as a compliment or not.

'Would you sign here?' Mrs Patel asked. And Minnie signed with a flourish. A. Utox-Smythe.

Not by the flicker of an eyelash did Mrs Patel betray her surprise and shock to hear the young lady's name. Unmarried and with a baby—called India—which suggested ...

'Thanks, 'bye,' Minnie called, while the boy strolled over to his mother and looked at the amount shown on the till and the open account book.

The door closed before he spoke. 'So she has a baby—fancy that,' he said. 'I bet her mother was a bit surprised.' But Mrs Patel rounded on him furiously.

'Don't be disrespectful!' she said. 'I don't like to hear the sort of things you say. And you must learn to mind your own business. It has nothing, absolutely nothing, to do with us, do you hear?'

He slouched off sulkily.

But Trishna had ambition, and thus it was that mulling it over, and being the good newshound that he was, he stored away this information in his agile brain. He knew Lady Utox-Smythe, of course, had often delivered groceries up to Clyde Lodge, while vowing to himself that it was the sort of place where he would live one day. After all, he never missed a trick. And Her Ladyship, he knew, was married to Sir John Utox-Smythe, a bigwig in the City or something like that.

Well, he thought, it might be an idea to investigate the family. He had no real desire to hurt anyone, but ferret-like wanted to learn more, to discover things, and put two and two together.

On his next excursion to the local library, he found *Who's Who*, which was a revelation. He had no idea that it would contain so much information. Having found it, he was completely and utterly hooked. Everyone was in there, everyone of importance, that was, including Sir John Utox-Smythe. Now he really *was* someone to contend with. Knighted ten years before, he had letters galore after his name, and held directorships of many companies, City-based firms. My word, he was quite something. There were so many inches given over to Sir John Utox-Smythe, there seemed to be no end to his achievements. 'Married to Jane, n. Purbright, one son, Graham, and daughter, Araminta'.

He closed the book thoughtfully and carried the heavy tome back to the reference shelf. Well, it would not be the last time he would refer to that magical book. Araminta, eh? With a baby daughter called India.

Still thinking, he rode home. Not exactly big news these days, an illegitimate baby. But it was wonderful what a bit of probing would do. He would store up the knowledge that he had gained for further use. You never knew.

A few days later, he parked his bicycle in the shed at the station at Cobbets Green. He was off to London, although his mother didn't know it. She thought he was going to see his cousins in Slough. He had bribed two of them to keep quiet and often went up to London, not to have the sort of evenings other boys might want but to scout around, to find out things.

That evening, he saw Sir John come out of the train and walk towards the car park. He knew him by sight, not only because he occasionally appeared in the village, a tall, well-built, commanding figure, but because he had seen innumerable photographs of him. He hung about until Sir John came out of the car park in his Bentley, his handsome face and fine head of hair unmistakable. The boy bent down to tie his shoelace, as a good reporter should, and glanced at his watch. Six-forty-five. The car drove out and up the hill towards Swansbridge.

So now he knew a bit more than he did yesterday.

On Friday he cycled down to the station and sat astride his bike, awaiting the six-forty-five train. And sure enough there was Sir John, emerging from the station and going into the car park. So now he knew Sir John was a creature of habit.

It was interesting following someone else's movements, and it was all good practice. He watched people for a while, and was just about to ride home when the Bentley passed him, but this time it went the other way into the village of Cobbets Green itself. It wasn't far, and following it he saw the car disappear down a slope which was obviously a car park for the shops. He waited with mounting interest in time to see Sir John emerge and walk up the slope to a line of shops, and press a button in a concealed doorway which opened to let him in. The doorway was the entrance to a flat above a dress shop. He made a mental note, then rode down the slope to the garages where there was no sign of Sir John's car.

Hmm, he thought again. I wonder what all that was about? Satisfied, he rode home. Well, it was all good fun ... it was good experience.

But the little scouting he had done had set him wanting more. Like a detective, he

189

found himself going into Cobbets Green and hanging about the parade of shops. The dress shop 'Tanya', was a very exclusive place and there was no way he could see inside. All very upmarket, he thought. What would Sir John be doing in a place like that?

The following Friday he went to the station again and saw Sir John do exactly the same thing. Up the slope and into the dress shop. He began putting two and two together. One evening, quite late, he walked around Cobbets Green, casually as any boy might, looking in the shops, up at the windows of the flat above the dress shop where a pretty lamp shone. Suddenly the door opened and a woman came out.

She was stunning, a real beauty, tall and elegant as you might expect the owner of a gown shop to be. She had with her a small dog on a lead. She strolled along, looking in the windows, while he went to the other side of the road. Finally, after half an hour, she went back inside.

Cor! No wonder Sir John went visiting the lady in the dress shop. His heart was pounding with excitement. It just showed what you could find out if you'd a mind. Still, it had only been an experiment. And in any case, you'd have to be a lot more sure of your facts than he was.

But, having started, he couldn't stop.

It was not difficult to find the name of the beautiful dress shop owner, nor to check up again and again on Sir John's movements. Then sometimes the Utox-Smythe girl came down to the shop and talked to his mother, who by now was insisting that he make up his mind about his future. July and August had gone by, and he was to start his accountancy course at the beginning of September. She would have to find someone else to help in the shop then. His father managed the larger branch, and was seldom on hand during the day to help in the small shop in Swansbridge.

'OK, OK,' he kept saying, causing her to wonder once again where they had gone wrong with his education. He was as different from his big brother as chalk from cheese—Big Brother who even now was married with a family and had his own string of shops in Southall.

Mrs Patel sighed.

By now every spare moment was given up to detective work.

He had it all placed together. City magnate having affair with owner of dress shop; high and mighty Lady Utox-Smythe, mother of daughter who had given birth to an illegitimate baby.

Well, the baby may not have been news, but the antics of Sir John certainly were.

However, he made doubly certain of his facts before going in to see the editor of the local newspaper, who agreed to give him an appointment when he was told he had an important item of news.

'Sit down,' he said to the boy, and knew by experience that the lad was the bearer of information that simply had to be told, so difficult was it for him to hide his excitement.

'What is it you wanted to see me about?' the editor asked. He had met them before, tellers of tales, but just here and there a good reporter came through, although he was not in the business of printing salacious gossip.

Trishna suddenly felt terrified of what he was doing. He certainly didn't want to hurt the girl, but he had no feelings either way for Sir John.

'I'd have to know that my name would not be mentioned?' And when he received no reply: 'I mean, I know something that would make a good story, but I wouldn't want anyone to know it came from me.'

'I'm sure,' the editor said. 'So what is it?'

'Suppose I could tell you about a famous man, really famous—I mean, a well-known financier and what he is getting up to? And his daughter—'

The editor had reached this exalted

position because he was a student of human nature, and not given to printing lurid details of human behaviour. The *Cobbet Times* was a nice little paper, suitable for local residents. It was more than his job was worth to try to emulate the *Sun.* Not only that, but before the lad had finished the editor had guessed to whom he was referring.

'Look, sonny,' he said, 'I don't want to know. If I printed everything that people got up to, famous or not, I'd be out of a job. We're not in the gutter press business here and I would advise you to keep your mouth shut. What did you hope to get out of it—money?'

'No, I wanted a job,' the boy said miserably. 'I did a lot of research into that story.'

'I'm sure you did,' the editor said. 'But stick to the rules, sonny. Just because you've unearthed what you think might be a story, doesn't mean anyone would want to print it. Go about it the right way. Take a commercial course, go to evening classes, try and get work on a good national newspaper—you never know. But this is not the way.'

Trishna seethed all the way home. Not only had he failed in his mission, he felt a fool. He had been shown up by that pompous little man! Not a story indeed—what did he think newspapers were for?

Well, he felt more than ever now that he must tell his story to the public, especially since he had verified all the facts. He knew he was right. In the right quarters a newspaper would give its eye teeth for a story like this. Why should Sir bloody John get away with it? He put his bike away and kicked the side door open.

'Is that you, Trishna?' his mother called. 'I've been looking for you everywhere. Where were you?'

'Had to get something for the bike.'

Well, he wasn't going to take this lying down. The *Sun* or the *Comet*—now they would be glad to hear from him, he'd bet. He hadn't done all that detective work for nothing. Yes, that's what he would do—and earn a few bob in the process.

It was some days later that Mrs Patel noticed that her son had become quiet, secretive, almost furtive. She spoke to her husband. 'You don't think he's on drugs, do you? He's behaving so strangely. Stays in his room, won't go out, and every time I speak to him he jumps. It's as if he's ashamed or something.'

'I expect he's a bit nervous about starting his course,' her husband said. 'He's sulking—it's not what he wanted to do—but he'll come round. He'll see it's for the best in the long run.'

Meantime, there was quite a bit of activity in Swansbridge and Cobbets Green. A nice man called one day when Janey was out, someone from the council with enquiries about who lived in the house, how many residents there were and their status. It had to do with a Register of Electors, apparently. Minnie was happy to oblige with the information. A nice polite man, unlike some she could mention.

Then there was the pretty girl who admired India in the village. 'Oh, how lucky you are,' she said. 'What a lovely baby.' And they got talking, Minnie happy to meet someone of her own age. She told the girl about India and Pakistan and Nepal, and the girl said she would love to go there.

In Cobbets Green it was the same, although they were not aware of what was going on around them, and they certainly were not aware of telephoto lenses trained on them. Once when Sir John left the flat a sudden flash startled him, but he disregarded it. Must have been lightning or a street lamp failing.

All in all, quite a bit of activity. Came the day when Mrs Patel, really worried by now about her son, went into his room but found nothing. Not until she searched his jacket pockets, and found there a cheque for five hundred pounds dated the previous day and issued by Comet Newspapers. She swayed slightly and telephoned her husband to come home at once.

The result for Trishna was that he was whisked off to Wolverhampton where another branch of the family lived. In fact his father drove him personally and left him there. On his return, he and his wife sat back to await events, sick to death with worry and remorse.

Chapter Twelve

As the days went by Minnie Utox-Smythe had to admit that she was secretly disappointed that the angry young man, as she termed him, had not returned. She had thought he would be back the same day, but evidently he had thought better of it.

Her mother led a very full life, if she wasn't at one meeting she was at another, and Minnie took advantage of the lull to think about what she was going to do.

She had no intention of staying on and being a burden to her parents. It wasn't just the money, for she knew they

196

were quite well off, but she wanted her independence. It had been wonderful to come home and be looked after but she had a responsibility to her daughter, and as the time wore on she felt it more keenly.

This morning, Becky Newman was coming in to see her and the baby. She liked Becky, always had. Becky just adored babies, and was a mine of information to the young mothers at the local baby clinic.

Janey had gone to court today, it being her day to sit as magistrate. Becky arrived about ten-thirty, an attractive woman with a mop of shiny dark curls, always beautifully cut, and serene grey eyes.

'How lovely to see you again!' she greeted Minnie warmly. 'My dear, I always envied you your trip to India, but I would never have had the nerve to go there myself.'

Minnie smiled and kissed her.

'Oh, it's warm today.' And Becky took off her cardigan. 'Now, where is she, baby India?'

'Outside in the garden,' Minnie told her. 'I put her out whenever, it's a nice day. The fresh air is good for her, I think.'

'Oh, you're absolutely right,' Becky said, following her outside. 'And the garden—so pretty. Ah, there she is!'

She looked down into the pram, and

India smiled up at her. Truth to tell India smiled at almost everyone, but it seemed Becky got a special grin.

'Oh, she's adorable!' she cried. 'You must be delighted with her.'

'I am,' Minnie said proudly. 'Now do sit down, what can I get you? Coffee? Mrs Nelson is in the kitchen, she'll make us some.'

'That would be lovely.' Becky smiled, seating herself in a garden chair near the baby's pram.

'Oh, I wish mine were that age again!' she said enviously, reaching out a finger for the baby to hold.

Minnie returned and sat next to her.

'I'd no idea that babies could be so time-consuming,' she said. 'It's a full-time job but I am enjoying it.'

'Well, this is a lovely age. But even so, there are compensations for any stage of their young lives.'

'How old are your children now?' Minnie asked.

'Irene is seven, David ten and Ben is twelve. I would have liked another,' Becky said wistfully, 'but, well, I must be satisfied. Now, do bring her down to the clinic, if you would like to. All babies are welcome, Thursdays from ten until four.' As Mrs Nelson appeared with the coffee and a tray of biscuits, she said, 'Good morning, Mrs Nelson, and how are you today?'

'I'm fine, Mrs Newman, and yourself?'

'Very well, thank you. Busy getting the children ready for going back to school.'

'Yes, there's a lot to do,' Mrs Nelson agreed. 'There you are then, Minnie.'

'Thanks, Mrs Nelson.'

'She's been with you a long time,' Becky observed. 'Ever since I came to live in Swansbridge.'

'Yes, forever. She came to us when I was very small.'

'Like an old family retainer,' Becky said, sipping her coffee.

'Mummy likes to think so.' And Minnie grinned.

'Tell me something about India. It always sounds so fascinating. I hope I haven't left it too late to visit. I'd like to go when the children are older—Srinagar and Kashmir—but I've been told Kashmir is not what it was. Did you go?'

'Yes, it was great, although I could see how much more wonderful it must have been before pollution set in and the troubles in the area—it must have been quite magical before the war and partition. But India is wonderful.'

'And did you go to Nepal?'

'Yes. I found that a little disappointing, full of climbers and back packers—lots of

English. But then, that's what it's all about now. For some reason I thought it would be covered in flowers but really it is very commercial. We didn't stay long there.'

'We?' Becky asked before she could stop herself.

'Yes, Tim and I—India's father.' And glancing at her, Becky saw that she hadn't flickered an eyelash.

If she wanted to say more, she would, thought Becky wisely as Minnie studied the herbaceous border.

'So—what are your plans now?' she asked, taking a biscuit, one of Mrs Nelson's homemades.

'Well ...' Minnie thought hard. 'I'd like to do something in a little while, when I've got used to being home, perhaps something where there would be a crèche for India. I would like to be self-supporting, if possible.'

'But your parents wouldn't want you to do that while the baby is so young, would they?' Becky asked gently.

'No, I expect not,' Minnie agreed. 'But I don't want them spoiling me. I would like a job, something to do, to bring in a little money. I have some from my grandmother, but I don't want to lean on them. I need a little place of my own—it's not fair on them to stay here too long.'

Becky could see her point.

'Yes, I know what you mean. It's not a good thing, living with parents. What could you do, Minnie?'

'I'm not suited for much, just traipsing around places, that sort of thing—travelling —that's all I've ever done since I left school!'

'But I expect it was good for you, helped you to be self-reliant, to look after yourself?'

'I don't think Daddy would agree with you.' And Minnie made a face. 'Seriously, yes, I could look after myself—I've had to one way and another. What do you think?'

'There are jobs of a sort in the village, light jobs, and after all, you wouldn't want to be tied down at this stage, just helping out, that sort of thing. Even my husband needs a young girl around the office. He has four members of staff, two men and two girls, but they need a general dogsbody. Of course, you would find an estate agent's rather boring after travelling.'

'I can't imagine it,' Minnie said honestly. 'Being tied down to an office. I've been fortunate, I suppose, never had to do that.'

'And there's always voluntary work?'

'No, I need—I want to earn some money.'

'Well, let's give it some thought. Oh, look she's dropped off to sleep, bless her little heart.'

Minnie rose and put a soft cover over the little girl's dimpled knees.

'You've made me feel quite envious,' Becky said wistfully.

They moved their chairs away from the pram and sat talking for a while. 'Where's your mother today?' Becky asked.

'At court.'

'Oh, she does work hard for this community. Gives unstintingly of her time.'

'I know,' Minnie said.

'And you heard about the row over the Butterfly Field?'

'Yes, awful.'

'Such a shock to everyone. Still, I expect it will sort itself out.'

They talked pleasantly until it was time for Becky to leave, and when India woke Minnie changed her and put her back in her pram until lunchtime.

When the doorbell rang just before twelve, Minnie was upstairs and heard Mrs Nelson answer it.

Presently, she called upstairs: 'It's a Mr Mathieson, Minnie.'

Her heart leapt. 'Oh! Er—I'll be right down, Mrs Nelson,' she called as she collected her thoughts.

Surprisingly, she had to tell herself not to

run down the stairs but to walk slowly and take her time. Arriving at the foot of them, she saw a very different David Mathieson from the man who had called previously.

'Good morning,' she said in level tones.

'Good morning,' he said, his expression pleasant. 'I—er wonder if I might have a word?'

'My mother is not at home just now,' Minnie said coldly.

'If I could have a word with you? It was you I really wanted to see.'

'You had better come in,' she said as Mrs Nelson waited. 'We shall be in the drawing room, Mrs Nelson,' she said, and led the way.

'Right you are,' Mrs Nelson said with a look which told Minnie she could rely on her being nearby.

Once in the drawing room, Minnie stood still.

'What was it you wanted?' she asked coolly, although her heart was pounding and it flashed through her mind what a presentable young man David Mathieson was.

'I really came ...' She waited. She could hear the tick-tock of the old grandfather clock. It sounded deafening.

'I came to apologise,' he said finally.

'Oh.' It was the last thing she had expected. 'You had better sit down,' she said, sounding almost like her mother dealing with a penitent.

When he sat down, she seated herself opposite him on the sofa.

'I realise how rude I was that day I called.'

'Good,' Minnie said shortly.

'But you see—'

'Is this a qualified apology?' she asked coldly.

And at this he gave the first glimmer of a smile.

'No, of course not. I was rude, I realise. But it was all a misunderstanding.'

'Was it?' Minnie said. She wasn't going to let him off the hook so lightly, remembering his scathing look at the baby and his stress on the word 'Miss'.

Pompous young man! He needed to be taken down a peg or two.

'Is that it?'

He got to his feet. 'I see you're not going to forgive me easily. Well, I don't blame you.'

But now that he was here, she had no desire to let him go. Perhaps she should hear him out? She was well aware of the mistake that had been made, but let him explain it.

'You see,' he began, and looked appealingly at her. Her staunch resolution suddenly died.

'Well, it's over now,' she said. 'I must admit I—'

'You must have thought me the most pigheaded fool?'

'I did. Do sit down. Would you like something? Sherry, perhaps?'

'No, thank you,' he said, but sat down again. 'I felt so awful afterwards when it was explained to me. Of course it had nothing to do with your mother, the building application, I mean—all she had done was put in an application for a community centre.'

'So I understand.' Minnie studied his shoes. Tan leather, so well-polished you could see your face in them, tweed jacket, cream shirt ... no Doc Martens or tee shirts.

'You see,' he began, 'the Butterfly Field has a special meaning for us as a family.'

Minnie looked up then. 'Yes?'

'My uncle farms at Hassington and I work for him as estate manager. It's quite an extensive holding.'

'Oh, I didn't know,' she said.

'My uncle is my mother's brother. There were just the two of them, and the Butterfly Field was my mother's favourite place to play in when she was a little girl. She died when I was born.' And suddenly Minnie felt very near to tears, as she quite often did these days since the birth of India.

205

'Oh, how sad,' she said, trying to imagine what it must be like to be brought up without a mother.

'My uncle adored her, and he—we have a picture of her at home, running through the Butterfly Field when she was about five. You can't imagine what it was like then with all those wild flowers, and the butterflies used to flock there in their hundreds: Purple Emperors, Painted Ladies, Peacocks and Brimstones. It's a treasured possession for me, too.'

'Oh, I can understand how you feel!' she cried. 'Of course you wouldn't want to give it up, not for any reason.'

'My uncle is feeling particularly vulnerable just now. His wife died some months ago, and they had no children, so I feel I have to be especially understanding. He has been so good to me.'

'What about your father?' Minnie asked.

'Oh, he went off and married someone else when I was two years old, but his new wife didn't want me so I stayed with Uncle Leo—they legally adopted me and I took the name of Mathieson.'

Minnie felt overwhelmed by the story. You never knew what went on in other people's lives.

'Anyway, enough of that,' said David. 'I'm glad we have cleared it up, and once again, I apologise.'

She smiled, showing her one dimple, then listened hard as she heard the baby cry out.

'Oh, I'm sorry, I must go. India's crying.'

'India?' he said. 'Is that her name? Delightful.'

'Well, she was born there, but that's another story,' Minnie said. 'I'm afraid I have to go.'

'I wondered if perhaps we could have dinner one evening?' His nice dark eyes searched her face, and she found herself blushing.

'Well—' She hesitated. 'How do you know I haven't a partner or a boyfriend?'

'Because I know your mother by reputation, and learned this morning that she was doing her good citizen bit as a magistrate. I went to the court very early, before it started, and asked her if it would be all right to call on you. I didn't want to mess up a second time.'

Well! she thought. You had to hand it to him for trying.

'Would you be agreeable?' he asked.

'Yes, I should like that,' she said, excitement already welling up inside her at the thought of it. But India's cries cut it short.

'I'll ring you,' he said. 'Thank you for seeing me, Araminta,'

'I'm always called Minnie,' she told him.

'Oh, I like Araminta better,' he said, and with a smile was gone.

'Oh, India, India,' she said, hugging her tightly, 'you won't believe it.' By now little India's tear-stained face was sunny with smiles. She had got what she wanted: attention.

The day started like any other for Sir John Utox-Smythe. He bathed and shaved, patted a very masculine cologne into his cheeks, peered at himself in the mirror, adjusted his tie, and was ready to start the day.

Going downstairs he found his wife in the kitchen before him, having already breakfasted. Janey was on her way to the study to do some preliminary work before going out. Minnie was upstairs seeing to the baby, and glancing at the kitchen clock he saw that it was seven-forty-five. He was due in the City for a very important meeting around ten and intended driving himself to the station and leaving the car there, for was it not Friday? His favourite day.

He was startled by the shrill buzz of the telephone. 'I'll get it,' he called, and picked up the kitchen extension.

'Dorothy, my dear.' It was his secretary.

Most unlike her to ring him except in an emergency.

'John, I don't know how to tell you this—'

'What is it?' He thought of banks tumbling, companies collapsing, Dow Jones, Wall Street, Lloyds ...

'It's the newspapers—at least, one of them. The *Comet*, I'm afraid.'

He became a little annoyed. 'Well, what about it?'

'It's an exposé,' she whispered for want of a better word. 'John, they've found out about, you know—her, Miss ... And there are pictures, and of Minnie and the baby.' His face drained of colour as the import of what she was saying sunk in.

'My God! Is this true?'

'I'm afraid so,' she said. 'Front-page stuff—oh, it's horrible. You can't believe what they're saying. Don't come in today, John, don't go to the station.'

He replaced the receiver without saying another word, and collapsed into a kitchen chair. He was shaking, and his heart was beating uncontrollably. His breathing was laboured and he sat for a moment or two to retain his composure. Christ! It couldn't be true. But what if it was? He floundered for a few moments, not knowing what to do for the best before leaving the house, calling out to Janey as he did so.

'I'm off now, Janey—I'll be back.' And getting out the car, he tried to steady his hands on the wheel. Best to drive to a shopping centre where he was not well-known. The electronic side gates of the drive opened for him.

Still trembling, he drove three miles before stopping and getting out of the car. He hurried into a newsagent's and bought a bundle of tabloids, throwing down a five-pound note and hurrying out of the shop.

'Hey! Your change.' But he had gone. Afterwards, the man said: 'That's him. That's Sir John what's 'is name. Gor, I wouldn't be in his shoes today.'

In the car he flopped back in his seat and drove on for a minute or two, stopping in a side road. Opening one after another of the papers he found that only the *Comet* was involved, though that was enough.

His own face greeted him on the front page: handsome, imperious. Beside him, smiling and lovely, was Melissa, looking up at him. They had never had their photograph taken together, how had the press managed that? Below, inset, was a photograph of Minnie with her baby, and then one of Janey, looking like everyone's idea of a determined do-gooder: worthy, but plain. And those headlines!

CITY FINANCIER'S LOVE NEST EXPOSED—in letters some three inches high.

ANOTHER WEALTHY TYCOON CHEATS ON WIFE. THE WIFE (inset) VERSUS THE MISTRESS (right). Janey looking dowdy as she never did. BELOW (inset) DAUGHTER ARAMINTA, MOTHER OF ILLEGITIMATE BABY BORN IN INDIA ...

He crumpled the paper and slumped back in the seat, not knowing which way to turn next.

After a few seconds, he picked up his mobile phone and telephoned Melissa.

'Is that you?' She could hardly hear him. 'Oh, John, I'm glad you phoned. I don't know what's going on, there's a group of men outside the shop and the front door—'

'Don't open it, whatever you do—they're reporters,' he whispered urgently. 'Melissa, it's out in the *Comet*, all over the front page: you, me, Janey, Minnie and the baby. God, it's sickening!'

There was a little wail from the other end.

'Oh, John, what are we going to do?'

'Sit tight,' he said. 'Nothing we can do now. It's too late. But don't move outside the house until I telephone.'

She sank back, too shocked even to cry.

That done, he telephoned Dorothy.

'I've seen it,' he said tersely. 'Now not a word, no interviews—nothing, you understand? I'm out of town for a few days and you don't know when I'll be back. In fact, I've gone abroad.'

A moment later, a call came through from Graham. 'Dad? What the hell is going on?'

He should ask, John thought grimly.

'Can't talk now,' he said, 'going home to see your mother.' And rang off.

He sat for a few moments feeling suddenly old and weary, for the first time in his life uncertain as to what to do next.

Facing Janey would be the worst thing. But there was no way this could be kept from her.

He turned round and drove back home and at the sight of the little group round the front door, opened the electric gates at the side of the house and drove in, letting himself in by the back door.

Janey was standing in the kitchen reading a copy of the *Comet* which someone obviously had stuffed through the letter box. There was no sign of Minnie.

She looked up over the paper, her expression inscrutable.

'Janey—' he began.

She put down the paper and looked at him squarely.

'I know,' she said. 'I've always known.'

Chapter Thirteen

For the second time that day, John sank into a kitchen chair, his head in his hands.

There was nothing Janey could say. When she saw his shoulders heave, she turned away.

'It's Minnie I'm worried about,' she said shortly. 'It's so unfair on her.'

He lifted his head. 'Has she seen it yet?'

'No, but she will, as soon as she comes down.'

'Janey—'

He still couldn't grasp it. His wife of thirty years, and she had known all along? This threw him almost as much as seeing the newspaper article. And she had never, by the slightest hint ...

'Hello, what's going on?'

It was Minnie, staring at them both. 'There's a crowd of men outside with cameras—what's all this about?' But she didn't look particularly concerned, just interested.

With a glance at John, Janey handed her the newspaper.

'There's no point in hiding it,' she said tersely to her husband. 'She's got to know sooner or later.'

Minnie stood, eyes wide, mouth open, scanning the article. Then, taking it with her, she rushed upstairs. John made as if to follow her.

'Leave her,' Janey ordered. 'You've done enough damage already.'

Upright and graceful as usual though she was, her shoulders sagged. Then John saw her straighten up, a look of determination on her face, as she took a deep breath and walked towards the door.

'Where are you going, Janey?' But she ignored him, and made straight for the front door, pulling it to behind her.

She walked the short distance to the front gate and stood, straight as a ramrod, facing them: four men and a young woman. They all began to talk at once.

'Lady Utox-Smythe! Could we ask—is it true—?'

'Shh,' she said gently. 'I can't hear you all at the same time. Now, what is your problem?' And she gave them one of her most gracious smiles.

'Have you read the paper? Has Sir John?' But she hushed them with a lifted hand and waited until they were silent.

'If you mean the newspaper article in the *Comet*—yes, I have read it, someone kindly put a copy through the letter box, but I have nothing to say on the matter, and must ask you to leave since we have a baby asleep in the house. Thank you, gentlemen.' And she smiled at them charmingly and, stately as a galleon, walked back to the front door, closing it firmly behind her. Once inside the house, she went straight upstairs to Minnie and found her in tears in her room. She instantly jumped up from the bed, and flung her arms around Janey.

'Oh, Mummy!' she cried. 'What a mess! What a bloody awful mess!'

Janey hugged her, looking over her shoulder and out into the fields beyond, her thoughts chasing each other around. So much misery, unnecessary misery, so much unhappiness, because people broke the rules. Someone always got hurt.

Minnie looked up, eyes red from weeping. Her mother looked so calm, almost as if she had been expecting it.

'Did you know?' she asked. 'About Daddy and—'

'Yes, Minnie, I did. A long time ago. You can't be married to someone as long as I have without knowing. I thought deeply about it, and decided no good would come of yelling and shouting. I hoped that after a time it would well, fizzle out. But there it is. In the event, it didn't.' And she looked grim.

'What are you going to do?' Minnie asked, almost fearfully as she saw the look of sheer determination on her mother's face.

'What I should have done a long time ago,' she said, giving a small smile of reassurance and going out of the room, closing the door behind her.

In John's dressing room, carefully and with precision, she began to lay clothes on the chaise longue. A City suit, sports jacket and trousers, the right shirts ... Where had she read of a wife tearing her husband's clothes to pieces? She wanted to do the same. She was more angry now than when she had read the article, more angry than when she had first discovered his secret—and that was nine years ago. She had been patient long enough. Grimly she took from the wardrobe a travelling bag and packed it neatly, adding toothpaste, toothbrush and hairbrush. There! That should do him temporarily. And with the satisfaction of a job well done, she walked down the stairs with her burden.

John was standing by the window, grim-faced. Turning as she approached, he was shocked by her appearance with the suitcase, which she let drop with a small thud.

'There, John!' she said, almost plea-santly. 'That should keep you going for a bit. I suggest you send for the rest of your things as soon as you can. Tomorrow, if possible.'

He was shocked to the core. 'Janey!'

'Are you surprised?' she asked. 'You shouldn't be. Even a worm will turn. And now I would like you to leave the house.'

'Janey, please—please think this over!'

'Oh, I've had lots of time to do that, John. Years, in fact. I should have done this before.'

Now he pleaded. 'You're not going to throw away thirty years of marriage?'

'You did!' she said, and he turned away, looking down at the suitcase as if realising its implication for the first time.

'Janey,' he pleaded, 'let's talk about it. Don't act hastily.'

'Please go,' she said. 'Now!' And he recognised the look: he had seen the light of battle in her eyes before and knew it was not to be ignored.

'I'll just go up—' he began.

'No, John.' And her voice cut him like a knife.

He picked up the suitcase without looking at her again and walked out of the kitchen door towards the garage.

Sally Sheffield saw the newspaper when Mrs Halliday brought it in, first thing in the morning, shocked disbelief on her face.

'You can't credit it, can you?' she said. 'Such goings on.'

Sally took the paper from her and her face paled. 'Oh!' She sat down abruptly. 'Poor Janey.'

'And respectable people too,' Mrs Halliday said. 'Makes you wonder, the things that go on.'

And Minnie—poor little Minnie. How on earth had they found out? And Sir John—someone had been doing a lot of detecting. Such a lovely-looking woman, that Melissa Wilding. She looked a nice person, not the floozy type at all. Oh, this awful gutter press! Who would be any the better for knowing all this? Full story, page two, she read.

She folded the paper, resisting all desire to read more. She would read the article later when Mrs Halliday had gone. She supposed Tessa and Tom would see it somewhere on the way to town. There had been no mention of it in their own newspaper.

Was there anything she could do? she wondered. But people were usually best left alone in these circumstances. They would need time to lick their wounds.

218

Yet it seemed necessary to offer them support. Later she would telephone Janey. She would need all her friends about her.

Mrs Halliday was unusually quiet—and somehow Sally didn't think that the revelations about the Utox-Smythes had anything to do with it.

She wandered off into the garden, still thinking about Janey, and with the sense of shock that she always felt now when she saw it, stared at the immense new conservatory which had appeared at The Mount and was near to completion. The skyline was blocked now, and although it was a splendid conservatory, nevertheless it stood where the old oak tree had been. Sally could hear the men working on the pool which must be on the other side of the house. They had made wonderful progress, and she would be pleased when it was all finished. Towards the end of September, Pauline had said. Well, she could be right. Sally felt she would give her eye teeth from sheer curiosity to see how much had been done to the house, for it had gone on all summer: demolition, lorries full of rubble, skips one after the other, smart designer gardening vans, to say nothing of the noise that they had been exposed to and the dust and dirt.

Tom had been furious, not only because of that but because of the shock of seeing the application for developing the Butterfly Field. He had put a note through the door asking Ron Carpenter to give him a call, but so far nothing had happened, though it was all over Swansbridge that the new people at The Mount had applied for planning permission to develop the Butterfly Field.

Sally sighed once more, thinking of Janey. How hard it would be for her to accept—for any woman—that her husband had a mistress. But the piece about Minnie was the unkindest cut of all. Poor little soul! And she would feel so guilty. Perhaps it would never have come out if someone had not investigated Sir John. It was a sad thing, she thought, that the more successful a man was, the more the media wanted to pull him down. On the other hand, in his position, it was a stupid thing to do, taking a mistress so near home. She wondered idly how the whole story had come out. Well, she decided, there were always people with information to sell, at a price.

Back in the house, she heard Mrs Halliday upstairs in William's room. He was off to agricultural college at long last and was excited about it. The only thing he didn't like was that he wouldn't see so much of Suzie. But she would come up to see him, she said. He was already looking forward to that.

When Mrs Halliday came down, she was no more pleased with life than she had been first thing, and Sally guessed it was her sister Mandy again.

'How's your sister getting on?' she asked.

'Oh, the council's found her a flat—nice one in Moresby Court. I don't s'pose you know it?'

'Yes, I do. That's good,' Sally said, pleased for Mrs Halliday's sake.

'It's a lovely flat—smashing bathroom and kitchen.'

'So it makes no difference that she didn't come from this area?' Sally asked, puzzled.

'What do you mean?'

'Well,' Sally felt a bit confused, 'I thought there was a council list of local people waiting to be housed?'

'Oh, not these days—seems you can push yourself in wherever,' Mrs Halliday said. ''Course, they would feel sorry for Mandy. I mean, she's such a pretty thing, and her being kicked out with a little girl and that—and nowhere to go.'

'Yes, I see what you mean. Well, I'm sure you're pleased.'

'Oh, yes, and it's a lovely flat—behind the old church.'

'Yes, I know where it is,' Sally added.

Janey had had a lot to do with that development, she knew. Fighting for single mothers and homeless people.

Oh, well, she hoped people would stick by her now. Janey had certainly done her bit for other people.

She was looking forward to Tessa's coming home, for the excitement about the Goyas was mounting daily. She sometimes wished her daughter had more friends. If only she would get over her infatuation with Hugo Blanchard, for that's what it seemed to be. And Sally was upset for Tessa that the man showed no interest in her while he certainly appeared to have fallen for the beautiful Spanish Contessa.

Yesterday there had been an unusual air of activity at MacBane's. Not for a long time had there been such excitement as at the arrival of the two Goyas, due that evening. They were being brought into the country under strict security, although the news of their arrival, indeed their existence, had not so far been released to the press.

In the staff room Tessa drank a late cup of coffee, waiting for Hugo to come in. When he did, she could tell by the set of his jaw that he was tense with excitement.

'Big day, Hugo?' Geoff Harker called out. Everyone was envious yet pleased at Hugo's success.

'Fingers crossed,' he replied. 'Tessa, how are you?' He took a seat beside her. It had been a long time since she had seen him—so many journeys to Spain. 'How is the Contessa? Is she coming over?' she made herself ask.

'No, actually,' he said. 'Her father's condition has deteriorated and she wishes to be with him. I don't blame her. She says she is happy to leave it with me—after all, she is only selling the pictures in order to pay for his medical treatment, and provided they reach the reserve, all well and good.'

Tessa put out a hand and touched his arm. 'I'm pleased for you, Hugo,' she said. 'It was quite a find. I'm thrilled that I was one of the first to see them.'

He looked at her in surprise.

'Oh, yes, I'd forgotten that,' he said. 'So you did. We went together, didn't we?'

Tessa showed none of the chagrin she felt. 'He didn't even remember,' she told Sally later.

'Well, I must fly,' she said, without any real need to do so. 'Good luck with them.' And was gone.

Alistair MacBane met her on the stairs.

'Are you on your way home, Tessa?'

She glanced at her watch.

'Yes, it's almost six.'

'I just wondered if you would like to

have dinner with me sometime?'

'Yes, that would be nice,' she said. 'What did you have in mind?'

'Towards the end of the week?' And she nodded.

'I'll be in touch,' he said.

Handsome devil, she thought. She would have liked to stay on until the Goyas arrived. Still, it might be quite late, and what was the point?

The next morning, however, it was as if a pall of silence hung over MacBane's. In the great auction room itself, all was quiet. Everyone seemed to be upstairs. It was still early, before the premises opened, and after taking off her jacket and sprucing herself up, Tessa made her way to the main office. She saw that the door into Alistair's special sanctum was open. Seeing her, he beckoned. 'Come in, Tessa, and close the door behind you.'

There were about six members of staff inside, and you could have heard a pin drop as the two porters stood waiting for the signal to remove the cloth covers from two paintings standing ready on matching easels.

'Right, George, whenever you like,' Alistair said, and Tessa saw that his face was flushed with excitement. The covers came off slowly, to reveal the two exquisite paintings.

A murmur ran through the little gathering.

They were magnificent, even more wonderful than Tessa remembered. In the modern functional setting the colours stood out and the figures seemed to come alive. She looked at Hugo and saw the beads of perspiration on his forehead. What a day for him! The excitement he must be feeling. Everyone was silent, drinking in the beauty of the paintings, and then everyone seemed to talk at once.

'Magnificent! What a find!'

'Well done, Hugo. Lucky devil!' and Tessa saw him take a deep breath and begin to relax.

'Not bad, eh?'

Even Alistair smiled at him. 'Great,' he said. 'Well done.' Which was praise indeed.

Then everyone went over to get a closer look, commenting and peering through magnifying glasses, while Hugo stood by, arms folded, enjoying his moment of glory.

'They should fetch a fortune,' everyone agreed. 'Wait until the press here gets a whiff of this.'

'And New York,' someone said.

'Not to mention Paris and Madrid.'

The talk went on for some time, and presently Tessa moved away to leave Hugo to his moment of glory.

Going along to her room, she heard footsteps behind her and turned to find Alistair there, with his long stride soon catching her up.

'You must have been astonished to see those two in Madrid,' he said, in his usual friendly fashion. 'It's a great day for MacBane's.'

At least, she thought, *he* remembered she had been there on that occasion.

'Yes, it was. The only thing that upset me was the client's refusal to proceed with the sale of the textiles and fine ceramics.'

'Yes, that was a pity,' he agreed. 'Promising, was it?'

'Yes. And if the Goyas are anything to go by, you might know it was excellent stuff.'

'Swings and roundabouts,' he said. He smiled and looked at her. 'You haven't forgotten our dinner date?'

She had reached the door of her room. 'No.' She smiled, though wishing it was Hugo who had asked her.

Today, she decided, she would go through the collection in the basement and sort it out. It was due to come up for sale soon, and there was quite an interesting assortment of stuff there. She would get Lizzie to help her. Lizzie was the new girl, who was to learn everything there was to know in MacBane's. If you were in early enough in the day you could get her services.

She rang through to the main office.

'Would you see if Lizzie is available to give me some help in the basement? Please ring me back,' she said.

'Yes, surely, Miss Sheffield,' the voice said, and later called to say Lizzie had just arrived and would join her as soon as possible.

Down in the basement, Tessa was in her element. Early Brussels tapestries, a fragment of Flemish tapestry—the colours still so vivid it might have been made yesterday—and her favourite, a seventeenth-century Mortlake tapestry. What wouldn't she give to own that!

There was a knock at the door and Lizzie came in, breathless from hurrying. She was eighteen and as pretty as a picture with masses of red curly hair and lovely skin. She was as slim as a wand, today wearing a pleated skirt which barely reached to the top of her thighs. With her 'Follow Me' tights she was a sight for sore eyes, as many of the young men in MacBane's could have attested. She was also the daughter of an earl, with a voice to match. Under her arm she carried a newspaper.

'I say, Tessa,' she said, 'don't you live somewhere near Cobbets Green?'

'Hello, Lizzie,' she said. 'Yes, I do. Why?'

'Well, do you know this old goat?' And she thrust the paper into Tessa's hands.

She opened it, and her hand flew to her mouth.

'Sir John—oh, no, it can't be true!'

'Do you know him?' Lizzie asked, fascinated.

'Yes, they're friends of ours,' she said. 'And Minnie's a particular friend,' she added staunchly. 'She's a poppet.'

'And 'e's a bit of orlright,' Lizzie said in a put on cockney accent.

'Oh, how awful!' Tessa cried. She felt like weeping. 'Poor Aunt Janey.'

'Is she really your aunt?'

'No, but I've known her forever. Oh, how could they do this? It just makes me sick, this sort of thing.'

'Well, I just thought you might be interested.'

'Shocked is more the word,' Tessa said, outraged. She couldn't wait to get home. Poor Minnie!

The day wore on, with Tessa enveloped in clouds of expensive scent while Lizzie persevered with the rugs and tapestries—not her favourite items.

She wrinkled her nose.

'They smell so horrid. I'm sure I'm allergic to this ghastly dust.'

'Well, try and be brave about it—it's all part of the job.'

'Fancy you liking this sort of thing. I mean, it's not like china or silver, is it?'

'No, not in the least,' Tessa agreed. 'And now that you've had a bash at this, you will know that it's not what you want to specialise in.'

'I'm not mad keen to specialise in anything,' Lizzie told her. 'As long as I get to a few parties and meet some good-looking men.'

'Wouldn't you have been better off working in Harrods?'

'Oh, no, everyone does that. There's far more cachet in working in fine arts,' Lizzie said blithely.

Tessa caught the early train and hurried home from the station.

'Oh, Mummy!' she cried as soon as she got in the door, and Sally knew she had seen the article. 'Isn't it awful? Poor Aunt Janey.'

'And Minnie, too,' Sally said, taking off her oven gloves. 'I telephoned Janey. She said if you can bear it, she thought Minnie might like a visitor this evening. The crowd round the front door has melted away apparently.'

'Golly!' Tessa cried. 'And Sir John?'

Sally looked grim.

'Janey didn't say.'

Chapter Fourteen

Sir John Utox-Smythe made his way across to the garage, where his car stood waiting. Throwing his small suitcase on to the back seat, he climbed in and slowly let the car out on to the drive. The electronic gates would open for him automatically, but he was unsure what was awaiting him at the front of the house. He could see two members of the press still outside the front door. He drove through, the gates closing after him, and in the mirror saw one of the men hurrying after his car, camera at the ready.

He drove on, almost blindly, until he came to the crossroads with Cobbets Green, and only when he had passed through the village and out the other side did he stop. Picking up his mobile phone, he put through a call to Melissa.

'John!' Her voice was low. 'It's you, I've been waiting for your call.'

'Listen,' he said. 'Don't say anything. I'm on my way to Gloucestershire—not the hotel where we usually stay. Drive on to the next village, and you'll find me there in the little hotel opposite the garage. John Hutton. I'll have booked a double room.'

He thought she was weeping softly.

'Melissa?'

He heard a faint intake of breath.

'Just join me whenever you can—tonight, tomorrow, whenever—but be sure you're safe and out of contact. This can only be a temporary nuisance. See you then.'

He heard the phone click as she put down the receiver. Stashing away his phone in the dash compartment, he drove on. He would make for the Cotswolds. Unfortunately he couldn't remember the name of the small hostelry in the next village, but he would have to take a chance and make for it. An hour or so's drive in which to go over the events of the last few hours. He was still unable to believe he was in this situation. This morning he had risen as usual, totally unaware of what was in store for him, and now here he was, thrown out of his house, not to put too fine an interpretation on it, and on his way to some obscure village where he had no idea if he might find a room for the night.

What had been the alternative? He certainly could not have stayed at Clyde

Lodge—Janey had been within her rights to tell him to go, and she had been as furious as he'd ever remembered seeing her. Not unnaturally. But then, why the fury if, as she said, she had known all along?

He was more shocked than he could say at the thought that she had known all this time. He felt such a fool, imagining that everything was a well-kept secret. And he wondered why she had kept it to herself when she first discovered it. Had she visited the shop? Had she recognised Melissa who had once been his secretary? She must have done. He gave a deep sigh. Well, he would have to wait for Melissa to reach him before deciding what to do next.

He was almost at his destination, going over and over the events of the past few hours, before he finally realised he was free. Free from marital ties, free from domestic encumbrances. He had been given his liberty, and could now live with Melissa openly and without restrictions.

But over and above that was the business of the revelations to all his business friends and contacts, and he was sorry for Minnie. Some of them might have guessed, after all it was not unusual for a successful businessman to take a mistress, but there might be some who would say: If you can't trust him as a husband, how else can you trust him?

That blasted paper had certainly opened up a can of worms. And who had discovered Melissa's hideaway? Well, it was done now.

It was dusk when he reached the village, and found his way to The George and Dragon. Yes, luckily they had a double room. For how long?

He was not sure, but his wife would be arriving later. Would there be a meal?

'Yes, of course, sir,' the woman said, and waited for him to sign the register.

Mr and Mrs John Hutton of London, apparently. Not that she believed that for a moment.

She slid the book back into place and, ringing the bell, waited for a porter to help the guest with his suitcase.

Once inside the room, he flopped on to the bed. This, of course, was a business hotel with perhaps a few tourists. It would not be immediately obvious who he was, he hoped. Nothing at all like the little love nest of a hotel which he and Melissa had stayed in previously, but it would have to do.

The room was small, with single beds, and certainly not designer furnished, but he was beyond thinking about that.

'Dinner at seven-thirty,' the porter said, disappearing down the narrow staircase, leaving Sir John alone with his thoughts.

It was midnight before Melissa could be sure the coast was clear. Then, having packed a small overnight bag, she called a local taxi service to drive her to Euston Station. In case the taxi driver felt like betraying her, she would exercise caution. Getting out at Euston, she took another cab to Paddington.

She had missed the last train out of Paddington and would have to wait until the following morning, so she stayed overnight at the nearest hotel and took a train out to Gloucestershire around seven, then waited for a cab to take her to the village.

Tired and dishevelled, she finally reached the hotel at ten-thirty in the morning, and fell into John's arms. She looked ghastly, and he felt a moment of compunction for putting her through all this. He asked for coffee to be sent up to their room, and then told Melissa all that had happened. It was only when the girl brought up the coffee that he realised the hotel receptionist may have recognised them, for the waitress behaved in a slightly embarrassed way. When she left, he asked if his bill could be made up immediately.

She looked surprised.

'Yes, sir. Of course, sir.'

'John?' Melissa looked at him, startled.

'They're on to us,' he said. 'Come on,

drink up, we're leaving.'

The woman at the desk looked guilty.

'We serve a very good home-cooked lunch, sir,' she said as he paid the bill in cash.

'Thank you, some other time,' he said, and walking through the portico to the garage, got into the Bentley and drove away, Melissa at his side.

He drove north for an hour before stopping in a layby and telling her all about it in detail.

She was shocked and horrified.

'Well, it can't be helped,' he said. 'I suppose it was bound to come out sooner or later.'

'But it's been so long, and no one ...'

'Well, my pet, someone gave us away,' he said. 'But that's done with. No use crying over spilt milk. We have to decide what's best for us to do now, until it all blows over. Thinking about it, perhaps we should stay away for a few days? Rent somewhere in the Yorkshire Dales. This time of year it should be easy.'

'Whatever you say, John,' Melissa said wearily. 'What do you think Janey will do now?'

'God knows,' he said grimly. 'Sue for divorce, I expect.'

Janey surprised herself. She was shaking

with anger, had never felt so furious or so helpless in her life. She had wanted to fling John's things after him, like any fishwife, she was in such a temper. But trying to pull herself together, she flopped into a chair and breathed deeply. That was how Minnie found her when she tiptoed downstairs. She had seen her father's car disappearing from the bedroom window, and although not wanting to interfere, could not resist coming down to see what was happening.

Janey was white-faced.

'Where's Daddy?' Minnie asked.

'Gone,' she said, staring into space.

'What do you mean—gone? I saw the car.'

'I asked him to leave,' Janey said. 'I packed a few things for him.'

'Mummy—you didn't!' Minnie's hand was over her mouth.

'Yes, I did.' Janey spoke clearly.

'But he'll be back?' Minnie said, in a doubtful voice.

'I hope not,' her mother said ominously, and got up. 'I'm just going to make some tea. Like some?'

Minnie nodded. 'India's asleep.'

'Good,' Janey said, and then the telephone rang.

'Oh, Graham, it's you ... yes, I'm fine—yes, if you like. It's up to you.'

She put the receiver down.

'It's Graham—he's coming down later this morning. If you'd make the tea, Minnie, I have to get some things sorted out.'

She disappeared and Minnie made the tea, looking out of the window every so often as if she expected her father to reappear.

Oh, what a mess! What would they do now? She had never seen her parents like this—they'd never quarrelled. Perhaps it would have been better if they had? Janey was always so busy with things to do, good works and that sort of thing, while Sir John had spent his time in the City—and elsewhere, apparently, Minnie thought with a little curl to her lip. Who would have thought it? She'd never expected such a thing. Somehow one didn't. A father was—well, a father, part of the family unit, and that woman she was sure had been his secretary years ago. Oh, how could he?

Sipping her tea, Janey was making notes, glancing outside to where the little group of reporters had dwindled to two. What did they hope to get out of her now? Once or twice the bell rang but she made no attempt to answer it.

Minnie pulled back a curtain in time to see a car coming up the drive from the side entrance.

'Isn't that Auntie Becky's car?'

'Yes, so it is,' Janey said, and went to open the kitchen door.

Becky's dark eyes were full of concern, and when Janey opened the door, she threw her arms around her. 'Oh, Janey my dear,' she said. 'I am so sorry.'

The two women stood together for a moment or two, and Minnie bit her lip. It always seemed much worse when older people were distressed.

'Cup of tea, Aunt Becky?' she asked.

'Love one, dear.' Becky turned to Janey. 'I can't possibly imagine how you must be feeling,' she said, 'but you must let me know if there is anything I can do. As a matter of fact, I have had an idea, but I don't know how you'll feel about it ...'

'That's very kind of you,' Janey said. 'But really, how does one behave in a situation like this?'

'Well, you know what they say: "If you don't like the heat, get out of the kitchen." And, I must say, that's what I would do.'

'What do you mean?'

'Janey, dear, don't you think you—you and Minnie, perhaps—should go away for a few days until all this mess dies down? It's simply frightful being hounded like this.'

'Oh, no.' Janey shook her head vigorously. 'I couldn't do that, there is so much to do. I need to be—'

'Janey, you don't,' Becky said. 'There is nothing that can't be taken care of Mrs Nelson is a strong capable woman, and you can leave the house in her hands. She won't stand any nonsense from anyone. Think of Minnie and India. Now I've an idea. A friend of mine owns a cottage in Wiltshire, lets it out to friends as a matter of fact. I've been on to her already.'

Janey shook her head, but Becky went on: 'You don't have to decide right away, but think about it. It's a darling cottage, we've been there and it's so cosy. There would even be a cot for India and you could rest there for a week or so, get the shopping in the village, look after yourselves, be away from all this awful hullabaloo. Oh, Janey, don't you see ...'

'But I have to be in court tomorrow, and there's a council meeting on Thursday.'

'Oh, blow the court and the council!' Becky said in a rare outburst. 'No one, pardon me, Janey, is indispensable.'

'You're right there,' she said, and swallowed hard.

Becky went over to her. 'You've had an awful shock. Think about what I've said—the cottage is vacant until the end of September, so you could certainly have a few days there. Give me a ring.'

Janey seemed calmer now. 'Becky, you

are good. I don't know if I'm on my head or my heels.'

'Where is John now?' her friend asked.

'I have no idea,' Janey said. 'I asked him to leave, packed his bag, and that was that.'

'Janey!'

'Well?' She looked belligerent.

'My dear, I can't imagine—I mean, who knows how one would react in similar circumstances?'

'Well, we're all different, Becky,' Janey said, 'and that was my reaction. You see, I knew—I had known all along—and I'd hoped—'

'Janey, how awful! So at least it wasn't a shock. But you believed he might come back, or give her up.'

'Yes. Wishful thinking, I suppose. But when the news broke, I was so mad at him for involving the family—'

'Of course you were,' Becky said, giving Minnie a nod to go upstairs to India.

When the door closed after her, Becky pulled up a chair next to her friend. 'What can I do?'

'Nothing, my dear,' Janey said. 'Graham is coming round later this morning. I do hope he doesn't say anything to those men outside. You can always trust him to put his foot in it.'

'Yes, I saw them as I came in. Perhaps

he'll come by the side door?'

'If he has any sense, he will.'

'Now, you will let me know about going down to Wiltshire? I honestly think you should, Janey.'

'I'll think about it.'

'I can do all the cancelling—nothing matters when you have a situation like this,' Becky said. 'Charity begins at home, Janey.'

It grieved her more than she could say to see her friend sitting so still, all the life gone out of her. Yet she had kept it to herself all this time.

'I'll be off then. Don't forget, pick up the phone.'

No sooner had she gone than Graham rang again.

'Mother? Are you all right?'

'Yes, dear.'

'I was thinking ... are the reporters guys still there?'

'Yes, a couple of them.'

'Well, I wonder if you'd give me a ring when the coast is clear? I don't want to get into any hassle with them. No point.'

'No dear,' she said. Typical Graham!

Seeing Becky's car disappear down the drive, Minnie once more made her way downstairs. How strange the house seemed, not a bit like her usual home—everything was different somehow.

'Mummy—'

Janey turned such a tired and strained face to her that Minnie could have wept. How could this nightmare have come about? And yet, what a good thing she was home. At least she could be with her mother.

'Did you think any more about Aunt Becky's suggestion?'

'I am thinking about it,' Janey said. 'And I must say, the idea of getting out of the way of it all is very appealing.'

'I wish you would,' Minnie said in heart-felt tones.

'Do you? Do you think we should?'

'It's for you to say. I'm sure it would be the best thing, but there's no point if half your mind is back here when you're away.'

'True. I feel I want to run away anywhere, just to get out of the house.'

She peered through the kitchen window and now there were no cars parked outside.

'Run into the hall and see if there's anyone at the front, Minnie.'

'They've gone,' she said, when she returned.

'But they'll be back,' Janey sighed. 'At least for a day or two. Look, I'm going upstairs to the study—I've a few calls to make. Are you agreeable to coming with me to Becky's cottage? If so, I'll ring her and arrange it.'

'I think it's a splendid idea.'

Janey made her way upstairs to her study and picked up the phone.

'Becky, I've decided to take you up on your offer of the cottage. Is that all right?'

'My dear, I am delighted. Much the best thing to do,' Becky said. 'Now, I'll tell you where it is, and ring Carla to let her know you'll be coming—when do you think ... ?'

'I think as soon as it's dark we'll make our way there. Shouldn't be so much traffic the later I make it. Will the cottage be ready?'

'Oh, yes, it's always ready for emergencies like this one,' Becky said kindly. 'I'll ring you back, Janey.'

Then a long call to Sally who was terribly upset about it all, and anxious to do anything to help. Janey explained what she was doing and promised to get in touch from there. Then a call to the social department of the local council, and a member of the Women's Guild, gradually working through all her connections until the last one. They had obviously all heard about the newspaper report for they were very sympathetic and fully in agreement to her going away. 'Don't worry, Janey, we'll manage,' they said. The last call was to Neil Bentinck, a fellow magistrate who sat on the bench with her.

'Neil?'

'Janey, my dear, I hoped you would ring.'

'Of course you've heard?' she began.

'Yes,' he said. 'I'm afraid so, Janey. Is there anything I can do?'

'Bless you, no. But, Neil, I've decided to go away for a few days—will you make my apologies?'

'Of course I will, Janey, and it's a good idea. You know you can rely on me.'

He'd been a good friend. His wife had died two years before, and he had been devastated. Neil would understand, she thought, he had had to face life on his own. Now she thought she understood how *he* must have felt; what it had meant after a long marriage.

'I shall probably be away a week or so, and I'm taking Minnie and her baby with me.'

'Don't worry about a thing, my dear,' he said. 'Everything will be quite all right here. You look after yourself, Janey, and that new grand-daughter of yours.'

Yes, she thought, putting down the phone. It was good to have friends. And it would be nice to have time to concentrate on Minnie and the baby without being so involved in other matters.

Now for Mrs Nelson. She dialled the

number and waited.

'Off you go, My Lady, and you can rely on me,' Mrs Nelson said stoutly. 'It'll all die a death in a day or two and when you come back people will hardly remember it happened.'

'Bless you.'

Wishful thinking, Janey thought. Still ...

'And I'll keep them reporters out of the way, never you fear,' Mrs Nelson said. 'You go off and have a good rest, and take care of your Minnie and the baby.'

'I'll phone you,' Janey said.

For the first time that day she felt a spark of hope.

By the time they had everything ready, and had received and made several more telephone calls, they were packed and ready to go: India in her sleeping basket, with clothes, nappies and blankets, Janey and Minnie with the least possible luggage.

'Everything is there,' Janey said. 'Someone will have put sheets on the beds, isn't that wonderful?

'Still no sign of Graham,' Minnie said.

'I'm not surprised,' her mother said. 'It's not his strong point. He's hardly a tower of strength in times of trouble.'

It was almost midnight when they left the house. As Janey drove down the drive and the gates clicked behind her, she thought: Things will never be the same again. That part of my life is over.

'All right?' she asked Minnie sitting beside her.

'Just fine, Mummy,' she said, swallowing hard.

'Good thing you're nursing India yourself,' Janey said practically. 'Saves no end of trouble.'

But Minnie was wondering bleakly where her father was.

Chapter Fifteen

It was a lovely September evening when Sally and Tom walked to the top of the garden, stopping now and again to look at something that caught their eye, for the garden, thanks to William, was still colourful.

'What are those?' Tom said, pointing to a brilliant clump of flowers by the hedge.

'Asters,' Sally said. 'Aren't the colours lovely?' There was every shade of mauve and pink, vibrant colours which merged well with the tints of the shrubs and trees now beginning to change with the onset of autumn. 'They remind me of when I was a little girl—when we had Brickhurst Hall and there were gardeners. There were always asters at this time of year, and dahlias. All the brilliant things.'

'It's nice you can remember those days,' he said. 'Life has changed a lot for you, one way and another.'

'Yes, but for the better, I think,' she said, putting an arm through his.

He squeezed her closer to him.

'Aren't we lucky, Tom?' she said. 'When I think of Janey and John—'

'Yes, I know—' But he stopped short as they beheld the overwhelming conservatory, towering above the landscape. 'I suppose the Carpenters will be back soon? Late September, wasn't it?'

'Yes, and those builders have made tremendous strides. I can't wait to see it all. What will you do, Tom, about the application to develop the field?'

'Go to see Ron,' Tom said. 'Strictly speaking, it's none of my business if a neighbour wants to apply for planning permission for a field that doesn't belong to him. It doesn't to me, for that matter. Still, it matters to the community, so I certainly would like an explanation. And it'd better be a good one,' he said grimly. 'Though actually I am more interested in how he has been able to do all this work on The Mount ...'

It was lovely in London the next day,

too, as Auguste Vandenburg walked out of Claridges on his way to MacBane's for the sale of Spanish and Italian paintings. He enjoyed coming to London; had been doing so since his father brought him as a young man way back in the sixties. His father, Klaus Vandenburg, the renowned authority on Old Masters, had died some years before and Auguste now carried on the Vandenburg tradition. Good as he was in his field—and there was none currently better—Auguste realised and accepted the fact that he had none of his father's genius. He had an instinctive love of fine art, had been trained by his father and gained experience all over the world, but did not possess the spark to propel him into the realms of the great. His father could look at a picture and tell you when and where it had been painted, and was seldom if ever wrong.

Nevertheless, Auguste was revered, not only out of deference to his father, but because he was a thoroughly likeable man in his own right. He came to London several times a year, and there was nothing he liked more than to be here strolling down Bond Street on a morning which, although still late-summer, already had an autumnal feel to it. And he liked MacBane's—liked the way they did business. He had his eye on four paintings today, already had buyers who were prepared to go to almost any price to get what they wanted. Nevertheless, he frowned on anyone who thought such commissions came easily. It was a huge responsibility to purchase on anyone's behalf, especially in the field of fine art. It was a highly profitable yet dangerous business, especially today with prices soaring sky high and the competition so fierce.

There was a special treat in store for him later. Young MacBane had told him he was in for a surprise. After the sale, he was to see something special, apparently. Auguste could hardly wait.

He took his own special seat, the one he always had, and though he barely turned his head, his sharp eyes missed nothing. He knew them all: the foreign dealers, the buyers, the bidders for the wealthy men who never visited a sale themselves, and a smattering of oddbods as he called them, who were new to the game and fascinated by the drama being enacted in front of them. Sometimes he wished he was back in that state of ignorance again, when auctions were magical events. But really, after all this time, he recognised them for what they were: business pure and simple.

He secured three of the paintings and lost the fourth to a Japanese gentleman bidding on behalf of a big conglomerate. A pity, it was his favourite.

He went up to verify his purchases, nodding pleasantly to old friends, being congratulated on his success, enjoying the moment.

Business over, he made his way to Alistair MacBane's sanctum. Alistair replied to his knock, and seeing who it was, rose to his feet and came forward, gripping the Dutchman's hand.

'Great to see you, Auguste,' he said. 'Were you lucky?'

'Yes, three out of four,' he said. 'I can't complain.'

'Sit down,' Alistair said. 'Your usual?'

'Please.' Auguste hitched his immaculate trousers and made himself comfortable.

Alistair poured two tiny glasses of liqueur and handed one to Auguste, who downed it in a single gulp.

Then, beaming, he rubbed his hands together and put down his glass.

'So what have you to show me?' he asked.

'I think I'll leave you guessing,' Alistair said. 'Your pleasure will be even greater when you realise what they are.'

They talked pleasantly for a time until Alistair pushed back his chair and led the way down through a maze of dark little passages and the smell of which he never tired: the smell of antiquity.

Alistair unlocked a door and led the way. The room was very dark, a long narrow window being covered by a heavy curtain to keep out the light. He switched on low spotlights and rang a bell. Two porters appeared. Seating Auguste some way from a central dais, Alistair asked for the lights to be switched on. On the dais stood two great easels over which hung floor-length drapes. At Alistair's bidding, the porter removed one of the heavy covers and exposed in all its glory was a Goya: rich dark jewel colours immediately recognisable, brooding yet vibrant.

Auguste made no sign, not a movement of his fingers or a flicker of his eyes, but the light in them was unmistakable. The sight of the painting had evoked incredulity and wonder.

Then he slumped back and let out a slow breath, with a slight nod letting Alistair know he was ready for the next one.

This was even more impressive: a portrait of a nobleman with cloak wrapped about him, hat at a rakish angle, a distant landscape stretching away behind him. The background was so vivid one wanted to walk into the picture, to be a part of it, to tread that road that led so invitingly into the unknown.

Glancing at him, Alistair saw that his friend's forehead was beaded with sweat, such an impact had the paintings had on him.

They said nothing for a time, then as if summoning his strength, Auguste got up and moved towards the dais as Alistair motioned the two porters to leave.

Auguste moved the bright lamps to his liking, taking out his special glass and peering through it, moving round to the back of the canvasses. With arms folded, Alistair stood watching him. He liked to see a professional at work, admired the absorption and concentration needed.

It must have been all of twenty minutes that Alistair waited, and then Auguste stood up and dabbed at his forehead.

'Shall we sit down?' he asked.

Alistair led the way back to the seat.

'Magnificent,' Auguste said reverently.

Alistair smiled proudly.

'But—' Auguste said softly, so quietly that Alistair hardly heard him.

He turned round sharply.

'What?'

'My friend,' Auguste said, 'you won't often hear me say this—but I should like a second opinion.'

'Good God!' Alistair said, shocked at the implication.

'Well, even I am not infallible.' And

Auguste gave a wry smile. 'May I ask where you obtained them?'

'You may,' Alistair said grimly. 'Spain.' And saw Auguste's eyebrows raise very slightly. 'Madrid.'

'Then I think—no, it is not possible. There is only one man who could have done this—if they are not genuine, that is—and he is dead long since.'

'My God!' Alistair said. 'What are you saying?'

'Look.' Auguste tried to calm him down. 'You and I know how careful we have to be if there is the slightest doubt. And I say there is a tiny, very tiny, suspicion in my mind.'

'But what did you see? What are you looking for?'

Auguste got up and went over to the picture again. He looked into the extreme bottom corner with a finger just pressing the canvas, so lightly as hardly to touch it.

'I should get Landvet over, he's in New York at the moment.'

'Landvet? You think it's that serious?'

'I do, though you know how I hate asking a second opinion. I have to be sure, so much is at stake. I would like them to be genuine for your sake, as well as for the future of MacBane's.'

Alistair stood by his side, tight-lipped.

'They will need a great deal of vetting,' Auguste said. 'Not only because there is this slight doubt in my mind ... but because they are perfect—almost—and let us admit—I could be wrong. I hope I am—'

'But could anyone really copy—'

'Yes—of course—if he was good enough. These are perhaps by Goya—perhaps not—get Landvet—oh, and MacBane—find out more about where you obtained them. Who did you send?'

'Blanchard.'

'Well, he's a good man. He should know a Goya when he sees one. I'll be in touch again. Give me a call if you need me. You know where I am.'

Alistair sat back and thought hard. Down here it was quiet. Only muffled sounds came through the thick walls, and the heavy sonorous ticking of the old German clock bought by his grandfather many years before had never seemed so loud. After fifteen minutes, he had made up his mind.

He dialled the number of Tessa's office, and when she did not reply eventually managed to contact her on her mobile phone.

'Tessa—Alistair. Look, could we have dinner this evening?' He sensed the hesitation when she took her time in answering.

'Er—well—'

'I wish you would. I've found this nice little place in Kensington.'

'Yes, all right, I can manage that.'

'Good,' he said. 'I'll see you around six-thirty—we'll have a drink first.'

Well, why not? Tessa thought, putting down the phone. Otherwise, it was just another quiet evening at home.

Alistair waited for her by the reception desk, a tall good-looking man in an impeccably cut suit, his profile against the light showing a strong, slightly beaked nose and well-shaped mouth. He turned as Tessa came towards him, and as always his heart leaped on seeing her. He had begun to wish now that he didn't feel this way about her, for she obviously had no interest in him. Still, tonight was different. She was not to know there was another purpose behind his invitation.

'Tessa,' He smiled at her, his deep-set grey eyes meeting hers, drinking in the heart-shaped face, the swing of shiny dark hair against her cheek.

When she smiled, it lit up her face. In repose she was inclined to look serious.

'I thought we'd take a taxi to the park and walk across it's such a lovely evening,' he said. 'Is that all right with you?'

'I'd love a walk,' she said, and meant it. After working in dark dusty rooms all day there was a desperate need for sun and air.

Alistair hailed a taxi which dropped them at the entrance to the park and then they stepped out, seeing the homegoing crowds, young lovers meeting, and the flower beds still full of colour on this late-summer's evening. The Serpentine shone like glass reflecting the setting sun. Dogs being led by their owners went slightly mad when they were let off the lead. Small boys were looking for conkers, and against the setting sun the tall buildings of Park Lane shone red against the sky. Alistair wished with all his heart that he could put his arm through hers but knew that this move would not be appreciated. Tessa did not grant such favours lightly.

They talked of this and that, and by the time they had reached the Prince of Wales gate, were both slightly flushed with the walk and the fresh air. Alistair hailed a taxi which drove them to a quiet Kensington backwater.

Tessa was impressed. She had never been to this restaurant before, and it was fairly obvious that it was discreet and quite luxurious.

'We'll have a drink before eating, shall we?' he asked as the waiter stood by. Tessa nodded.

'Certainly, sir.' The waiter led them to a

small alcove where a low table sat in front of curved cushioned seats.

He waited until Tessa was comfortable before asking. 'What will you have? Sherry, dry martini, cocktail?'

'A dry martini, please,' she said.

'Make that two,' Alistair agreed, looking around to see who was there. Then he glanced at Tessa again. How lovely she looked. He wondered if she knew just how appealing she was to the rest of the male staff. She had a slightly imperious air, although his word for it would have been shy, and was not at all the sort of girl who would exchange jokes with the rest of the staff. A serious-minded girl, he would have said, and yet there was something about her that indicated she might not be all she seemed. Perhaps underneath the cool exterior lay an undiscovered warmth, passion even—or was that wishful thinking? At all events, the centre of her interest was certainly Blanchard—and, manlike, Alistair could never understand why. Why delectable women like her fell for—well, men who fell short by other men's standards. Still, this wasn't why he had asked her out. He had something much more important on his mind. They sat and admired the decor: the good pictures that adorned the walls, and the magnificent flowers arranged in great urns.

They had finished the main course before Alistair decided to mention what was on his mind. By then he hoped the excellent red wine and the intimate atmosphere would have melted her coolness a little. Fortunately for him, Tessa was the first to mention the subject which was on his mind.

'I expect you're looking forward to announcing the arrival of the Goyas to the press?' she said, smiling across at him.

'Yes, I am,' he said. 'It's quite an event for MacBane's—for any fine arts auctioneers.'

'What did Herr Vandenburg have to say? I bet he did a double take when he saw them.'

'Mmm.' Alistair nodded, sipping his wine.

They waited while the waiter cleared away.

'You know, I miss getting around as I used to—it can be quite dull, being home-based,' he said. 'I enjoyed my training. I spent eight years out and about, under my father's supervision of course. But that was before you joined the firm. I think we started in London around the same time.'

'Two years ago,' she said. 'Yes, I

suppose you must do. Being able to get out and buy is great fun—one of the perks, I always think.' It was true. She hadn't realised that nowadays he was mostly cooped up in London, running the business.

'I'm sure you enjoyed Madrid,' he said. 'Had you been before?'

'No, never. It was wonderful. I certainly want to go back.'

They ordered a pudding, and Alistair went on.

'I suppose we were lucky they chose us—the Contessa's family. You must tell me about it? I'd like to get the background, it sounds most interesting.'

Pleased to relive her trip to Madrid, Tessa was only too glad to talk about it.

'Where did they live? In the centre of Madrid?'

'Yes, a delightful old house—tall and timbered with wrought-iron balconies. It was a joy. And the Contessa gave us lunch.'

'What was she like—the Contessa?' he asked casually.

'Oh, simply beautiful. Young and Italian-looking, rather than Spanish.'

And that would have pleased Blanchard, thought Alistair. He probably fell for her hook, line and sinker.

'And then there were these wonderful tapestries, wall hangings, quite a collection of stuff—Turkish rugs and artefacts. I was simply furious when she decided not to sell.'

Alistair thought hard. Yes, why had she changed her mind?

A delicious confection arrived for pudding, followed by cheese and coffee, and by now Tessa had relaxed and was enjoying herself.

'And her father was a sweetie.'

'Her father?'

She frowned. 'I think so—he could have been her grandfather. No, her father, she said. Perhaps he was quite old when she was born. Anyway he was in a wheelchair and quite frail. It was for him, of course, that she was getting rid of the Goyas—to pay for his treatment which they get in America. It's very expensive, I understand.'

'I'm sure,' Alistair said seriously. 'Well, she certainly owned them, that much we had to make sure of.'

'Why—was there some doubt?' Tessa asked curiously.

'No, of course not—just that there has to be proof of ownership when something as valuable as this is at stake.'

'Oh, of course, I realise that.'

'So, how interesting it must have been. And I am sure Blan—Hugo must have enjoyed the visit. A lovely young Contessa.'

You don't like him, Tessa thought, you're jealous. But really I mustn't be unfair. You are quite nice, and good company. It's just you don't have the charm and magnetism of Hugo ...

They finished their coffee, talking of other things: the business, Tessa's interest in textiles.

'And so you go home most evenings to—where is it?'

'Sorry,' she said. 'Yes, I still live at home, in a place called Swansbridge—it's not much more than a village.'

He smiled across at her, his grey eyes meeting hers.

'And you take the train home, I suppose?'

She nodded, picking up her handbag.

'We'll get a taxi to Waterloo.'

'No, there's no need. I can get a tube.'

'Indeed you won't,' he said.

'Thank you for a lovely evening,' she said. 'I thought the dinner was perfect.'

'Yes, we must do it again sometime,' he said.

'I did enjoy it,' Tessa said, and to her surprise found she meant it.

Leaving her, Alistair took a taxi back to MacBane's and let himself into his flat at the top of the building.

It was spacious with wonderful views. He

sank back into a chair and sat thinking for some time. Then, glancing at his watch, he moved into the study where he picked up the telephone and dialled a New York number.

'Will you ask Mr Landvet to telephone me in London? He has my number. Tell him it's urgent.' And putting the phone down, he sat back and looked out over the lights of London.

Well, he had done all he could for now. Calling in Landvet was expensive but needs must. There must have been real doubt in Vandenburg's mind for him to have suggested it. And Tessa—what he wouldn't give to be on the receiving end of one of those lovely smiles she gave Blanchard whenever they were together. But try as he might to focus now on her loveliness, what kept him awake were the Goyas ...

Tessa, on her way home, and the late train was fairly full, thought about her evening with Alistair. She supposed he wasn't bad-looking. He had nice grey eyes that looked straight at you. Disconcerting sometimes—it wouldn't be easy to lie. But then, she had nothing to hide except her infatuation with Hugo—which, if she faced up to it, was a waste of time. He obviously cared nothing for her, never had, and now that he had the lovely Contessa—or Tessa supposed that he had—why waste any further thoughts on him?

But he was so handsome with those black unruly curls, the dark eyes that smouldered—he surely wasn't completely English? He was a sort of Heathcliff, with a brooding quality. She shivered slightly. Well, she must be drawn to that type of man, and Alistair MacBane was so boringly English, or Scottish if the truth were told. Dependable, though. Kind. And it had been a treat to be taken out to dinner. She should do it more often—accept more invitations. It wasn't as if she was never asked. Her mother would be pleased too. She always said: 'All work and no play, makes Jill a dull girl.'

Tessa wondered how Minnie was getting on in Wiltshire. What an awful thing to have happened to the Utox-Smythe family. And that lovely baby ... As soon as they returned home she would telephone Minnie, perhaps take her out for lunch or dinner if Janey didn't mind baby sitting.

And now Cobbets Green station where several people got out. Tessa made for the car park where her little Renault was waiting for her.

Yes, all in all it had been a very good evening.

Chapter Sixteen

It was dark when Janey drove through the little Wiltshire village, but thanks to a very carefully drawn map from Becky, she was able to find the cottage easily. Driving through the entrance to Besford Farm, then up a winding drive, she saw the low timbered building. When she stopped the car, Minnie, who had been sleeping, woke drowsily, sitting up straight and looking about her. 'Can't see a thing.' She squinted. 'Are we there?' She turned round to look on the back seat where India lay in her carry cot, oblivious to the world.

Minnie rubbed her eyes. 'Well, this looks interesting,' she said. 'Mummy, what a brick you are. All that way while I slept.'

'No problem, the roads were clear,' Janey said, although in truth she was somewhat stiff and anxious to get out and stretch her legs.

'Let me open the door and let you in. We'll just take the overnight bag and India's things and leave the rest until morning. Thank goodness we didn't bring much—we'll take her in last.'

Once inside with the lights switched on,

it was bright and cosy. Warm, too, for someone had put the heating on, and there was a note from the owners telling them to ring if they should need anything, and some milk and tea and coffee.

'Oh!' Janey said. 'Aren't people kind?'

Minnie could see that she was on the verge of tears. 'Look, let's get India in and then we can close the door. I should think the car's all right there for the night.'

They could see nothing outside in the dark. With the door closed and the curtains pulled, they looked briefly around the kitchen and went upstairs. Two pretty bedrooms, with a cot in one for the baby, and wonder of wonders—hot water bottles in the bed. Cool now but the clothes were aired.

'Oh!' Janey cried. 'Bliss!' And kicking off her shoes, she lay back quietly for a moment or two.

'I'll go downstairs and make us a hot drink,' Minnie said. Thank God for Becky, she thought. Her mother was all in.

They slept like the proverbial log, and woke to India's cry and a lovely October morning. Stepping out of bed, Janey pulled back the curtains to look at her surroundings. It was like something out of a picture book, grounds sweeping away before her to a big Georgian house set in open countryside. But the real glory was the river—could it be the Avon, Janey wondered?—which ran past the house, and curved back round an island to flow in front of the cottage. There was a slight mist, the sun breaking through, the water gleaming, and she caught her breath at its beauty. A tranquil setting if ever there was one. She unlocked the front door and went outside, walking down to the river's edge where two fine ducks sailed past. What bliss, she thought, to be away from everything if only for a few days. She must make the most of it. And then, sailing round a bend in the river, a swan came gliding by, her wings half open, head held high, and Janey felt a lump in her throat. Somehow she just knew it was a female. The swan sailed up to her and stopped, regarding Janey, her feathers as white as snow, before moving off again to the opposite side of the river.

Janey felt she could stay here and watch this scene forever—such perfect peace and tranquillity. Then she was interrupted by Minnie's call. 'Mummy, where are you?'

'Coming, darling.' And she retraced her steps to the house.

After breakfast they unpacked, and Janey looked around the cottage. It was a dear little house, just such a refuge as one might want in times of stress. Stress, Janey thought, and bit her lip. She had never imagined it would be like this. She had seen her life continuing in the future in much the same way it had done for the past few years. At first she had imagined that John would tire of Melissa—for it was Melissa, of course, she had always known that. Ever since a nosy neighbour had said she had seen them dining, John and his secretary, in a little tucked away place in the Cotswolds when he should have been in Brussels. The woman had moved away since then, and Janey had kept the secret to herself. She had met Melissa once or twice at business functions when she was John's secretary and thought then how beautiful she was. Never dreaming when John said she was leaving that she was doing anything other than finding another high-powered job.

She'd never imagined that the woman ran a little high-class gown shop in Cobbets Green. So near! All that time and she had never known. What if she had gone into the shop? But it wasn't likely. She usually shopped in town, and John knew that.

She sighed deeply, and while Minnie unpacked the food, broke off a piece of bread from the loaf and strolled out into the garden, breathing deeply of the scented air, and wandering down to the river. It was an idyllic spot. As she arrived at the water's edge, the swan glided swiftly towards her and Janey broke the bread into pieces and threw it to the bird. She wasn't young, Janey guessed. And where is your partner? she wanted to ask, knowing that swans mate for life. But the swan looked down, her slim neck curved, and moved away to the far bank.

Every day, Janey took a chair to the side of the river and rested, her thoughts gradually settling, the sense of disbelief and shock and horror slowly becoming easier to bear. And every day the swan glided towards her and Janey fed her. Once or twice the bird came out of the water to stand at her side. She had never been that close to a swan before and kept very still, for she had heard that a swan could lash out with a wing and break an arm, but she felt no fear, just a warm feeling of companionship.

'Mummy,' Minnie said one day, coming over to her, 'you've really made a friend there, haven't you?' And she smiled. She felt even more sorry for her mother now that she was away from home, realising how deep the hurt had been, how wonderfully brave Janey had been throughout it all.

'What say we go down to the village? It's not far, we can walk.'

'Good idea,' Janey said, and they set out with the baby's little pushchair.

'I'm so glad you came back safely

from India,' Janey said presently. 'I really missed you.'

'Did you?' And Minnie turned a glowing face towards her.

'Of course,' said Janey.

'We haven't seen Graham yet, have we? I wonder how he's taken it?' Minnie commented.

'Oh, he'll survive,' Janey said grimly. She had no illusions about her only son. What she was wondering most acutely was where John had got to with his paramour. They would have had to leave the shop, and had obviously gone to ground somewhere. Once, years ago, he had had a small flat in town, but that had been sold. Well, he had Melissa to himself now. No more lies, no more double standards, no need for pretence. And she realised painfully that she wished things could have gone on as they were—at least then she'd had a husband of sorts.

But it was a calmer Janey who left the cottage and the swan on the last day. This tranquil space of time had done her good, enabled her to see things more clearly—awful though they were. She even found herself wondering on the way back home if John might be there, at home in Swansbridge, begging for forgiveness, asking her to start again.

'Hmm!' A small sound escaped her.

Such stuff as dreams are made of, she thought harshly, her face grim, causing Minnie to throw a sidelong glance at her.

'All right, Mummy? Would you like me to take over?'

'No, I'm fine, darling,' Janey lied. 'Just fine.'

John and Melissa stayed four days in the small hotel they found in South Yorkshire, but the accommodation was small and the cloud that hung over them did nothing to help relations between them. John finally suggested they should make tracks for London where they would find a flat.

'Oh,' Melissa said softly. 'Do you think we should?'

'Look, it's out now—no need for any more secrecy. We'll have to face up to it. Have you any other suggestions?'

Strange, Melissa thought, he would never have spoken so sharply to her before it all happened. But the strain was beginning to tell. They neither of them wanted it to be like this.

'No, darling, as you say we can be lost in London—no one will even notice us.' And she smiled at him brightly.

They booked into an obscure hotel and went flat hunting, finding a luxury apartment in Chelsea. Fourth-floor, large, with gracious rooms and a view over the river.

She put her arms around him, her head on his chest. 'Darling, this is lovely. Just to be together.'

He kissed her, holding her tight, his beautiful Melissa. Now at last they were free.

'I'll notify people gradually,' he said. 'Those who matter. We can't expect the fuss to die down straight away but people have short memories. It will be forgotten in a little while.'

Melissa wondered if Janey intended to divorce him. She had nothing to lose herself, had already lost her reputation such as it was, and there would be nothing she would like more, but she had a shrewd suspicion that although Janey wanted John out of her life, she was not going to divorce him.

But Melissa at least was happy. She had John to herself now, and it was not as if they were new to the situation. They had been lovers for nine years, and even before that, when she had first come as a young girl of twenty-one to be his private secretary's assistant, she had fallen in love with him. When Miss Banks had retired, Melissa had stepped into her shoes, openly adoring her employer. He was twice her age, a famous figure—how could she have dreamed it would ever end like this? It was more than she'd dared hope for.

It seemed so strange to be sitting at breakfast together, with no fear of being discovered. It was almost as good as being his wife and Melissa felt a sense of relief that it was all out in the open at last. John had put his things in the small dressing room that led off the main bedroom, his personal belongings, leather holdalls and silver brushes—but no photographs. She had half expected to see one of Minnie, his daughter. One day when he was in the City she looked in the drawers, but there were only neatly folded clothes in there, where she had put them when they were laundered. A man without possessions, she thought. Did he miss them, his family? There had been no word from Graham—and for that she was relieved. She had never liked the sound of his son, had been shocked to hear of the antics of that spoilt young man.

It was one early evening in October when the doorbell rang and John went to answer it. Over his shoulder, Melissa saw a man a little taller than John, a younger version of him, and realised with a shock that this was his son.

'Graham!' John was obviously surprised, but Graham held out his hand. 'Dad, it's great to see you. I'd have come before but—'

'How did you know I was here?' John asked, closing the door behind them.

'I rang Asher and he told me—you don't mind, my finding your hideaway?' And he gave a conspiratorial grin, looking sidelong at Melissa with more than a little interest.

John crossed the room. 'I'd like you to meet Melissa,' he said, not best pleased at his son's arrival, she could see. 'Melissa Wilding—my son, Graham.'

Melissa found her hand grasped warmly and was surprised, close to, to see how like his father Graham was. A striking resemblance, yet John was by far the more imposing figure. She realised the son was but a pale imitation of his father.

'Sit down,' John said, though Melissa could tell he was quite put out by his son's arrival. 'What can I get you to drink?'

He moved over to the drinks cabinet.

'A whisky would be fine,' Graham said, making himself comfortable on the sofa and staring across at Melissa quite openly now.

'You don't mind my coming, I hope?' he asked her.

'No, not at all,' she said politely.

'What for you, Melissa?'

'A dry sherry, please, John.' And there was an awkward silence as he came over with the tray.

'There we are,' he said stiffly, and sat himself down at Melissa's side. 'And to what do we owe this honour?' he asked, taking his glass from the tray.

'Well—' And Graham hesitated. 'I thought I'd come to pay my—respects. Or is that the wrong word?'

But John ignored the question. 'How are you?' he asked. 'Business good?'

'Yes, thanks.'

'Will you excuse me?' Melissa said, making a quiet exit and going into the kitchen to find something to eat with the drinks.

Cheese biscuits, she thought, nuts—and now they can say what they like to each other. Will John ask after Janey? What sort of awkward conversation will there be?

She wasted a few moments finding bowls and dishes and finally went back into the drawing room.

'Ah, thanks,' Graham said gratefully, helping himself, while John sat with a scowl on his face.

Graham sat back with a grin. 'Look,' he said, 'I know I've rather burst in unannounced but quite frankly, I was worried.'

'Well, no need to be,' John said. 'And

I don't want this address bandied about, Graham.'

'Of course not,' he said in a man to man voice. 'I quite understand.' He turned to Melissa. 'I expect you know all about me,' he said. 'I know you and Dad have been friends for a long time.'

'Yes, we have,' John said.

'Look, Dad,' Graham continued, 'you don't want to worry about me. I quite understand—I won't say a word. I mean, if there is anything I can do—'

'Have you seen your mother?' John asked abruptly.

Graham looked down. 'No, I haven't as a matter of fact. I think she's been away.'

'Well, you might give her a call, if you're not too busy,' John said. 'She'd be glad of a word.'

'Yes, I will,' Graham said, and hastily downing his drink, stood up.

'Well, I'd best be off. I only called in to see you were all right.'

'Yes, thanks,' his father said. 'I'll see you out.' And walked him across to the door.

Graham held out his hand. 'Goodbye, Melissa,' he said, and for a moment she thought he was going to take her hand to his lips. 'I'll be off now. Nice to have met you.'

'Cheerio, Dad.' And he was gone.

John's face was livid when he came back. He clenched and unclenched his fists.

'John, he meant well—he just wanted to see you. It's not going to be easy—'

'No one said it was,' John said testily. 'I could have done without it, that's all. He's as useless as a—'

'Finish your drink,' she urged.

Well, Graham thought smugly, getting out of the lift. What a turn up for the book! My word, the old man was a rum one and all those years ... And she was a real good looker—well, Dad certainly knew how to pick them. And, humming to himself, he called a taxi.

After he had gone, John was quieter than usual. All through the meal, he seemed preoccupied. When Melissa had cleared away the dinner things and disappeared into the kitchen, he stood looking out of the window far into the distance, where the lights of London began to go on and the Thames shone like glass. It was a beautiful scene, but John saw none of it.

When Melissa returned, he stood silently for a while and she picked up a magazine and browsed through it, knowing he was best left alone with his thoughts. When he did finally turn round, she saw that he was tense and his eyes anxious.

He came to her and sat down.

'I'm going to have to see Janey.'

'Of course,' Melissa said softly. 'Of course you must see her.'

'There's a lot to discuss, and I hope we can do so like sensible adults,' he said. 'After all, I have a family to consider, and there's the house and the business.'

'You don't have to explain to me, John,' Melissa said quietly. 'I do understand. It is only fair—you can't just walk out and leave it at that.'

He turned to face her and covered her hand with his.

'Thank you, my dear,' he said. 'It can't have been easy for her, any more than it was for us.'

'No, we mustn't lose sight of that,' Melissa agreed.

'So I'll set the wheels in motion. I have no idea if she'll want a divorce.'

Melissa refrained from asking the question she was longing to ask. Would you, John? Want a divorce? No, best leave it unsaid.

'Well, you must see her,' she said firmly. After all, she could afford to be generous. She had got what she'd always wanted.

John waited until he knew it was a day when Janey would be home and Mrs Nelson not there. He waited for her to answer the phone with an accustomed feeling of trepidation. When he finally heard her voice, it seemed the most natural thing in the world. 'Janey Utox-Smythe.'

'Janey—it's John.' It seemed ages before she answered.

'Oh, John ...'

'Janey, I—we have to talk. May I see you sometime?'

'I don't think there is anything we have to say to each other,' she said in a firm voice. 'Nothing that could not be said in front of a solicitor anyway.'

'Janey, is that what you want—a divorce?'

'Isn't that the sensible thing to do?' she asked. 'In all fairness to everyone.'

'Well, I'd like to see you about it, talk about it—it's no good saying I'm sorry.'

'No,' she said coolly.

'So what about—shall I come to the house?'

'Well ...'

'Why not?'

'I suppose there's no good reason.' She didn't add: 'Because I don't want to see you—ever again. I couldn't bear it.'

'You're not still being plagued by reporters, are you?' He sounded anxious.

'No, mercifully. They've gone away.'

'Janey, I'm really sorry about the way it happened. I had no idea ...'

'Shall we say next Tuesday evening?' she said. 'Would that be convenient?'

'Yes, of course. Around eight o'clock— will that suit you?'

'I'll see you then.'

Janey put the phone back on its hook, her heart thumping wildly. She wondered if she could persuade Minnie to go to visit Tessa Sheffield after she had put India to bed. She didn't want any complications. It would be simpler that way, just herself and John, though already she found herself dreading it.

If only she could put back the clock ...

Chapter Seventeen

'How was Gran?' Sally asked William when he arrived back late on Sunday evening from visiting her mother.

'Oh, simply great—she looks wonderful. She gave us a super tea, made the cake herself, and says she is looking forward to her eightieth birthday. We will all be going, won't we, Mum?'

'Of course, William,' said Sally staunchly. 'Time was when Gran would have come here for a few days, but I don't think she could do it now, the journey both ways. It would tire her too much. Anyway, we'll all go up and make a weekend of it, perhaps. An eightieth birthday is something of a celebration, after all.'

'She'll love that. We could stay in that little hotel in the village.'

'Well, it's not until December, so we'll work something out. Did you give her the flowers and the book?'

'Yes, she was pleased with them. She had had her hair done, said someone from the village, a hairdresser girl, comes in.'

'That's nice,' Sally said, giving the draining board a final wipe down.

Imagine her mother being eighty! Perhaps it was time to make some other arrangements for her. She was getting too old to run that little house herself—but she had help and was happy, living in a place she loved ...

Yes, Sally thought, they would make a wonderful occasion of Emily's eightieth birthday and she promised herself she would get down to making plans for it as soon as possible.

When the telephone rang that evening it turned out to be Minnie wanting to speak to Tessa.

'Minnie would like to come round on Tuesday,' she said, coming back into the kitchen. 'After she's put India to bed. Her mother will look after her.'

'Oh, that'll be nice. Minnie will be glad of a break.'

'And I'd like to hear how they got on in Wiltshire,' Tessa said. 'Apparently it's a lovely little cottage, and she would thoroughly recommend it.'

Monday brought a dull wet day and it was soon fairly obvious that the Carpenters had arrived back home, judging by the cars in the drive and the lights on all over the house, including the vast conservatory. Tom said it looked like Piccadilly Circus.

'They've certainly put The Mount on the map,' he said. 'Aren't they new, those lights down the drive? I don't remember seeing them before.' Tall lamp standards were strung along the drive, each hung with a pair of huge glass globes.

'Yes, they're new,' Sally said. 'I haven't seen them lit up yet.'

'It's a pity, I think,' he said. 'The illusion of living in the countryside has gone. It used to be so nice with just the occasional light showing through the trees.'

'Perhaps they feel more lights will put off intruders and burglars?' Sally said. 'There's always two sides to everything.'

'Well, I'd rather have it as it was,' her husband grumbled. 'Nothing's been the same since that lot moved in.'

Sally knew what he meant, and that evening when Tessa arrived home it was obvious she felt the same as her father.

'Have you seen next door?' she cried. 'The lights almost blinded me! How could they do that—it's like the Christmas illuminations in Regent Street!'

Sally laughed. 'How did you get on today?' she asked.

'Well, funny you should ask but there was a rather odd atmosphere about MacBane's today. When Alistair passed me on the stairs he just nodded, and I couldn't seem to get a word out of Hugo.' She shrugged. 'Anyway, for my part I was quite pleased. A dear old soul brought in some fabulous pottery—a pair of Egyptian vases, absolutely wonderful. She said her husband had had them since before World War One. Imagine—he was an archaeologist, long dead now, and she was hard up and needed the money. I was able to tell her they were quite valuable. I love it when something like that happens, it makes it so worthwhile.'

She flung her jacket down on a chair. 'So the Carpenters are back. Can we look forward to that awful girl, what's-her-name, joining us on the train to town—or have Daddy and I now got to play hide-and-seek again?'

'Oh, come on, she can't be that bad!' Sally cried. 'Incidentally, Pauline phoned and asked us in on Saturday for drinks at lunchtime.'

'Sorry,' Tessa said, studying her nails. 'I won't be able to join you.'

'Why? Where are you going?' Sally asked suspiciously.

'Don't know yet,' her daughter said with a grin, 'but it won't be next door to the Carpenters.' And she picked up her jacket and made for the hall.

Sally sighed, and checked the casserole. What a pity the Carpenters were as they were—and yet they were friendly and likeable enough. But not to Tessa, she thought, and certainly not to Tom.

When Tessa opened the door on Tuesday evening to Minnie Utox-Smythe, she was delighted to see her.

'Come on upstairs,' she said, 'to my room—we can talk up there. Oh, it is good to see you! Sit down there—that's a comfortable chair. I'll get us some coffee later. How's India?'

'She's great,' Minnie said, blissfully sinking into the small but comfortable chair, 'but I'll let you into a little secret. Dad is coming to visit Mother this evening!' And she waited for the news to sink in.

'No!' Tessa said, open-mouthed. 'Really?'

'Mummy only told me just as I was leaving. I was furious. "So that's why you were trying to get rid of me," I said. But she explained that he was coming to talk things over.'

'Oh! You don't think ...'

'No such luck, I'm afraid. He's coming to talk about the separation or divorce or whatever is on the cards. And when you think about it, there must be lots to talk about. I suppose she thought I would be better out of the way.'

'That's true,' Tessa agreed. 'So, besides that, how's it all going?'

'Well, we had a wonderful week in Wiltshire and I'm sure it did Mummy a world of good. As much as anything could. She misses him, Tess.'

'Of course she does! They've been married forever, haven't they?'

'Yes.'

'Even longer than my parents,' Tessa said. 'You know, he was a pig, behaving like that, Minnie.'

'I know—I do know, Tessa. But, well, he's my dad, and I do love him. I wish I could have seen him.'

'You will,' Tessa assured her. 'It'll work out, you'll see.'

'Yes—to her benefit, Melissa thing, whatever her name is,' Minnie said crossly. 'You know, you won't believe it, but when we got back we had some awful post, quite abusive letters.'

'Golly!'

'Mummy chucked most of them in the waste paper bin without reading them.

You could tell after a time what they were.'

What Minnie didn't say was that she'd hoped there might have been a letter from David Mathieson and she hoped her mother hadn't thrown it away with the others. But that was just wishful thinking, as she realised when she was honest with herself Why would he get in touch with her? He'd have read all the scandal in the papers like everyone else, and he was rather a conventional young man ...

'But why would people be so awful to you? It wasn't your fault.'

'Well, one letter said if Mummy hadn't been such a do-gooder and had looked after her family properly, her husband would have had no need to find consolation elsewhere.'

'Oh, what beasts people are!' cried Tessa. 'That's simply despicable.'

'Well, there you go,' Minnie said. 'Heavens, this is such a pretty room,' she said, anxious to change the subject. 'I remember it when you had little girl's wallpaper, you know, and pop stars all over.'

'Well, I grew out of that stage—thankfully,' Tessa said. 'Look, let's go down and get some coffee. We can talk in the kitchen, it's lovely and warm down there.'

Just before ten o'clock, Minnie said she must be going.

'I must get back, just in case India wakes—she often does around this time.'

'Do you think your father will still be there?'

Minnie shrugged. 'I expect it would be better if he weren't but I would like to see him. It's a funny thing, Tess, but I feel furious that that woman has him and we haven't—so just imagine how Mummy must feel. Oh, well,' she said, 'see you.' And getting into Janey's small car, drove away. She had reached the gates of Clyde Lodge when a car pulled out and she recognised her father's Bentley. She had just missed him!

'Well, what did Daddy have to say?' she asked as soon as she got indoors.

But Janey was very subdued. 'Not a lot,' she said. 'We discussed the finances, that sort of thing. There's an enormous amount of paperwork to be dealt with.'

Minnie could see that her mother was visibly shaken. She would talk about it when she wanted.

'It's a funny thing,' Janey said slowly, 'but I have helped so many women—at least I hope I have—to deal with separation and divorce, but when it comes to your own marriage break up, it's quite a different ball game.'

She stood with her back to the window, her fine eyes troubled. Janey had rather nice grey eyes. Minnie wished there was something she could do, but she felt helpless.

'How about a hot drink?' she said.

'Lovely. How was Tessa?'

'Great,' Minnie said, reaching for a saucepan.

'I think I'll take mine up with me,' her mother said. 'I'm all in.'

Minnie could have wept. How absolutely awful it all was. How could her father have behaved so badly? Her own eyes filled with tears.

'You go on up and I'll bring it upstairs,' she said. 'We'll have a chat in the morning. Was India all right?'

'Yes, fine, darling. Not a peep out of her.' And wearily Janey made her way up the stairs.

In the morning, she seemed calmer and more accepting of the situation.

'Did Daddy seem happy?' Minnie asked.

'No, I wouldn't say that—but then he could hardly show his feelings to me, could he? We have so much to talk about. He has to put his affairs in order, and of course take us all into consideration.'

'Did he mention divorce?'

'Yes, he asked me if I wanted it, and I said I thought it was the only solution.'

'Mummy, you didn't!'

'Of course I did. Do you suppose I want to go on like this—with your father living with another woman that he has been seeing for the past nine years?'

'No, of course you don't,' Minnie said. 'I'm sorry.'

'Oh, darling, it's not your fault. But I have a life to get on with too.'

'I know, Mummy, I know.' And Minnie went upstairs to bring India down.

It crossed her mind to wonder how the story had come out in the first place. She shrugged. What did it matter now? It was all water under the bridge.

Would they go on living here? she wondered.

After all, if one day she got married or found someone to live with, her mother would be left on her own. The house was too large for her as a single person, but she would hate to leave it. It was difficult to imagine not living at Clyde Lodge, but then that's what happened when marriages broke up. What was Graham doing about it? she wondered. They had heard nothing from him since they had been back. But what could he do? Sometimes she felt she would like to go and visit her father, talk some common sense into him, but she knew that would be the last thing she would, or should, do. What happened between two people was their own affair—even parents. She and Graham had long passed the stage of needing them—except, she thought now, what would she have done if they hadn't been there for her when she got back from India?

Round and round the thoughts went, and all to no good purpose. She would achieve more if she found something better to do. Such as? she wondered. And was back to square one again.

In the meantime, Janey had her work to do: council meetings, women's clubs, charity work and school visiting, all of which she had taken up again as if nothing untoward had happened. People were very kind, all those who knew her, that was, and greeted her like the friendly souls they were. It is only the people who don't know me who throw stones, she decided, taking comfort from the fact that she was going to be allowed to carry on as normal, that her life had not been completely shattered. Well, she decided, they say working for others takes one's mind off oneself, and she was not unused to it, knowing as she had for a long time that her husband of thirty years had been unfaithful to her.

The local council meeting held once a month on a Thursday was to take place this week. Neil Bentinck had offered to give her a lift. 'No problem at all, Janey,' he had assured her. 'It's on my way to the Town Hall.'

'Oh, Neil, that would be terrific,' she said. 'Just before eight then.'

'So what are you discussing this evening?' Minnie asked when Thursday came around. Somehow without realising it she was taking her father's place, thinking now that perhaps he would once have asked Janey the same thing.

'Well, the Butterfly Field is on the agenda, particularly a discussion of the application made by the Carpenters. Incidentally, I hear they're back. I meant to ring Sally and ask her if Tom has done anything about tackling them.'

'Yes, they are, I saw the lights on when I went to Tessa's on Tuesday,' Minnie said. 'You should just see them!'

'So I've heard,' her mother said darkly. She glanced at her watch. 'Ten to—' And the doorbell rang.

'I'll go, it'll be Neil. He's a little early.'

At her usual stately pace, she went to the front door, a smile on her face—only to be greeted by John standing under the light in the porch, a large official-looking envelope in his hand.

'Have I called at an awkward time?'

'I'm sorry, John, I was just going out. It's a council meeting this evening.'

'Oh! I completely forgot. I really came

to give you this by hand. Somehow, I just don't trust important documents in the post.'

He handed it to her just as a car arrived and parked behind his and he saw who it was: Neil Bentinck.

'I won't keep you,' he said stiffly, handing the envelope to Janey. 'Just wanted you to have these.'

He hurried down the path to his Bentley, passing Neil who was just getting out.

'Evening, John.'

'Evening,' he said shortly, and in a flash was back in his car, speeding down the road, shocked to find himself in such a temper. Why the hell had he taken the petition by hand? And Janey—what was the idea? Was she not capable of driving herself to the council meeting? She always had unless they'd gone together. He set off on the road to town, not easing up until he almost went through a red light.

Easy does it, he told himself. What did you expect her to do? Sit at home in tears, feeling sorry for herself?

'Come in, Neil, I won't be a moment,' Janey said. 'I just want to put this safely upstairs in the study out of everyone's way. John and I have a lot of sorting out to do, as you may imagine.'

'Naturally,' he said. 'No hurry.'

She came back downstairs followed by Minnie.

'Oh, hello, Mr Bentinck,' the girl said.

'Hello, Minnie—how's the baby?'

'She's fine, thanks.'

'Well, off now,' Janey said. 'I won't be late.'

Neil thought: She didn't tell Minnie John called.

On Friday morning, Tessa arrived at MacBane's to find instead of the usual bustle at the start of a working day, a pall of silence. 'What's wrong?' she asked the commissionaire. 'Everything is so quiet.'

'Don't know, miss,' he said. 'But Mr MacBane is in his office, and from what I've been told, not in the best of moods.'

She hung up her jacket but before she could do anything else, her telephone bleeped. It was Alistair.

'Tessa—would you come along to my office, please?'

'Certainly, Alistair,' she said, wondering what was wrong.

'Good morning,' he greeted her, in such a stern voice, she wondered what she had done.

'Good morning, Alistair—is something up?'

'Most definitely,' he said. 'I'm telling you first, because you were in at the beginning. I'm afraid we have had some bad news.'

'What is it?' For a moment she wondered whether anything had happened at home since she'd left early this morning.

He came straight to the point.

'The Goyas are fakes.'

She slumped back in her chair. 'Fakes! But they can't be!' She knew by his face that it was true, though. 'Oh, Alistair!'

Poor Hugo, she thought.

Chapter Eighteen

Anger, Tessa decided, added a new dimension to Alistair. His grey eyes were like steel as they met hers, and she saw that he was having difficulty in holding back his feelings. Not surprisingly, she thought though, considering.

'How did you discover that they were fakes?' she asked. 'I thought Herr Vandenburg had seen them?'

'He had,' Alistair said grimly. 'What you didn't know was that he wasn't one hundred per cent happy with them.'

Tessa was shocked.

'I can't imagine their not being genuine,' she began. 'But then, I'm no expert on oils.

I thought they were wonderful.'

'They are,' Alistair said, 'In that sense. But they are still forgeries. I had to call Landvet in from New York.'

'Golly!' Tessa said, impressed.

'He arrived on Wednesday evening. I met him at Heathrow and we spent the evening here. The upshot was that Vandenburg's suspicions were proved correct—they are quite simply, fakes.'

'Oh, what a disappointment for poor Hugo,' she said. 'He was so—'

Alistair's eyes blazed with feeling.

'Is that all you can think about—poor Hugo?' he said. 'What about the damage to MacBane's?'

Tessa sprang instantly to her own defence.

'You hadn't released the news to the press,' she retorted.

'But quite a few people knew that we had them. It's difficult to keep something like that quiet. Poor Hugo be damned! What about MacBane's—what about our reputation?'

'I still think it must have been a big disappointment to him, just when he thought he had made a world discovery.'

'Yes, I can see you would,' said Alistair, and his lip curled. 'Of course you would. Well, I'm not sure your precious Hugo is completely in the clear.'

Tessa's dark eyes were blazing as she got to her feet. 'What are you saying?' she said hotly. 'Are you suggesting—'

He gave no answer but sat staring at her. She could almost see the thoughts going round in his head.

'You've never liked him, have you?' she said now accusingly. 'All along you've had it in for him.'

'Don't be ridiculous!'

How could she accuse him of jealousy, Tessa thought, without suggesting that there might be something between her and Hugo?

'That's why you asked me to dinner that night,' she said slowly as the penny dropped. 'You were quizzing me.' And knew by the look on his face that she was right. 'What a despicable thing to do!' she cried. 'Why couldn't you have asked Hugo himself? He was the one who actually negotiated the deal. You were using me to see what the set up was, and you're using this as an excuse to get rid of him.'

'I don't need an excuse,' Alistair said, and seemed to take hold of himself, toying with a paperweight on his desk. 'Look, Tessa, there's more to this than you know. It is more serious than you imagine.'

'Yes, you're right, I don't know—I am as shocked as you are. I am sorry for MacBane's. As for Hugo—well, I think you're being a bit hasty in your judgement.' She stopped as the telephone rang shrilly, making her jump. He picked it up automatically. 'MacBane.' And put his hand over the receiver.

'If you will excuse me,' Tessa said, 'I'll get back to work. I'm sure you have lots to do.' And head held high, she walked out, back to her own room, and sat down at her desk to mull over what she had been told.

Well, Alistair was right, it was a bad day for MacBane's—but it wasn't the end of the world. And what did he mean by putting the blame on Hugo? After all, he wasn't a world-class expert on paintings—but probably the best MacBane's could afford ...

She began checking her inventories but her heart wasn't in it. She was relieved when a tap came on her door around ten.

'Come in,' she called, and saw Lizzie standing there, looking unusually serious.

'I say, Tess,' she said, 'it's jolly rotten about the Goyas, isn't it? And Hugo—' She bit her lip. Most of the female staff had a soft spot for Hugo.

'What about him?' Tessa said sharply.

'Well, he's gone.'

'What do you mean, gone?'

'He hasn't turned up. He had an appointment at nine-thirty and when we rang his flat, there was no reply.'

'Well, I'm sure there's a perfectly logical explanation.'

'I dunno. It's funny, isn't it? Everyone's talking about it.'

'Well, I think they should all have something better to do,' Tessa snapped, feeling twice her age as she fought to take in the information.

'See if there's any late post, will you?' she said. 'And close the door when you go out.'

She sat back in her chair. What did it all mean?

Was Hugo ... had he ... but the idea was absolute nonsense. How could he have had any part in it? She went back in her mind to that weekend in Madrid, and relived again those momentous two days.

What did Alistair mean: Hugo knew more than he said? That was tantamount to saying that he was involved in fraud. Tessa shivered. It was such an ugly word ... and terrifying when it came to a fine arts house, even a small one like MacBane's.

Fraud—well, whoever thought that one up, faking Goyas, must have known what he was doing. But what about the Contessa and her father? It didn't bear thinking about. Poor things, they must have thought they were on to a great deal of money, and now—nothing.

There was an air of doom around the premises today. Not unnaturally—anything like this was bound to have an effect on everyone.

But Hugo—why had he not come in? Surely he was man enough to face the music? After all, it wasn't his fault. One would need exceptional expertise to know for sure. Alistair had had to call in Vandenburg and Landvet, the latter was a world authority on certain artists.

She sighed. Oh, how dreary it all seemed—a pall seemed to hang over everything. As for Alistair, well, she had never seen him like that before, and somehow she liked him better for it—it showed another side to his character even though his anger had been directed at her. So he could be quite nasty when pushed? And she pulled a little face.

Well, she thought, I'm quite sure there was nothing I said about the trip to Madrid that pointed towards Hugo being at fault. Had he really gone for good? Did it mean she would never see him again? Those dark eyes, the gypsy-like good looks, the hair that would always fall over his eyes. And yet he had never given her the slightest hint that she was any more to him than any other member of staff. Sometimes she wondered if he had a girlfriend, but after meeting the Contessa, whoever she was would have had to take a back seat. Poor Contessa, and poor Hugo— and damn Alistair, she thought. Rude devil.

It was around three in the afternoon when he rang through.

'Tessa—I apologise for this morning.'

'Oh.'

'There was no need to rant at you—it was nothing to do with you.'

She stayed silent.

'I have a lot of explaining to do—between ourselves that is. I certainly do not want the rest of the staff to be aware of the facts. You are only involved because you were there on that weekend in Madrid and have a right to know.'

'Thank you.'

'I would like you to cancel anything you have on for this afternoon and come into my office at four.'

'Of course, Alistair. I'll be there.'

It was with some trepidation that she knocked on his door before going in.

He was more relaxed now, but still serious as he asked her to sit down opposite him.

'I'll start off by saying that you are not going to like any of this, Tessa,' he said, 'but it has to be done. We simply must get to the bottom of things, and I need your help.'

'Of course.'

He handed her a newspaper cutting of the photograph of a man.

'Does that mean anything to you?' he asked.

She saw a handsome man of around sixty, with long curly dark hair and goatee beard, and a pair of humorous dark eyes. Somehow he didn't look English. She shook her head although there was something faintly familiar about him. An ageing film star?

Alistair passed over another newspaper cutting and it too contained a similar photograph of this man, beneath the heading: ALBERT COMERA DIES AT SIXTY FIVE.

The date on the newspaper was the 11th of January 1986.

There were other similar cuttings.

'GREAT FRAUDSTER DIES. The man who was called the most brilliant conman of them all, Albert Comera ...' She thumbed through them.

'You don't recognise him?' Alistair asked.

'No,' Tessa said. 'Should I? There's something a little familiar about him, yet I can't place him.'

'You don't see a likeness between him

and Señor Perez, the Contessa's father?'

Her heart jumped and began beating fast as she began to get the connection.

'Oh, no! No—of course not! No And yet, she told herself, there was something, just something. Given white hair, a white goatee beard, was it possible that it could be?

'But this man is dead,' she said slowly.

'Is he? Just suppose he is not,' Alistair said grimly.

'Do you think you could start at the beginning?' Tessa asked. She felt numb, her thoughts in a whirl.

'When Landvet saw the Goyas, he was mystified. He said there was only one man who could have done them and he died ten years ago.'

'So these could be the work of this man, Albert Comera? It happens, doesn't it?'

'Ah—but Landvet says these have been painted in the last ten years, and he is the expert.'

'How can that be?' asked Tessa.

'We haven't finished all our enquiries yet, but we have started on what could turn out to be the biggest fraud inquiry of them all,' Alistair said. 'What I have done is enquire into the Madrid background, and so far I have come up with some interesting facts.

'It seems that the residence of the Perez

family where you went to spend your weekend in Madrid was a rented property.'

'Well?'

He put up his hand. 'It was hired for just two months by the Contessa, her father and two family retainers.' Slowly Tessa began to realise what he was getting at.

'Once there, they established themselves as well-to-do Spanish aristocrats—the sick father, the old retainer, the maid.'

'I don't understand?'

'Bear with me. In reality it was our friend Albert Comera up to his old tricks. It was convenient to have him thought dead, that was why they announced it, but in fact he went into hiding, and now we see him pretending to be a member of this family coming to Madrid from the south—where he presumably did the paintings—and asking a representative of a British fine arts house to come and see the treasures.'

'But there were the tapestries, the textiles, the pottery—I saw them.'

'Yes, all put there to give credibility to the story of a once wealthy family.'

'Oh, I can't believe this!'

Alistair raised his eyebrows. 'The Contessa did cancel the sale of your artefacts, didn't she? Why?'

Tessa shrugged.

'Well—'

It was all coming together now though it seemed to her a highly improbable story.

'You would have to be awfully sure of your facts.'

'I am ninety per cent sure,' he said. 'I am only waiting for confirmation of certain aspects to come in.'

'I have to say, I hardly believe a word of it.'

'I think you are forgetting that there were huge sums of money at stake—millions of dollars. Some people will do anything for money—lots of money—and for love, too, of course.'

And Tessa blushed to the roots of her hair.

'Yes, well.' Then asking the question that had been uppermost in her mind all along: 'And where does Hugo fit in to all this?'

'You won't like this, but we have established that he met "the Contessa" previously in Spain and fell in love with her. A year or more ago, or perhaps before. Whether she engineered the whole thing or if it was an accidental meeting we shall never know, but at that first encounter he fell in love with her and became a perhaps unwilling member of the gang, for that's what it was.'

Tessa bit her lip. 'I'm sorry, but I can't

go along with any of it. You have no proof, only suspicions.'

'I do know a little of it. I know, for instance, that Hugo has been going to Spain regularly for the past two years—not to Madrid, but to a little town in the south.'

'How do you know that? And it's not unusual is it? Thousands of people go to Spain every year.'

'Yes, but this is to the same place. Two years ago, just about the time you started here, Hugo went on holiday to Spain with Jeff Legget—an ex-employee of MacBane's. While they were there they met two girls, one of whom I believe was your Contessa.'

Disbelief was plain in Tessa's face.

'I remembered this and recalled that Legget had some holiday snapshots which he showed me at the time—he left MacBane's soon after. I am waiting to receive one or two of them which he has promised to turf out, if he still has them. I think we will find it is the Contessa—taken two years ago. She will hardly have changed and I would like you to identify her.'

'You are placing a great deal of responsibility on my shoulders.'

'Oh, it's only one clue in a highly complex business,' Alistair said. 'Of course, if you'd rather not—'

'No, no. But what will happen to Hugo if it is all true?' she asked.

'Nothing we can do,' he said. 'Unfortunately. Nothing came of the plan. It was only an attempt at fraud—MacBane's is the loser, having to transport the paintings over and pay Landvet's fee, but that is nothing compared with what we might have lost had it all come out after a sale.'

Tessa slumped back in her chair.

'I can't bear to think I actually took part in a plot.'

'But unknowingly,' Alistair assured her. 'It had nothing to do with you, was not your fault. Still, I hope you will be prepared to give all the help you can to us?'

'Of course,' she said. 'Although I still—'

'I know. But all sorts of things, unpleasant as well as pleasant, happen in a business like ours, and everything is for a purpose: to teach us to be aware, that no one is above suspicion.'

'Not even me?' She gave a weak attempt at a smile.

He looked across at her, and his feelings for her were exposed as openly as if he had just told her he loved her.

'Yes, well,' she said, getting up. 'I'm glad you have put me in the picture even though I can hardly credit it. Perhaps I am naive—too naive to be in this business. But as you say, you live and learn.'

He smiled at her, back to the usual status quo of employer and employee.

'Get off home now, and have a good night's rest. It may be that on going over it something will jog your memory. But in any case, I think I have it worked out. There's just one last link—the photographs.

'And, Tessa—people aren't always what they seem. My father taught me to trust no one, and I thought it was a very hard and unpleasant way to go through life. But I do think, in business, it might be as well to remember that.'

She left in a daze. Inside Alistair's office it had seemed a plausible tale: outside, it had the elements of an improbable TV script.

And Hugo? she thought. No matter what, willing or unwilling, he had just been a pawn in the game.

She sat in the train, eyes closed, thinking over what Alistair had said. Going over that weekend in Madrid, she could see it was possible—but probable? Surely not? And yet the two paintings were fakes. Alistair had not imagined that.

She decided to say nothing to her parents, it was all too stressful to talk of as yet. Once it was known for certain, she might tell them then.

The next morning, Alistair asked to see her straight away.

On his desk was a manilla envelope, and instinctively she knew that the photographs had arrived.

'Morning, Tessa,' he said. 'Well, they're here. I've already seen them, but of course they mean nothing to me. Perhaps to you?' And he drew out four colour photographs.

One was of a foursome, standing facing the camera, arms linked around each other; two of a couple, arms entwined; and yet another of the same couple, sipping drinks at a bar on a terrace, looking into each other's eyes. There was no doubting their feelings for each other.

Trying to hide his anxiety, Alistair said casually: 'Well? What do you think?'

She looked at them all again then raised dark troubled eyes to his.

'Yes, it's her—the Contessa,' she said. 'And Hugo.' For some reason she felt like weeping.

Tessa placed the photos back on the desk silently. In a flash, Alistair was at her side. He put his arms around her.

'Tessa,' he said, but she broke away and fled from the room.

'Oh, leave me alone!' she cried.

Alistair sat for a long time after she had gone. Well, you certainly ballsed that up, he told himself. He had for one brief overwhelming moment believed he might be able to comfort her, knowing what she must be feeling—the shock of the disclosure that Hugo was not the man she had thought him; had had someone like the Contessa in the background all the time.

He felt old, at thirty, compared to Tessa, who was twenty-one. She was young and romantic, while he was a staid businessman—he had no place in her life.

Leave her alone, he told himself. Let her get on with living. She's not for you.

But it was hard to take, just the same.

Chapter Nineteen

'Are you sure you won't come with us to the Carpenters'?' Sally asked Tessa, who had come down to breakfast this morning looking pale and washed out with dark rings around her eyes.

'Oh, no, really,' she said. That was the last thing she wanted to do.

She had seemed tired when she'd arrived home the night before, Sally thought. Oh, well, if something were wrong, she would tell them when she was ready.

'I'm making more coffee—do you want some?' Tessa asked.

'No, thank you, dear. We shall be leaving in a hour or so to go next door.'

Sally could hardly wait, being curious to know just what the Carpenters had done to The Mount. It had been frustrating to live next door while it was going on. Tom, on the other hand, had a more important reason to visit. He was about to tackle the subject of the Carpenters' application to develop the Butterfly Field.

They walked slowly along the lane until they reached the drive leading to The Mount, and walked past the lamp posts with their intrusive globes and up to the flight of steps which led to the house. Before they could ring Pauline was there in the open doorway, a vision in a cream trouser suit, as brown as a berry, eyes sparkling with sheer good health.

'Oh, come on in! It's lovely to see you again!' She embraced Sally warmly as Beattie came up to the door behind her, like a little wrinkled walnut, her bright blue eyes darting from one of them to the other.

When Sally emerged from the hug, she was amazed to see that what had originally been the hall, which had been large enough, was now open straight through to the huge reception room, the dividing point now being a line of faux marble pillars.

'Oh!' she said. There was not much more you could say, for the enormous expanse of drawing room, combined with the hall, seemed to go on forever, while from dramatic floor-length windows a pool could be seen shimmering in the midday sun.

'Oh, Pauline,' she said. 'It's well— wonderful! Imagine, I had no idea. It doesn't look like the same house.'

'Well, it isn't!' Pauline laughed. 'At least, I hope not!' And she glanced at Tom, who was inspecting the ceiling, as an architect might, for signs that all had been done properly.

'Well, what do you think?' she asked, while Beattie stood by as proud as a little peacock.

'Amazing,' he said. 'They've done a good job.'

'Oh, nothing but the best,' she said. 'Well, come through, Ron's in the garden.' She led the way to the dining room, now splendid with ornate furniture, the doors of which stood open to the new conservatory which stretched upwards and outwards, filled with exotic plants, small trees, climbing vines. It looked a little like the hothouse in Kew Gardens, Sally thought. No wonder they could see it from

Christmas Cottage.

'We'll have drinks in here presently,' Pauline said, 'after you've seen the pool.'

Sally lagged behind, looking at the wonderful display of plants and flowers before catching up with Pauline and Tom. The pool, quite the largest private one she had ever seen, shimmered in the sun, blue and green tiles all round, a trimmed hedge separating it from an enormous summerhouse and terrace.

'Come inside and look,' Pauline said, and they dutifully followed her in to where tables and chairs stood on the tiled floor, a bar held every conceivable kind of drink and two telephones sat just waiting for calls.

'And these are the changing rooms,' she said proudly, leading the way to a row of chalets, brightly painted. As they looked on admiringly Ron emerged from one holding a skimmer for the pool, a wide grin on his face, eyes twinkling.

'Hi, there!' he called. 'Well, what's the verdict?'

'Wonderful,' they both said at once.

'We're still trying to get our bearings,' Sally said, looking round. From where she stood, Christmas Cottage looked like an oversized shed in the distance.

'Yes, bloody marvellous, isn't it?' He put down the skimmer and came towards them with outstretched hands.

He shook hands with Tom and kissed Sally lightly.

'Why don't you go in, darlin', and see to the drinks? Tom and I want to have a look around. I want to show him the works.'

'Yes, of course,' Pauline said, linking her arm through Sally's. 'I'd like you to see the bedrooms and bathrooms—men aren't interested in that sort of thing, are they?' she asked confidentially. 'All right, Mum?' she called out as they went through the conservatory.

'Yes, I'm fine, darlin',' called Beattie. 'You take yer time.'

Up the wide staircase, where Sally's feet sank into the soft carpet. Immaculately painted doors on the wide landing led to the six bedrooms—now each with en suite bathroom. Each had its four poster bed, and each was in a different colour scheme. The richness of the curtains dazzled Sally, and the quantity of material used (acres, she told Tom afterwards), with pleats and frills and tie backs. 'Draped pelmets big enough to make our curtains,' she said. 'You wouldn't believe it, Tom. So rich and expensive—I couldn't take it all in.' She caught her breath as each door was opened, wondering what was coming next. Designer it certainly was.

Imagine, she thought, being able to go away and return to find it all done—just like that. Still, they were unusual people, these Carpenters, different.

'I'm quite pleased,' Pauline said, apropos of nothing, closing each door after her. 'They did a good job.' There were fine paintings upstairs in the hall, and on the way downstairs. Genuine? Sally wondered.

'Well, here we are,' Pauline said, reaching the bottom. 'That's why I didn't want you to see it before it was done. Wouldn't recognise it now, would you?'

'Good Lord, no!' Sally said, as they went into the conservatory where Beattie sat with a cold drink reading the *Mirror*.

'Ah, there you are,' she said, folding the paper and stuffing it down the side of one of the cane chairs. 'Well, what do you think? Lovely, innit? Did you see my room—the yeller one?'

'Oh, the sunny one? Yes, I did. It's lovely, Beattie.'

'And yeller bathroom to match—I'm tickled pink,' she said, and looked it.

'Now what would you like, Sally?' Pauline asked, her almond-shaped eyes warm with friendship and good humour. 'I see you helped yourself, Mum,' she admonished with a wagging finger, but only as a joke. 'Wine or sherry?'

'I really don't mind.'

'We have everything,' Pauline said. 'White wine might be nice, and I've made some canapes.' She pronounced it 'canaps.' 'Oh, and some *tapas*—that's what we eat in Spain.'

'Oh, lovely,' Sally said.

'Well, ain't she done well?' Beattie asked confidentially as Pauline disappeared into the dining room.

'Yes, it's amazing,' Sally said.

'She's a clever gel and no mistake, my Pauly,' Beattie said.

'And did you enjoy Spain?'

'Oh, yes, it was lovely—they've got a terrific 'ouse there. Look, I'll show you the picture.' And she walked over to a small table where stood a framed photograph of a fabulous white house set on a hillside, surrounded by cherry and lemon trees, and a gleaming blue pool.

'Oh—is this it?' Sally said.

'Yes, that's it,' Beattie said, taking the photo back to the table. '"Mon Repos" it's called. And how've you been?' she went on, ''Ad a busy summer, 'ave you?'

'Yes, I suppose we have, one way and another.'

'Where's your daughter today? I was hopin' to see her—lovely girl.'

'She had a previous appointment with a friend otherwise she would have come,'

Sally said. 'And where's Sandra?'

'Oh, naughty girl!' Beattie said with mock severity. 'She's stayed out there. Met this chap—nice enough but Spanish. You know 'ow they are. 'Course, they're as thick as thieves and we couldn't get 'er to come back.' And she clucked like an old hen. 'Oh, she'll be all right—got 'er 'ead screwed on right, our Sandra.'

Pauline came in with a tray of drinks and a trolley with food. 'Now, here you are, Sally. Good health. Ah, here are the men.'

'Did you see the workshop area where the machinery is? Isn't it wonderful?' Pauline asked. 'It's Ron's pride and joy.' And she looked at him lovingly.

'Yes, I showed him around. What'll you have, Tom?'

'I'll join you,' he said. 'Wine, I think.'

'Tom's just been telling me about the fuss over the application for the—what's it called?—the Butterfly Field. He was quite worried there for a minute, weren't you, old man?'

Pauline busied herself getting the men glasses of wine and passing round plates.

'But as I told him, it's the usual procedure in the property business.'

'I don't think I realised you *were* in the property business?' Tom said.

'Oh, yes, Carpenter's. I wonder you

haven't heard of us. She's a director,' he said, pointing to Pauline, 'and Beattie too. It's a family business.'

'But in the unlikely event that you obtain planning permission, would you go ahead and build?'

'It's not likely, first time round, but it's useful to have on hand. Permission lasts five years, and after all, it's in our area. We want to know what's going on in our own neck of the woods, don't we?' And Ron raised his glass cheerfully.

'And when you get us as neighbours,' Pauline declared, 'you get us for keeps. We're not movers.'

Sally didn't know whether to be upset with this statement or pleased.

'So—have you heard?' Tom asked.

'Not yet,' Ron said, 'but these things take time.' And he took a swig of his wine.

'I must say, I took a poor view of the application coming from a neighbour, and a new neighbour at that. It came as a shock, a complete surprise.'

'Oh, don't you worry about that,' Ron said reassuringly. 'It's just routine procedure so far as we're concerned. By the way, you didn't tell me what you do, Tom, although I made enquiries naturally. You're an architect, I understand?'

Tom nodded, outmanoeuvred.

'Ah—then you'll be well versed in council procedure. If I didn't make the application, mate, someone else would.'

Sally suddenly felt rather annoyed and looked at Pauline. 'Did you tell Ron about Janey's hard work, trying to get the field for a community centre?' she said, daring to put her spoke in.

'Yes, well, we don't want that on our doorstep, do we?' he said. 'Bring your drink, Tom, you haven't seen the billiard room yet. Do you play?'

They were smooth, the pair of them, Sally decided. A couple of smoothies. Could gloss over and dispense with a problem just like that, whereas she and Tom had spent anxious hours wondering what exactly was going on.

'How's Janey?' Pauline asked, looking quite concerned.

'She's fine,' Sally answered.

'I heard about the break up—and I'm not surprised,' Pauline said. 'Some friends of ours told us. They came out to Spain to stay. What a shock for old Janey. Still, on the other hand, these women who spend all their time doing good works, instead of looking after their own families. Well ...'

'Yes,' Beattie said disapprovingly, 'I never liked her.'

'Oh, Mum, now then,' Pauline said with a twinkle.

Sally sat thinking. Was that all that was going to be said about the Butterfly Field? She had expected more of a row about it, although Tom wasn't a man to lose his temper. Whatever he was thinking he would keep to himself—for the moment. But he would go on looking into it, in his own way.

'Yes, all that terrible publicity in the newspapers—it's a shame, though,' Pauline was saying. 'You don't like to hear of people breaking up, do you?'

'Well, darlin', not everyone has such a perfect marriage as you and Ron,' her mother said.

Yes, Sally reflected, they do seem a well-matched pair.

'When's our next meeting?' Pauline asked. 'Has Janey taken up her good works again? Poor thing.'

'Yes, she keeps busy,' Sally said, and was glad when Tom came back.

'Our Sandra stayed out in Spain,' Pauline said.

'Yes, your mother said.'

'He's a lovely boy—Spanish, of course. She'll end up marrying a Spanish boy, I expect.'

But Ron hadn't missed a word.

'Over my dead body!' he said. 'You was saying, Tom?'

'I was sorry you had to cut down the

old oak tree. I believe it was three hundred years old.'

'Yes, pity that,' Ron said. 'I asked the landscape gardeners to go into it—get in touch with the council, I knew it was protected. But before they could do anything it was down. Case of "Oops, sorry!" But apparently it was rotten and quite dangerous—so having it down was a good thing. Probably saved you unnecessary trouble in the future if it fell on your side, eh, Tom?' And he laughed out loud.

Tom didn't believe a word of it. This man, he thought, has friends in high places—at least high up in council offices. After what he had seen, he was more than ever convinced that there had been a contravention of the building laws and, in all conscience, Ron Carpenter could not be allowed to get away with it.

He glanced at his watch.

'Sorry, darling,' he said to Sally, 'but I promised to remind you when it was one-forty-five.'

She thought swiftly. 'So you did! Yes, I have a casserole in the oven for lunch.'

'Haven't you got an automatic timer?' Pauline asked.

'No, I'm afraid my cooker is quite old-fashioned. It's an Aga, one of the old ones,' Sally said.

'My dear, I wouldn't give them house room,' Pauline announced grandly.

'Yes, well ...' And somehow they found themselves at the front door, thanking their hosts and repeating how wonderful it all was, with promises from the Carpenters to stop in for a reciprocal drink. Then at last they were walking down the drive, and Tom was holding Sally's arm.

'Tom,' she giggled, 'whatever made you think of that?'

'Couldn't stand any more of it,' he said. 'God, what a shower! You know he's trampled across building regulations and broken every rule in the book, I daresay.'

'And what about the Butterfly Field?'

Tom looked grim. 'Yes, well, we'll see about that.'

When they reached the end of the drive, Sally stopped. 'I've had an idea ... I wonder what Janey and Minnie are doing tomorrow? Why don't we invite them to Sunday lunch?'

'Why not?' Tom said. 'It's a bit late, though.'

'I'll give Janey a ring when we get back. I've got a leg of lamb.'

Once in the hall, she picked up the telephone.

'Janey—are you doing anything at lunch-time tomorrow?'

'No, nothing that I can think of.' Janey did sound down.

'Come and have lunch with us, you and Minnie and the baby.'

'Oh, Sally, are you sure?'

'Yes, quite sure. We'd love to see you. Around twelve-thirty?' she said.

'Lovely.' Janey sounded pleased.

'Well,' Tessa said, coming down the stairs, 'how was it?'

'Ghastly,' her father said.

'Well, you would say that.' And she grinned. 'Mummy?'

'First of all, the wall has been knocked down between the hall and the drawing room ...' And she went on to describe the rest of it.

'Must have cost a fortune,' Tessa said.

'And by the way, I've asked Janey and Minnie to lunch tomorrow.'

Tessa's face brightened.

'Super,' she said. 'What are we having?'

'Leg of lamb, and there are plenty of vegetables in the garden. We have those Victoria plums from the tree and I'll make a lemon tart.'

'Good, I shall look forward to that.'

Tessa was in the kitchen the next morning helping to prepare lunch: the vegetables done, the joint in, the mint chopped for mint sauce, and the table laid in the dining room. Her mother took off her oven gloves and apron.

'Well, that's that,' she said. 'Nothing to do now but tidy myself up.'

When she came back into the kitchen, hair brushed, a clean blouse and skirt on, she looked very youthful. Tessa had spent most of the morning thinking about MacBane's, and on the spur of the moment decided this was the time to come clean.

'I've got something to tell you,' she said, and Sally was not surprised. Tessa was like that. It had to be in her own time.

'Well!' she said, when her daughter had come to the end of the saga about the Goyas. 'No wonder you've been looking a bit peaky. What an awful shock! It's almost unbelievable. Now that you've had time to think it over, what conclusion have you come to?'

'Sadly, that Alistair is probably right— and that Hugo did know all along. But it's an awful business just the same. And I feel such a fool.' She looked so miserable that Sally longed to comfort her.

'Oh, darling, why should you? You weren't to know.'

'But springing to his defence like that. Alistair was furious with me.'

'He'll get over it,' Sally said. 'And do you think he has left? Hugo?'

'We shall know tomorrow,' Tessa said.

'Goodness, I must fly upstairs. They'll be here in a moment.'

They heard Janey's car outside, and presently she sailed up the path with Minnie in tow, holding the baby who grinned at Sally like a long-lost friend.

'Oh, you poppet!' she said, holding her. 'Isn't she gorgeous? She's like you Minnie.'

'Is she?' Minnie said, looking pleased.

'Come on through, she can have that tiny chair that used to be Tessa's—I brought it down from upstairs.'

Sally left the girls talking while she and Janey went into the kitchen, Sally to check the lunch.

'It's almost ready,' she said. 'Tom will be in from the garden soon. We'll have a glass of wine while we're waiting.'

They joined the girls sitting on the window seat in the dining room.

'So what happened next door?' Janey asked. 'Did you get round to the Butterfly Field?'

'Yes, we did, or Tom did,' Sally said. 'You wouldn't believe the casual way they took it—as if what they had done was the most ordinary thing in the world.'

'We discussed it at the meeting on Thursday,' Janey said. 'Of course we got nowhere, but still, David Mathieson did put in an appearance.'

The name penetrated even above the girls' conversation and India's giggles.

'David Mathieson?' Minnie asked. 'Was he there? You didn't tell me.'

'It slipped my mind, Minnie, I've been thinking about so many other things.'

And one in particular, Sally thought sadly.

Chapter Twenty

Sir John Utox-Smythe stood by the picture windows of his luxury apartment overlooking the river. It was a bright morning but cold, and Melissa had taken her Yorkshire terrier out for a stroll. The little thing had been in kennels all this time, and was delighted to be reunited with his mistress.

John couldn't help reflecting how different his lifestyle was now from what it had once been.

He moved over from the window to where a simulated log fire burned bright in the Adam-style fireplace. At home—and he always called Clyde Lodge that to himself—there would have been logs in the great brick fireplace, home-felled logs, for Roddis would have been busy in the autumn making sure they were well set up for the winter.

No good thinking about it, he decided. He had burned his boats. He often used to think, in the years when Melissa had been his mistress, if only they could be together always. Now that wish had come true, he spent a lot of his time thinking about his home, and Janey, and Minnie—he seldom thought about Graham, finding it better not to.

Yes, Clyde Lodge *was* his home, had been for thirty years. Why did he have to leave it before he realised how much it meant to him?

He had his work, he was still a busy man, thank goodness, but had to admit that this place didn't feel like home. Perhaps on reflection he and Melissa would have been better off in a town house—but he always saw himself in a country home somehow, surrounded by gardens. He had loved his garden at Clyde Lodge. He wondered now whether Roddis had put out the tulips yet, if Janey had the hyacinth bulbs planted in the bowls that she liked to have ready for Christmas.

No good thinking about it. That was then. Perhaps he and Melissa would be better in a little house with a small garden, something he could get his teeth into. Gardening was therapeutic. It had been one of the delights of his life to come home and walk around, see how everything was doing. He was a gardener by nature, he decided. Unfortunately he had wanted it all. A home, a garden, a wife, children—and a mistress. But fate usually decreed that wasn't possible without someone having to suffer.

He sighed heavily. Well, Janey was happy enough with her good works, the children were off hand, this was a good time to break up—that is if any time was a good one for a marital break up.

He and Melissa could move out of town, to a large cottage, perhaps. He liked space. Bucks, perhaps, or Gloucestershire. He would have to commute for a while although as he got older, he would cut down on the pressures of City life.

The trouble was, he could not envisage Melissa living that kind of life. The life that suited Janey—a country life. Melissa was basically a businesswoman, had a sharp brain. And face it, he told himself, she is still only thirty-six—time enough for her to have a family if she's so inclined. It wasn't fair to tie her down to an old man. He corrected himself. An older man. Perhaps she did not want children? They had never discussed it. He only knew she was at her best in the City, or running her little shop, which had come a poor second.

He would mention it to her—buying a house somewhere in the country, not too far from London—see what her reaction was.

Melissa came in and wiped the little dog's paws before taking him in the kitchen and giving him a drink. Then she went into the large drawing room, where John sat reading the business news.

He looked up at her pretty face, flushed now from walking in the cold air, eyes bright and warm with affection at the sight of him.

Going over to him, she kissed him and he felt her hands.

'Oh, you're freezing!'

'I know, it's cold out—although I had gloves on.' She sat down beside him. 'Well, you've a free day, John. What would you like to do? No, wait, I'll make some coffee first then you can tell me.'

When she returned with the steaming coffee, he sat back, watching her reaction.

'Do you fancy a drive into the country for lunch?'

She raised sparkling eyes to his.

'That's a nice thought,' she said. 'It's a lovely day.'

'What do you think of the idea of looking for somewhere to live—a house, I mean?' He saw her eyes cloud over and her face grow serious.

'Oh, John! You're not happy here, are you? Poor darling ...'

'Yes, it's nice enough, but—'

She wanted to add: But you miss Clyde Lodge. Instead she kept quiet and waited for him to go on.

'I suppose really I'm a country person at heart. Town is all right in its place—'

'But not for you,' she finished gently.

'Well, I don't like to think we would be here for good,' he said. 'It's all right as a stop gap, for being near the City, but not otherwise.'

She said nothing.

'But how do you feel?' he asked her. 'Does the idea appeal to you?'

'I've always lived in towns,' she said. 'I was brought up in London, and I love it. I like the country just for visiting. Apart from my long stint in Cobbets Green, I've never lived anywhere else.'

'And how did that suit you—Cobbets Green?'

'Well, darling, I had the shop and I had you so I was happy.'

'Then perhaps you could do something like that again? What do you think?'

'We could look around,' she said. She would always put him first, he knew that.

They drove off towards Marlow, and then on to Henley, a beautiful stretch of road where the views were magnificent.

The wooded slopes dropped steeply into great wide valleys, and the colours of the leaves were splendid in their brilliance. John knew that in the spring there were carpets of bluebells on this road for he had been born and brought up in the area and had often cycled this route as a teenager.

As they neared Henley he suggested they should stop for lunch by the river. Although it looked cold, a misty sun shone over the wintry scene.

Melissa shivered, but it was warm and friendly inside the small hotel, which had a large fire blazing in the hearth.

John looked across at Melissa. She looked pale, almost fragile, her blonde hair a halo around her face, her skin as fair and smooth as a child's. Who would imagine, he thought wonderingly, that someone as attractive as she would have a razor sharp brain and business acumen? She had been the most efficient secretary he had ever had.

'Would you like to live around here, John?' she asked presently.

'The Thames Valley? Yes, I would. I spent—or mis-spent many years here as a young man. It's one of my favourite parts of the world. I love the villages that sprawl behind the road we were on: Hambledon, Fingest, Weston Turville.'

Was that, Melissa, wondered, why he

had suggested the run out today? He was obviously serious about looking for somewhere to live—and not in London.

'Can we go back that way?' she asked.

'Yes, of course, and we had best set off soon. It gets dark so quickly at this time of year.'

They drove back slowly, up and down the lanes, occasionally coming across a picture postcard village. The views were enchanting, the little country churches sitting so quietly amid the green fields. No wonder Americans loved it, Melissa thought, it was how they liked to think of England.

They were halfway home on the slow road when they saw the house with the FOR SALE board, and John stopped the car outside.

She glanced at his face and saw the excitement there, the pleasurable anticipation. Then she looked at the house. Very pretty, a large cottage surrounded by clipped yew trees and a magnificent garden kept in pristine condition.

'Well—how does that appeal to you?' he asked. 'Let's have a look.' And before she could say anything was outside the car, waiting for her.

'But, John, someone may be at home.'

'Oh, they won't mind us looking around. I'm not asking to go over it.'

He locked the car and she followed him up the short drive that led to the house. Close to, it was even nicer, sitting above the road, with wonderful views from the front. It had large windows downstairs to either side of a front door, a pair of box trees flanking the porch. He peered through a window, much to Melissa's embarrassment.

'John, perhaps ...'

'I don't think there's anyone at home,' he said, walking round to the back.

Melissa had to admit it was a dream home. A closely cut lawn stretched away into the distance. There was a terrace with pots full of box trees and clipped yew; large French windows opened on to the terrace. There was even a pool, small and covered now. It was a home that asked to be lived in and loved. John walked about in great excitement. Presently, he took hold of Melissa's arm. 'What a find,' he said with enthusiasm. 'What do you think? Isn't that a bit of luck—just coming across it like this?'

Her heart sank.

'I'll ring the agents in the morning and we'll make an appointment to view.'

He was in a good mood on the way home, chatting of this and that, so much so that it didn't penetrate in his euphoric state just how quiet Melissa was. He was working out how long it would take him to get to the City, what kind of help they would need, what the owners would be asking ... while all the time Melissa sat quietly beside him.

Both tired from their day out, he from excitement, Melissa from trying to keep up a cheerful front, they had a light supper and went to bed.

But she was awake until three in the morning, tossing and turning, her clenched fist stuffed into her mouth to stop her from weeping. I can't, I can't, she told herself over and over again. I can't live there, lovely though it is, not even for John. What would I do while he was away or at the office? Cut off, away from her roots—it wasn't as if she were like Janey, anxious to help others, and she had to admit, she missed the shop. Her dear little shop, with the customers constantly coming in, then going to the warehouses and choosing the right things, items that would sell, and watching the business tick over. How could she bear to be buried in the country? Did John want to start another family? The thought appalled her. I never really wanted children, she thought, and never realised it until now. I have reached a turning point. That's what this is all about. Have I the courage to go through with it, the move to a country home? And she knew she hadn't. Wearily, she turned over again. Perhaps she would feel better in the morning. But sleep just wouldn't come. It was past three when she finally fell into a doze.

In the morning, John was up and about first as usual, making coffee, preparing breakfast. Melissa was never at her best in the morning, but woke to the fact that she felt awful, drained, and in no mood to make decisions. But could she let John down? Was he not her life? Hadn't she given up everything to be with him? How would she live without him? Anything was better, even living in the country. With John beside her, she could cope.

The appointment was made for eleven-thirty, and the estate agent was to meet them there. She was quiet on the journey, but John knew she often was. Melissa wasn't a chatterer, a maker of conversation for the sake of it. He could hardly keep his excitement at bay, for all that, and when they reached the house, the agent's car was already outside.

Inside, the house fulfilled all its exterior promise. Gracious, spacious, and if that were the sort of house one wanted, it was perfect. Cosy and inviting, the kitchen was a dream. Someone had spent a great deal of money on it. Early-Victorian, the agent thought, with its high ceilings and deep skirting boards and plasterwork on the ceilings, nice wide doors ... it was all John could want. Upstairs, four bedrooms and two bathrooms, all done in a taste that anyone could live with.

Melissa felt like wringing her hands. What were the alternatives? Losing John, or giving in and living a life for which she knew she was not suited?

'We'll be in touch,' John said when they left. Driving on, they stopped after a while at a small picturesque pub for coffee.

'Well?' he asked. 'What did you think?' It had not escaped his notice how subdued Melissa was. Going around the house he had tried to imagine them living there, and somehow failed to come up with a convincing picture. Melissa in the drawing room ... cooking in the kitchen while he was in the garden ... but the images escaped him.

Somehow it wasn't right. There was nothing wrong with the house—only the idea of himself and Melissa living in it.

'Well,' she said brightly, 'it was certainly lovely.' I must think, she told herself. Think hard, think of all it means and what the future could hold for us.

John was quiet on the way home, from time to time mentioning something they had seen. 'I liked that bathroom idea—the shape of the bath and the fitments.'

'Yes, the colours inside the house were nice.'

But it was a desultory conversation with no life to it.

Are we, Melissa wondered, living in a fool's paradise? If we don't find a house for John to live in, will he stay?

That's what he's missing, his home and his family, and he's trying to make do with another house and his mistress. But it's not the same. Even if we did move there, it wouldn't last. I should be unhappy, and John would know I was. I couldn't hide it from him. He's missing his family, the things that have accumulated round him over thirty years. It was all right as long as he had Janey as well but—and she faced it—this is not enough. She gave a groan deep inside her. Better to face the facts. The thing she had been dreading all along had finally surfaced.

When they reached home, John changed and freshened up, and poured himself a whisky. She noticed it was a large one.

'I'll have a martini, John,' she said, and as their eyes met over their glasses, they locked for an instant until John looked away and Melissa recognised the moment of truth.

'It's not going to work, John, is it?' she asked.

'What?' But there was no fooling Melissa.

She was too honest herself.

'You mean the house?'

'No, John. Us.'

'My dear Melissa,' he began.

'John, let's have no secrets between us. We never have. I've known for some time how you must be feeling. You gave up a family for me, while I gave up nothing except a job.'

He was moved almost to tears, and went over and sat by her side and took her hand.

'I suppose it's because I love you that I know what you must be going through. Oh, I know family life is different—not as exciting as what we had before we came here, I mean. But it has changed for you, hasn't it?'

What would be the point of lying? he thought.

'It was stupid of me to want a house like that,' he said. 'You would be lost there, and so would I.'

'You were just trying to replace Clyde Lodge,' she said gently.

'Perhaps,' he said. 'Let's talk about it.'

And they talked far into the night, of the pros and cons, as they had on many such occasions.

'You see, John, you're of an age where your family is important to you: a suitable wife and background, things around you to which you are accustomed.'

'And you are young,' he said, as he stopped her. 'So young compared to me. And that is important.'

'What would you like to do, John?' she said.

'I'd like to be back where we were.'

She smiled ruefully. 'Have your cake and eating it? Oh, John!'

'I never deserved you,' he admitted.

'You've given me the happiest years of my life.'

He tried to imagine life without her, and failed. She had been part of his life for so long, but that was the answer, he decided. Part of his life. Was their feeling for each other enough to see them through the rest of their lives? Most of the time these days he wanted to be back home with Janey—with everything that was so familiar. He missed the security, his study full of personal things, and the answer was not just to move them here. He missed the work he did for charity, the work he and Janey did together, even the Butterfly Field project—he and Janey had been involved in so many things. But most of all, he felt it was wrong to inflict a life on Melissa that was alien to her. She could have settled in this flat but he never could in a month of Sundays, and that was the first bone of contention. He was getting old, he thought. Perhaps that was it?

'Of course, we don't know what Janey wants,' he said. 'Whether she would be agreeable to have me back.'

'Oh, John! Of course she would.' And Melissa gave a tremulous smile. 'Janey still loves you, I'm sure.'

'I'm a lucky man, then,' he said.

'Yes' she said slowly. 'I would say you are.' She got up. 'I'll make some coffee. And, John, don't worry about me. Honestly. I have had a wonderful time, and what's more it was worth it. I never really wanted to hurt Janey, but out of sight was out of mind.'

She wondered nevertheless what his wife's reaction would be.

They let the matter rest for a few days, then came the day when John thought he had enough courage to tackle Janey.

'We'll see what she says.'

Melissa saw that he was nervous about the outcome.

'Are you going to ring her to see if she's prepared to see you?'

'No, I'm going to take the bull by the horns,' he said. 'It's always better that way. Suppose she's not agreeable?' he asked. 'She may hate my guts for what I've done—and I wouldn't blame her.'

Melissa was serious. 'I'm banking on the fact that she has known about us all these years, and said nothing. Now don't worry about me—I'm going up to Knightsbridge to do some shopping.'

He was glad she was going to be busy while he drove out to Swansbridge. Who would have thought a week ago I would be doing this? he thought as the miles slipped past. If it hadn't been for wanting that house ...

Janey saw his car coming up the lane, and her heart skipped a beat. What could he want? More papers about the divorce? He could have done it all through his solicitor. Upstairs she could hear Minnie with the baby.

When the doorbell rang she went to answer it. Confronted by her, John found her expression unfathomable—whether she was pleased to see him, or angry, he couldn't tell. Janey saw a man in turmoil, and something told her that things had changed.

'May I come in?' he asked.

'Of course,' she said, standing aside to let him pass and closing the door behind him.

'Where's Minnie?' he asked.

'Upstairs with the baby'

He followed her along the hall, seeing her upright carriage, the way she danced along, despite her size, and noting that she had lost weight. Her well-turned ankles were still slim, and he had a sudden longing to put his arms around her.

'In here,' she said, going into the drawing room and closing the door behind them.

'Sit down, John.' She sat herself down opposite him, the coffee table in between. She seemed so much in charge of herself, the way she would at any council meeting, while he was losing confidence by the minute.

He decided to speak without delay.

'Janey,' be began, 'I want to come back.'

Now her heart lurched strangely. It was the last thing she had expected. She felt a surge of elation, followed by a feeling of pity for Melissa.

'And what does your mistress have to say about that?' she asked as coolly as she could in the circumstances. None of this conversation seemed real so far.

'We talked it over together,' he said. 'She knows.'

What was the good, Janey thought, of making catty and sarcastic remarks? So, she's finished with you, has she? You've become bored ... it wasn't quite what you expected. But even if all that were true, here was her husband of thirty years' standing asking to come back home. And the girl—for girl she was compared to Janey—what were her thoughts on the

340

matter? Where did she come in? Nine years was a long time for an affair. What had happened? Janey had worked among women with sad and tragic backgrounds, and there were always two sides to every broken marriage. She could find it in her heart to spare some sympathy for Melissa. The saving grace of it was that Melissa was still young. She could make another life for herself, while John at fifty-six ...

'Do you want to talk about it?' she asked.

'Not if you're averse to the idea,' he said. 'I'm not keen on baring my soul only to be thrown out at the end of it.'

They were both silent, and then Janey, looking down at his well-polished shoes and knowing how he liked his pure wool fine Scottish socks, made an observation.

'You've got thin silk socks on.'

They stared at each other, then John was across at her side, burying his head in her ample lap as, tentatively at first, she stroked his grey hair.

It wasn't going to be easy, she thought, but anything was worth having him back again. He had given the apartment to Melissa and made sure that she would lose nothing financially. Janey could cope with wagging tongues, she decided. Hadn't she had enough of them already?

She smiled at the china swan she had

bought which now sat on the mantelpiece. She wouldn't do so much voluntary work as she had done in the past. Only as much as John wanted her to. Enough to keep them busy and happy. Oh, and the Butterfly Field project. Yes, she hadn't finished with that yet.

A few days later, Sir John moved back into Clyde Lodge, and a delighted Minnie welcomed him with open arms. Later she was on the phone upstairs to her brother Graham. 'Can't talk now,' she whispered, 'but Daddy's back.'

'What?' he asked. 'Back home at Clyde Lodge?'

'Yes, 'bye,' Minnie said, putting down the receiver.

Well, Graham decided, after giving it a little thought. What a turn up for the book. And humming a little tune, he shaved and changed into a dark grey lounge suit and selected a rather nice tie.

Then he caught a taxi.

When the front doorbell rang at the apartment, Melissa was browsing through a business journal and listening to one of her favourite cassettes.

Going to the door, she opened it and saw Graham Utox-Smythe. Her heart turned over, he looked so like his father.

'Graham!'

He came in and walked towards her, his arms open, and she walked into them like a child.

Holding her tightly, he looked above her head into the gilded mirror over the fireplace, and saw there a tall, powerful young man, his arms around a woman whose pretty blonde head lay against his manly chest, while a triumphant smile played around his mouth.

Chapter Twenty-One

The village soon got used to the idea that Sir John Utox-Smythe was back with his wife. From the moment the newsagent began delivering the financial papers and the business periodicals to Clyde Lodge again, the news quickly spread, and despite the *frisson* of excitement the separation had caused, most people were relieved. Janey had lost none of her dignity throughout, and as a consequence was more respected than ever.

Today was a raw, end-of-November day. There had been a sharp frost, and only the chrysanthemums still showed some colour. Minnie decided to push the pram to the village shops. She had kept a low profile during the separation, but now felt able to face everyone again. She had not forgotten the devious reporters who had waylaid her and extracted information, which had left her feeling raw and used.

India, in a woolly outfit, was delighted with the whole idea. She sat looking to either side of her at everything that was going on. There were leaves blowing off the trees and skimming the pavement to settle into little piles, birds high up in the sky, a car or two, a passer by—life was full of interest.

Minnie made for Patel's where she was greeted warmly by Mrs Patel, who had seemed rather subdued of late. Now she placed her hands together in greeting, and showed her splendid teeth in a wide smile.

It passed through Minnie's mind that Mrs Patel had behaved strangely from the time her father had moved out. Then she had hardly looked up or spoken when Minnie entered the shop. Now, apparently, all was well.

Minnie collected a few things for her mother and stayed chatting for a few moments.

'Your baba is lovely,' Mrs Patel cooed. 'So pretty, like her mother.'

'And how is your family?' Minnie asked. 'Your son—has he settled after leaving school? What was he going to do—an accountancy course?' But a shut down look had come over Mrs Patel's normally pleasant features.

'Yes—yes, he is away on a course. Now is there anything else I can get you?'

'No, I think that's all,' Minnie said as Mrs Patel handed her the stacked box which she put underneath the pram in the basket.

'Remember me to your mother!' Mrs Patel called after her.

Thank God it was all over, Minnie decided.

She walked round the green so that India could see the two ducks, the trees—cherry and pear—bereft now of their leaves, while the birds pecked about for crumbs and Minnie dived into her basket and came up with some stale bread. She crumbled it before throwing pieces to the hungry sparrows and a blackbird who seemed determined that his wife shouldn't have any.

She was enjoying her morning walk, feeling free for the first time since the break up. The row of cottages stood as they had done for the past two hundred years. There was a lot of history in Swansbridge and the little almshouses were always keenly sought after.

The local council kept the green immaculate. There were always one or two gardeners to be seen clearing away odd pieces of paper or pruning a tree. They were very proud of Swansbridge village.

It was when she got up to leave the seat, for it was a little chilly for sitting out, that she saw a familiar figure coming towards her. A tall young man with a lock of dark hair falling over his forehead. His eyes were smiling as he recognised her.

It was David Mathieson, and she felt a stab of pleasure to see him.

'Hello.'

'It's Miss Utox-Smythe—Araminta, if I remember correctly?' He smiled, holding out his hand.

'Mr Math—'

'David.' He smiled. 'And this is India,' he said, bending down and smiling into the pram. 'You see, I remembered.' Of course India was delighted. She was always pleased to see any new face, particularly a smiling one.

'It was such a nice day, I decided to bring her to the village for a walk.'

'Good idea,' said David, straightening up. 'I had to come into Swansbridge for my uncle.' And his face grew grave. 'I'm sad to say he's ill. Very ill, in fact.'

'Oh, I am sorry,' Minnie said quickly.

'He has been ill for some time. If you

remember, that was why I didn't want him worried about the—well, we won't mention it now.' They both looked serious for a moment, until David smiled.

'No, best not.' Minnie smiled back at him.

'Shall we walk? I'm going back home,' she suggested.

'Yes, I'll come a little way. My car is parked down there.'

'It's none of my business,' he began after a minute or so, 'but a little bird told me that Sir John is home again?'

'Good Lord! How news gets about,' Minnie said. 'But, yes, he is—and I can't tell you how relieved we all are.'

David looked serious. 'It must have been an awful time for you. I did write.'

She flushed with pleasure. 'Really?' And she remembered Janey's tearing up of letters unopened.

'I never received it,' she said. 'So much was happening.'

'Yes, of course. Well, I did. In case you thought—'

'I never thought anything,' Minnie said defensively.

'Look, I have to get back but could we perhaps meet sometime? I can't make any definite arrangements at the moment, because of my uncle.'

'I do hope he gets well soon.'

David shook his head. 'No, I'm afraid he won't. We can only try to make his life as pleasant as we can, I'm sorry to say. May I ring you?'

'Yes, of course,' Minnie said, and he held out a finger to little India who grasped it tightly. 'Hey there, give it back.' He smiled, and then with a nod to her was gone.

'Goodbye for now, Araminta,' he called over his shoulder.

Minnie walked home on air. She felt overwhelmingly happy. Even if I am being ridiculous, she thought, it was great to see him, and to know that all that business with Daddy made no difference. And I thought he disapproved! 'Well, what did I know?' She tipped up the pram and bent low over India, who subsided into giggles which had no bearing on the matter at all.

'Guess who I saw in the village?' Minnie asked her mother when she brought the shopping into the kitchen.

Janey turned swiftly. 'Who?'

'David Mathieson,' Minnie answered, and there was no doubting the pleasure this had given her.

'Oh, how nice.'

'He said he did write, when—you know.'

'That was kind. But you know I threw so much stuff away. I got tired of reading offensive letters.'

348

'Never mind, he wrote,' Minnie said. 'By the way, did you know his uncle is very ill?'

Janey looked shocked. 'No, I didn't. Oh, what a shame! Of course, he's an old man,' she said. 'I only met him once, years ago, and he was getting on then. She was nice, his wife, a gentle person—but that was before the Butterfly Field project.'

She stood thoughtfully for a moment.

'Friday is a council meeting and it's on the agenda but I really think we must hold back a bit. It won't hurt to delay, it's taken ages already.'

'David said something about not wanting his uncle to be disturbed about it.'

'I don't suppose they would tell him.'

'He's terribly fond of his uncle.'

'Well, his uncle and aunt brought him up, after his mother died in childbirth and his father married again. His mother was Mr Mathieson's only sister, younger than he, and he adored her. They were known to be very close.'

'Yes, David told me. Is Daddy going with you on Friday evening to the council meeting?'

'Yes, why?'

'Oh, I don't know. It'll take some doing, to walk in as though nothing has happened.'

'Minnie, you will learn as you grow older

349

that it is better to tackle a problem right away and not let it simmer. Far better to face up to things, distasteful though it may be. Putting off the evil day is never a good thing.'

Minnie supposed she was right. Her mother was a wise old owl, had learned to be after all her experiences. In the meantime, John seemed as pleased as punch to be home again almost as if he had never been away. As for Graham, he had telephoned the previous evening to say he was off to Australia—though whether for a holiday or on business he didn't say. It had seemed to be urgent, anyway.

Well, they saw so little of him, it hardly mattered. As far as she was concerned, meeting David Mathieson had given her just the kind of fillip she needed. Not that she intended to read more into it than she should, but she needed someone of her own age to talk to. That was one of the difficulties of being an unmarried mother, especially if you still lived at home.

'I've been thinking,' Janey said, coming into the room after being on the telephone, almost as if she had been reading Minnie's thoughts, 'your father and I feel it would be a good idea to go out to dinner tomorrow evening.'

'Yes, it would,' Minnie said.

'I mean, the three of us,' Janey said. 'It

would do you good, too.'

'Oh, no,' she said, but pleased just the same. 'You and Daddy go.'

'But, I've just been on the phone to Mrs Nelson and she's happy to babysit for India—now what do you think?'

'Oh, that's a wonderful idea!' Minnie said, more pleased that she would have imagined. Something to look forward to.

'That's all right, then,' Janey said. 'I thought we would go to The Plough. They do a good meal there.'

'Thanks,' Minnie said. 'I'll look forward to it.'

Janey meantime was racking her brains to think of something interesting for Minnie to do. A party, perhaps? They could hardly celebrate John's return—but a young people's party? The trouble was they had lost touch with so many of her daughter's contemporaries. Her going to India had made such a difference, just as they were all at a turning point in their lives. True, there was Tessa and even young William, perhaps David Mathieson ... but she thought she had better leave that. No point in pushing things.

It was when she had spent a day or so trying to work something out that the news came through of old Mr Mathieson's death. 'That's that, then,' Janey said to John, putting down the receiver thoughtfully.

'Oh, give it a week or two, then the lad will probably be glad to be out and about again.'

'Difficult, though,' she said slowly.

'Why?' John asked.

'Well, it's on the cards that the Butterfly Field will now belong to him,' she said.

John raised his eyebrows.

'Can't be seen to be currying favour.'

'Oh, see what you mean,' he said. 'Hmmm.'

Her parents, Minnie knew, would have sent a letter of condolence, but she wanted to do something herself. She had little idea of David's background. Did he live on an estate? He had said he was the estate manager. Were there many relatives? Lots of Mathiesons? No one really close, that was sure, if his uncle and aunt had been his guardians.

Minnie decided she must write. Condolence letters were so difficult. She knew her parents would be past masters at letters like that—knowing exactly what to say.

In her imagination she saw David in the middle of the Butterfly Field, with no one on whom to call. He stood in the centre, alone, the protector of all that his uncle had loved. Of course he felt passionately about it—why should he give it up in order to satisfy people who wanted to build on it and change it out of all recognition? Her sympathies were with him.

She liked him very much. Had done so from the beginning, despite his aggressive start, but she thought she recognised why that was. He had been kind, and what's more India liked him. That was all important.

Yes, she had to send a separate letter. It was the least she could do.

'Dear David', she began, but it wasn't easy. She did finally get it written and posted. Well, that was that.

Now she must make plans. With her father back home, she would try to find somewhere else to live. Then a job. Perhaps, her mother would help her there? But she wanted her freedom, nice though living at home was. They needed the house to themselves and she wanted her own home. It needn't be much, perhaps in Cobbets Green or farther away? Not Swansbridge, her family was too well-known there.

Becky would help. She knew everyone, and was a tower of strength.

It was three weeks later when the bouquet arrived. A bunch of red roses. Minnie buried her face in them.

Janey took it very coolly, or pretended she did.

'Lovely, darling. Who are they from?' she asked.

'David—David Mathieson,' said Minnie, her heart thumping oddly.

'Oh, how kind,' Janey said. 'Look, here's a vase. Give them a long drink.'

They were perfect, Minnie thought. Especially the message, which she kept hidden.

'To Araminta—with love from David.'

Janey was as happy as she had ever been. Her husband back at her side, and now Minnie with a boyfriend—and who knew what might become of that?

She fingered the little swan she had bought in the village in Wiltshire. She thought of it often, and those days when she had sat alone by the riverbank and the swan had glided by, like a friend.

The telephone rang and she answered it.

'Becky, my dear, nice to hear from you. Is all well?'

'Just thought I'd have a word—have you a moment?'

'Yes, of course.'

'Well, between you and me, I don't think we shall have much trouble from the Carpenters about the Butterfly Field, Janey.'

'Oh? Why's that?'

'Well, my dear, as you know I'm not supposed to discuss Lewis's business matters—they are strictly private. But, keep it under your hat, he is co-agenting with a very prestigious outfit in town the sale of The Mount.'

'No!' Janey gasped.

'They are asking one point five million for it.'

'But I heard her distinctly say that they were not movers. Once here it was for life, sort of thing.'

'If you'll believe that, you'll believe anything,' Becky said coolly. 'Apparently, this is what they do—move in to a nice residence, spend a small fortune on it and get a large fortune back at the end of it. Not bad, eh?'

'Well!'

'They've done it many times, Lewis said. So they were out to make a quick buck on the Butterfly Field too. I don't imagine we shall hear any more about that now.'

'I'm delighted to hear it,' Janey said. 'I must ring Sally. Is that all right?'

'Yes, I don't suppose she knows yet. Although it will be all over the place by tomorrow, you can bet. The adverts have gone out. And, by the way, how are Minnie and the baby?'

'Absolutely fine,' Janey said. 'They're both extremely well.' Her fingers were crossed behind her back.

They had turned a rather difficult corner, she realised.

Chapter Twenty-Two

For Sally Sheffield, it started like any other Monday.

She sat over her breakfast coffee after Tom and Tessa and William had left, one of her favourite times of the day when she could glance through the paper and collect herself before beginning the household chores. Monday was the one morning Mrs Halliday came for three hours so there was no great hurry as on a usual day.

William had left almost at daybreak to get back to college after his weekend at home, but not before reminding her to organise Grandma Pargeter's eightieth birthday. Suzie had come to lunch on Sunday and Sally smiled as she thought of how inseparable she and William were. What with William and his flowers and vegetables, and Suzie with her eccentric dress sense, they made an odd pair. But then, she thought, Suzie would have dressed oddly whatever age she had been born into.

She planned to telephone the hotel in the village near where her mother lived. They would stay overnight, and take Emily out to lunch on Sunday—she would like that. In early December it should not be too difficult to get a booking.

She heard the front gate click, and glanced at the clock. On the dot of eight-thirty. She cleared the table and stacked the dirty dishes on the draining board for her cleaner to put in the dishwasher. But it was a troubled Mrs Halliday who finally let herself in.

'Morning,' she called out as she usually did, but it was in nothing like her usual voice. Barely audible, in fact. Sally looked up to see Mrs Halliday putting on her apron, and it was obvious she had been crying. Her eyes were red and puffy, and she looked awful.

'Mrs Halliday! Are you all right?'

She looked at Sally as though finding it difficult to explain. Eventually she found her voice.

'Mrs Sheffield, you're never going to believe this. It's Mandy—she's gone.'

'Gone? What do you mean—gone where?'

'Friday,' she said. 'I'd just got in from Mrs Bignell's—I finish there about five—and in come this woman. I'd never seen her before in my life—a big woman, blonde. And she starts shouting at me ...'

'Sit down,' Sally said, pushing a chair

forward. It was obvious Mrs Halliday was under great stress, and she would need to take her time. She looked awful.

'Here, drink this,' said Sally, pouring a strong cup of coffee from the pot.

'Oh, dear, I—'

'Come on, you've obviously had a shock,' Sally said sympathetically. 'Take your time, there's no hurry.'

Mrs Halliday grasped the cup in both hands as if to warm them.

'It seems this woman was Mandy's next-door neighbour and—well, to cut a long story short, said Mandy had gone off with her husband.'

'Oh, my goodness!' Sally said. 'And is it true?'

'Oh, it's true all right,' Mrs Halliday said grimly. 'I went round later—Eric come with me—and of course there's no sign of her. It was a furnished flat, see, and all her personal stuff had gone. Kylie, too, all her toys and things.' And she wiped away a tear.

Somewhere at the back of her mind Sally wasn't surprised. From the beginning warning bells had rung about Mandy.

'Well, I couldn't believe it at first, although I could see by this woman that it was true. And the language! I needn't tell you what she called my sister.'

Sally could imagine.

'And you can guess what Eric is saying: I told you so.'

'Yes, well,' Sally said. There was not much comfort she could give Mrs Halliday, short of sending her home.

'I am sorry, I don't know what to say.'

'No more do I,' she sobbed.

'Look, would you like to go home? There's no need for you to stay—I can manage.'

'To what?' Mrs Halliday said bitterly. 'No, I'm better off working.'

'Saturday,' she went on, 'I bumped into one of the other people at the flats, and she said everyone knew about it except the man's wife. It seems he was out of work, a layabout, and they were off everywhere together, him and Mandy. Years younger than our Mandy too. Oh, I felt so ashamed. I'll never hold my head up again.'

'Yes, you will,' Sally said staunchly. 'After all, it's not your fault. You can't be responsible for what your sister does and how she behaves.'

This Mandy had a lot to answer for, Sally thought, feeling quite bitter about all she had heard of the woman. The sort, obviously, that makes trouble wherever she goes—sadly for Mrs Halliday who was such a nice little woman, and a hard worker.

She began stacking the dishwasher.

'I'll do that, Mrs Sheffield,' Mrs Halliday said, getting up and wiping her eyes. 'No need for you to do it—I'll be all right now. Eric said I was asking for trouble, letting her come in the first place, and I daresay he's right. But I never thought she'd do that right on my doorstep.'

She sniffed and blew her nose. 'Oh, well, I feel better now I've had my little moan. I'm sorry to have troubled you.'

'No trouble, it's you who has that. If I were you, I'd try to forget about it, concentrate on your own family—you sound as if you have a good husband, one with some sense. Don't feel you have to be responsible for this sister of yours. You're not, you know, you have your own family to look after.'

She went upstairs to William's room and turned the mattress on his bed, the better to give vent to her anger over Mrs Halliday's bad news. I suppose I knew from the beginning that that young woman meant trouble, she thought.

She opened the window wide to let in the fresh air and went into Tessa's room to make the bed. What troubles some people had. It made you realise how lucky you were. But then you never knew when your turn might come ...

What could she do for poor Mrs Halliday? What consolation could she give her? No good sending her home, she wanted something to do.

She picked up one of Tessa's gloves—she must have dropped it without knowing—and smoothed it, a soft navy doeskin glove. Tessa liked nice things. What would she find today at MacBane's after the weekend?

Tessa hurried along from the station to her office, having realised as soon as she left home and arrived at the station that she was missing a glove and hoping she hadn't lost it.

The cold air stung her face, but once inside MacBane's it was warm and cheerful. She greeted the doorman and checked at the reception desk. 'Any post for me?'

'Yes, miss, two.' And he handed them to her. Walking along the corridor to her office, she saw Alistair coming towards her, not with a smile and warm greeting, but a simple 'Good morning, Tessa' before walking on.

Oh, dear, she thought. Hasn't got over the Goyas yet.

Later she would have to tell him that the tapestries she had gone to see on Friday in Hampstead had turned out to be modern copies. A brother and sister, left various items in their mother's will, had thought mistakenly that the tapestries were original

Flemish. They had stood there with wide expectant eyes. She always felt sorry when she had to dash someone's expectations, but that was the way it was more often than not. Just occasionally she came up with a find which made it all worthwhile.

Tessa opened her letters. 'For the attention of Miss Sheffield.' These would be from people living out of town who, when telephoning, would have been given her name to write to and describe what they had for sale.

She sighed. It looked as if a visit to Derbyshire was on the cards, it sounded interesting, but the Egyptian pots ... well, she would have to see.

A knock came on the door and Lizzie stepped inside, as delectable-looking as ever in chestnut brown thigh-length skirt and polo neck sweater, her hair tied neatly back.

'Hi, Tessa,' she said. 'Have a nice weekend?'

'Yes, super,' she said. Well, it was, just seeing William and young Suzie—then she wondered what someone like Lizzie did on a Saturday night. At eighteen the world was her oyster. She probably went to rave clubs and danced all night. At twenty-one Tessa felt positively middle-aged beside her.

'I say,' Lizzie said, 'he hasn't come

back.' And she bit into a bright green apple.

'Who?' Tessa said, as if she didn't know.

'Hugo,' said Lizzie. 'Well, he won't come back now, will he? Especially when they've got a replacement.'

'Oh?' Tessa said, intrigued. 'Who is it?'

'I don't know—someone called Winterhalter,' Lizzie said.

Tessa turned laughing eyes to her. 'Did you make that up?'

'No,' said an aggrieved Lizzie. 'I saw it written down at reception.'

'That's the name of a famous artist,' Tessa said, 'but then I expect you knew that?'

''Course I did,' Lizzie lied, throwing her apple core into the waste paper basket. 'Well, see you later,' she said, and turned back at the door. 'Oh, anything for me to do this morning?'

'No, not at the moment, things are a bit quiet,' said Tessa.

An hour later, she took her files and walked along to Alistair's room, knocking gently on the door.

At his reply she walked in, but he hardly looked up, bent on riffling through some papers. 'Ah, Tessa.'

The truth was that the very sight of her—that fall of dark hair, her heart-shaped face and lovely eyes—made him determined to keep himself in check. Hadn't he promised himself he would? After all, there were other girls.

Still looking though his papers, he said, 'Yes?'

Tessa gave him a small smile. So that was the way of it. He was sulking about the Goyas.

'About those tapestries I went to see in Hampstead ...'

He looked up, grey eyes meeting hers very briefly.

'No good,' she said briefly.

'Oh, pity. Wasted journey then,' he said, going back to his papers. He usually liked to keep her hanging about for a spot of conversation—but not this morning.

'I've one or two other things to see, probably sometime today.'

'Yes, I'm sure you have lots to do.'

Tessa found the colour surging into her cheeks. Well, who did he think he was? Just because he'd had a disappointment over the Goyas.

'I'll see you then,' she said coolly, and was leaving when the door opened to admit a vision. There was no other word for it. Tall, fair and willowy, like a Pre-Raphaelite painting, she was dressed in long floating clothes.

'Ah,' said Alistair. 'Tamara.'

Tessa made to slide past, but he stopped

her. 'Tessa—meet the new member of our staff. Art expert and picture restorer, Tamara Winterhalter. Tamara, this is Tessa Sheffield, fine arts and textiles.'

'How do you do?' Tessa said briefly, while Tamara just smiled, a lovely vague smile.

Outside the door, Tessa bit her lip. Tamara Winterhalter, indeed! Where did she get a name like that? Oh, well, it seemed Alistair would be all right now. It would certainly get him off her back. And crossly she went back to her room. Winterhalter ... What nationality was she? It was well-known men were always impressed by a foreign accent.

She slammed about for a while, annoyed with Alistair, with herself, with the Goyas, with Hugo—until she settled down and got to work.

'Isn't she smashing?' Lizzie said, coming in with coffee a bit later. 'Have you seen her?'

'Yes,' Tessa answered briefly.

'Isn't she gorgeous? We can do with someone like that around. I don't know what she is—Czech? German, perhaps?'

'Russian, I would think.' And Lizzie turned startled eyes on her.

'Really?'

'I'm joking,' Tessa said.

'Would you like a sandwich—I'm just

going out?' Lizzie said.

'Yes, please. Ham and cheese with some tomato.'

She had decided to go this afternoon to Chelsea. Somehow the idea of Egyptian pots had begun to pall.

When Lizzie had gone, Tessa sat and thought about things. Herself in particular. Was she jealous of the delectable young woman who had come to work at MacBane's? Nonsense. Of course she wasn't. What was she jealous of then? Who was she jealous of?

It was just that Alistair ... And she faced up to the situation that yes, indeed, she was jealous of Tamara Winterhalter. She was so lovely, what man wouldn't fall for her?

You are a misery, Tessa Sheffield, she told herself in a moment of self-knowledge. Mooning about Hugo without the slightest reason except that you fancied him. Now you're jealous of Tamara Winterhalter. What is it you really want?

How would you feel if you heard that Alistair had asked the beautiful Tamara out to dinner? Say to that restaurant in Kensington? Or to his flat?

Furious, she thought. Absolutely furious.

And would you worry if you never saw him again?

Yes, I would, she thought honestly.

What about Hugo Blanchard?

Well, what about him? she asked herself.

It's time you took hold of yourself and asked what you want out of life. Is this job enough? Has Hugo's departure left you demoralised?

Would you worry if suddenly Alistair was ill? Or took Miss Hungary out to a meal?

Yes, yes, yes, she cried.

Or is this all because the lovely Miss Thing has arrived on the scene?

Well, in a way perhaps. But I do often feel Alistair's grey eyes on me, very intently, and it does make a kind of shiver go through me ...

It was going on for lunchtime when she finally finished cataloguing her next sale: Roman vases and early Turkish pots. A kind of peace had come over her, as it always did when she was working with things a thousand years old. She weighed a vase in her hand. Imagine the age of it. All those years, and the scene painted on it told of a man and a woman meeting, the moment strangely erotic even now ...

She traced it with her finger, and put it alongside the others—dreaming a little. And somehow it had fallen with an awful crash, breaking into a hundred fragments. She stood looking down at it, horrified, her hands over her mouth to prevent herself from crying out.

Lizzie had heard the crash and was there in an instant. She saw what had happened, looking down at the terracotta shards in horror.

'Christ!' she said. 'Oh, no.'

She looked at Tessa who seemed speechless.

'What shall I do?' she asked. 'I mean, clear it up?'

'No, no!' Tessa cried. 'Leave it there, I shall have to call Alistair.'

She wanted to die. If she could have faded away, fallen through the floor—she had never done such a thing in her life before. The value—how would she ever pay for it?

'I'll go,' Lizzie said sympathetically.

It seemed ages before he came, during which time, Tessa had died a thousand deaths, from shame and anger at herself. What had made her do such a thing?

Her heart leaped as she heard the handle of the door turn and Alistair came in, closing the door softly behind him. He could see the cause of the disaster there before him, a pile of broken pottery with pieces still dotted about the room where they had landed. He looked down at them, and then at Tessa's drained face.

'I'm sorry,' she whispered.

His face was grim. 'How did it happen?' he asked, and her temper rose.

'Oh, how do you think it happened? I dropped it!' she cried.

'I can see that.'

'Brilliant,' she said scathingly. 'Well, I shall pay for it, have no fear. Every penny piece. You can knock it off my salary.'

He looked at her. 'It will take rather a long time.'

'And while you're at it,' she said, 'you can keep your old job!'

When he didn't answer, she looked up and what she saw in his eyes took all the wind out of her sails.

'I'm sorry, Alistair,' she said. 'Truly, I am. I don't know how ...'

But he was there at her side, and his arms were round her, holding her close, and this time she didn't push him away.

'Darling, Tessa,' he said lovingly

Sally was sitting in the kitchen when she received the call from Tessa.

'I won't be home for dinner this evening.' She sounded quite excited. 'I'm going to dinner with Alistair so I may be late.'

'Oh, that's fine, darling,' Sally said, and sat back, eyes shining with pleasure.

Oh, wouldn't it be wonderful if this was the start of a romance? She had always liked the sound of Alistair MacBane. Then she heard a car drawing up outside the front door.

Now who could that be? She saw to her surprise her old friend Jessica walking up the path. Good Lord, she hadn't seen her since the hat sale! What a strange Monday, she thought.

'Darling Sally,' Jessica said, giving her a kiss on either cheek. She looked splendid in her usual cloak of black lined with scarlet and on her head wore the most beautiful mink hat Sally had ever seen.

'I can't stop,' Jessica said, 'but I thought you might like to see this. How's Tessa?'

'Your god-daughter is going out for the evening with her boss,' Sally said. 'Aren't you going to sit down? Have a sherry, some tea?'

'No, dear, I'm on my way to the Aeolian Hall, but I thought you might like to see this. But perhaps you know? It only came out today and I thought it looked familiar.'

It was a very upmarket magazine, geared to London properties, and Jessica had it folded back to a full-page advertisement of a house for sale, a rather splendid house.

Sally stared at it in disbelief.

GENTLEMAN'S FINE RESIDENCE

And there in all its glory was a photograph of The Mount.

'Close your mouth, dear,' Jessica said.

In the picture it looked superb—six bedrooms, six bathrooms, billiard room, swimming pool, conservatory.

'I don't believe it!' Sally said. 'It says price on application.'

'Which is why I rang them to ask,' Jessica said.

'You did?'

'It's one point five million,' her friend said. 'Aren't you surprised?'

'You know,' Sally said slowly, thinking of Pauline and Ron and Beattie, 'I don't think I am.'

Jessica was on the point of leaving when the telephone rang. Answering it, Sally heard a woman's voice, a neighbour of her mother's.

'It's Mrs Dalrymple, dear, Betty Dalrymple,' she said. 'I live next door to your mother. I'm afraid I have some bad news ...'

Chapter Twenty-Three

The dawn would be up in an hour or two and the fast-waning moon hung like pale grey silk in the lightening sky when Emily Pargeter awoke. The bird song had not yet begun and the owl who kept constant vigil in the oak tree which overhung The Close made no sound. Emily, who had awakened feeling most peculiar, realised with a slight sense of shock that today was the day of reckoning, at least for her. Fancy, she thought with a mild sense of surprise. Well, I never. And felt faintly irritated with her Lord.

'Lord,' she said a little plaintively, for she was given to having little conversations with him, 'in two weeks I shall be eighty years old. You could have waited, I so wanted to see my eightieth birthday.'

'The Lord works in mysterious ways,' her Lord said mildly.

'Poppycock!' Emily replied, for she had never been one to mince her words.

As a new wife to the Reverend Ernest Pargeter she had learned to pray beside him in darkest Africa, on the plains and hills of India, in the far-flung islands of the Dodecanese, and in other places long since forgotten. Prayed for guidance for herself and Ernest, whom she'd loved dearly. After a while, though, she'd felt the need for a more personal relationship and took to having little chats with her Lord—when she was quite alone, of course, for she had an idea that Ernest might not have approved.

Now, remembering the good advice she

had received over the years, and the battles she had fought—yes, literally waged, when she had lost her temper and argued—she had no regrets.

It was just like that, well, it was nice and tidy to reach one's eightieth birthday. There was a slight feeling of having not quite accomplished what one had set out to do, of strings left untied.

It didn't seem possible that one person could crowd so much into a life in so many different ways. And how lucky she had been that she retained an almost perfect memory. So many of her friends ... and the strange thing was she could remember what had happened all those years ago better than she could remember what she'd had for supper the night before.

Her thoughts were clear, like running water, like a stream burbling over polished stones. The stones were the people she'd met on the way.

'I would have liked William to be here,' she said.

'It would have distressed him,' her Lord said mildly, 'and you would not have wanted that. You were not envisaging a moving deathbed scene, were you?'

'Of course not,' she said sharply. 'You know me better than that.'

'Well, you always leaned slightly towards the theatrical, shall we say?'

'Me?' she cried ungrammatically. 'Never! Still, there is something I want to ask you.

'As you know, Lord, there are twenty-nine years to go on the lease of number two Abbey Close, which of course I bequeath to my beloved grandson. I have always thought he needed more help than Tessa, love her dearly though I do. Now, could you see your way clear to persuading him to come and live here? I don't want him to sell it, and I know that to most people it would be a godsend, if you will pardon the expression. Do you think it might be possible for him to carry on his modus operandi, so to speak, from here?'

'Mmmm ...' her Lord said.

'Then, of course, there's Suzie.'

'Yes, of course, there's Suzie,' her Lord said thoughtfully.

'You mustn't be too hard on them, Lord,' she said gently. 'Things have changed since you were here. It's different now, the whole world is changing.'

'Yes, I realise that,' her Lord said drily.

'So if you could see your way clear to—well, sort out things for me.' And she saw through the lace curtains the sudden glory of the dawn breaking, and smiled.

'I must just say,' she went on, 'there's one thing more.' For her thoughts had begun to wander. 'I never really understood why you didn't see fit to make Ernest a bishop? He was a good man, and would have done it so well.' But her Lord put a forefinger to her lips.

And in the glory of a new day, Emily Pargeter went to meet her Lord.

It was a misty December evening when the little gathering arrived home in Swansbridge after attending Emily's funeral.

Sally took off her hat and coat and hung them up in the cloakroom, washing her hands and staring hard at the mirror at her tear-stained face. Strange how much older you felt when you lost a parent. She went into the kitchen, automatically putting the kettle on to make them all a pot of tea.

Coming in after her, Tom threw her a glance.

'All right, Sally?'

'So many regrets,' she said, going over to him. 'That I didn't see her more often than I did. That she didn't have her birthday.'

He put his arms round her. 'Sally, dear, that's all part of the grieving, the sadness. But your mother was a very contented woman, she was happy, had lived a full life.'

'Yes, I have to remember that,' she said. 'And how nice of her to leave the unexpired lease of her house to William! Such a surprise—although I always knew

375

she was fond of him.' And she wiped away a tear.

The kettle boiled, and Tom turned. 'What's that for? Tea?' He took it off the Aga. 'No, we're going to have a drink, my dear Sally, a stiff one.'

In his pocket burned a letter he had received that morning, the contents of which he had kept secret until now. It was an answer to enquiries he had sent in a long time ago, and he had only just this morning received a reply. The contents excited him more than somewhat, and he could hardly wait to tell Sally.

For quite a few people had been interested in the December issue of *Country Life* magazine, not the least of whom was Sir Barnaby Parsons who now lived in London's Albany but had at one time owned a listed property in Swansbridge called The Mount. Staring hard at the photograph on the glossy page, he absorbed every little detail. And he wasn't the only one. The telephone lines of English Heritage, National Heritage, The Garden History Society and various other watchful bodies had also noticed, and not a few were shocked—to say nothing of the ripples that washed through the offices of the local council planning offices.

Tom had set in motion an enquiry which was to have far-reaching effects.

He went into the dining room and poured himself and Sally a drink, while William, and Tessa and Suzie sat excitedly discussing William's surprise inheritance in the drawing room.

In the kitchen, Tom and Sally were quiet until he pulled out the letter and showed his wife.

He saw her slight frown turn to a look of amazement, then disbelief.

'Tom!' she cried. 'What does this mean?'

'It means they're going to take up the whole question of planning permission for the work done at The Mount.'

Her eyes now were wide. 'But suppose it has all been done without proper planning permission?'

'Ah, then perhaps they will have to undo it all,' he said with great satisfaction.

'Oh, I can't believe that will happen!' Sally cried, half wishing it would and half that it wouldn't. 'How awful.'

'You see, I'm not the only one who is interested,' he explained. 'I had a call the other day from John Graveley—you know he is one of the Heritage lot. I knew him at university, and he looked me up and we had quite a chat.'

'Goodness,' Sally said, her mind now on Pauline and Beattie and the house next door. She shivered.

'Golly, I wouldn't like to be in their

shoes,' she said. 'I mean, if there is something wrong.'

'Well,' Tom said mildly, 'we shall see.'

It was the next morning that two well-dressed men drove up the wide drive to the front door of The Mount.

Beattie, who missed nothing, saw them get out of the car.

'Pauly!' she yelled. 'Two men at the front door!'

'Oh, I expect it's the men after the gardening jobs,' Pauline said, looking in the hall mirror and giving a swift pat to her silky black hair.

She looked a vision as usual as she stood there, smiling warmly at them.

'Good morning,' they said together. 'Mrs Carpenter?'

'Yes.' She smiled. These men didn't look like gardeners. 'What can I do for you?'

One of the men held out a card. 'We are from the council,' he said. 'Building inspectors.'

For once Pauline was disconcerted, but she quickly recovered.

'My husband isn't here just now but if ...'

'We would like to come in and look around,' one said.

'Oh, I'm afraid you can't do that. Not

without my husband being here. Could you show me your credentials—something to prove who you are?'

And they did so. Cards and letters from the council, regarding the work that had been done: plans and maps and official communications.

Pauline thought quickly. Far better they come in now when Ron wasn't here. He wouldn't like being surprised. He'd blow his top.

'Come in, gentlemen,' she said brightly. 'Make yourselves at home. Where would you like to start?'

''Oo are they?' Beattie asked, coming down the stairs to join her.

'Oh, just council men, checking, Mum,' she said. 'You go on up. Coffee, gentlemen?'

'No, thank you,' they said. 'May we—?'

'Sure,' Pauline said. 'Go ahead. Feel free.'

They were there three hours, during which time they extensively examined every change, addition, every RSJ, the pool, the hollow in the grass where the oak tree had been ...

'Thank you,' they said on leaving. 'We'll be in touch.'

With a warm smile. Pauline saw them off, and was straight on to Ron's mobile phone in a flash.

'Ron—building inspectors. They've been here, just left.'

'Christ!' he said, and went white, not wasting a moment before turning his car around and hurrying home.

He looked anxious when he came in, his face bathed in perspiration, small eyes glittering like coals.

'What did they say?'

'Nothing much, just spent three hours here.'

'You shouldn't have let them in.'

'Now, Ron,' she said gently.

'I just hope Tonkins got it right.'

'Tonkins?' Pauline asked.

'Oh, for Christ's sake, Pauly!' he said. 'Tonkins—he had a big enough bung.'

'Oh, him,' she said. 'Yes, well.'

It wouldn't be the first time they had come unstuck, she thought, and remembered that time in Bath when they bought the house in Royal Crescent. Oh, well, win some, lose some, she thought. They'd always have Spain, the house she really loved.

Ron paced around like a caged tiger until the telephone call came. It was requested that he should meet the building inspectors, at his house or the council offices.

He arranged to meet them the next day at the council offices.

They didn't beat around the bush.

There was no sign of Tonkins, he'd either done a bunk or been sacked, but the council authorities were anxious to put matters right. After giving him a list, and it was lengthy, of how much work he had done contravening the building regulations covering a listed property, and in order that they should clear themselves of corruption charges, it had been decided to serve enforcement notices on Ron Carpenter, ordering him to put the house back to its original state.

'I've spent more than half a million on that bloody place,' he spluttered. 'You'll be hearing from my solicitors! Let's face it, if you'd kept proper tabs on it—'

'I daresay, sir, but you should have gone through the regular channels,' they said.

'And what if I don't comply with the order?' he asked.

'Then we shall send enforcement officers round,' they said blandly. 'And that would be a pity, sir. A bit of a mess.'

In a lifetime of dodgy deals, this was the worst one yet.

'Which is it to be, sir?' they asked him.

'I'll see to it,' said Ron tersely.

'We'll be checking from time to time— sending our inspectors round.'

'I'll bet you will,' he hissed through clenched teeth.

A few days later Tom received a letter from the council authorities telling him what had happened, and the steps they had taken to put the matter to rights.

They apologised for the disruption and noise he would suffer, but felt sure he would approve of their measures to redress what had obviously been an oversight.

'That's a joke,' Tom said.

One day, a bitterly cold one in January, builders arrived once more at The Mount. By this time there was no sign of the Carpenters, and after a day or two it was obvious that they had moved out.

'Moved on, I think the expression is,' Tom said.

'And not a word from Pauline.'

'Well, you can understand that. It'll cost Ron a packet, but he will still own the place—what a waste of time when you think about it. All that noise and work.'

'It won't put back the oak tree,' she said.

'No, but we'll plant one,' Tom promised. 'We'll buy one from William's nursery.'

Six months later The Mount, without pool and conservatory, no lamps up the drive, was for sale once more, while public notices revealed that receivers had been called in to the development firm of Carpenter's.

Sally looked sad.

'I must say, I really quite liked Pauline.'

'I shouldn't waste your sympathy,' her husband said. 'People like that pop up again with very little trouble.'

'I wonder what happened to Sandra?' Tessa asked idly, using her left hand to pick up the milk jug so she could admire the single blazing stone on her engagement finger. 'Do you suppose she stayed in Spain or married her Spanish boy?'

'I wonder,' Sally said. 'It's been a strange year when you think of all that has happened. I'll bet Janey's pleased, too,' she said. 'It all came right for her in the end.'

Chapter Twenty-Four

Things had not been quiet in the Utox-Smythe household either, for David Mathieson had asked Minnie and India to lunch at the farm in Hassington for India's first birthday, and Minnie drove over there in a state of suppressed excitement. Since the New Year she and David had met several times, and each time she realised how much more she liked him, and the fact that he adored India just added to the warmth she felt whenever she saw him.

There had been a great deal for him to do after his uncle's death, for as farm and estate manager his days were full.

As she drove through the village towards the farm, she passed a row of farmworker's cottages and then the farmhouse itself appeared through the trees. It was just as she had imagined, looking as if it grew out of the landscape: quite old, a little tumbledown, with beams and wide gates. And although it was a working farm, it was beautifully kept, while in the distance sheep grazed and there was the sound of clucking geese from somewhere nearby.

Two collies sat in the porch, and ran towards the car as she drove in. An ancient Labrador got slowly to his feet, his days as a watchdog obviously over.

David came out to greet her, quieting the dogs and kissing her lightly on her cheek, much as he would any lady visitor. He put his arms out to hold India, who was delighted to see him. She adored David.

Inside the house was large and rambling, a fire burning in the brick fireplace on this cool March morning. Taking off India's outside clothes and her own, and putting them on an old oak settle, Minnie followed David through to the low-beamed drawing room.

'Oh,' she said. 'It's lovely.'

'I thought you would like it. It's been my home ever since I can remember,' he said. 'I've been lucky.'

There was another log fire in this room, and he saw them settled on a comfortable old sofa.

'We have a wonderful housekeeper. She used to be my nursemaid, and stayed on as housekeeper to Aunt Dorothy when my mother died.'

'Aunt Dorothy—was she your Uncle Leopold's wife?'

'Yes, she died last year.'

He went over to a small table and came back with a package which he handed to the baby.

'Happy birthday, India,' he said. 'I hadn't forgotten, you see, this is for you.'

She looked up at him with grave blue eyes, then at her mother. Minnie nodded.

'Yes. Say thank you, and you may open it.'

With a bit of help, India untied the ribbon and produced from the paper a soft brown teddy bear with such a lovely expression on his face that she hugged him to her.

Minnie smiled. 'How kind of you, David.'

'My pleasure,' he said, and looked at Minnie for what seemed like ages, so that she blushed and felt so warm she must be sitting too near the fire. It flashed through her mind how different this feeling was from her experience with Tim. Now it was history, something she could hardly remember, so thoroughly had she put it out of her mind. This feeling was different, exciting yet warm and friendly. She found herself wondering what it would be like to be really kissed by David Mathieson, found herself longing for him to put his arms around her and hold her close ...

'Ah, here's Mrs Tuttle.'

Mrs Tuttle beamed at them, a comfortably large lady, carrying an overladen tray which she put down on the table between them.

'This is Minnie Utox-Smythe and her baby daughter India,' David said, introducing them.

'So this is India—I've heard a lot about you, young lady!'

Mrs Tuttle said as the little girl hugged the teddy bear close. 'She's beautiful,' the housekeeper said approvingly to Minnie. 'And are you going to pour?' she asked.

'Yes, I'll do it,' Minnie said, and began to arrange the tea things about the low table.

What a strange life David must have had, with no mother, she was thinking. Mrs Tuttle and his aunt must have been like mothers to him, although he had been at boarding school for many years.

Over tea, they seemed to find no end of things to talk about, and when it was time to clear away, Mrs Tuttle appeared as if by magic and offered to look after India while David showed Minnie around the house and the rest of the farm.

She found herself wondering just exactly what David's intentions were. It was clear that he liked her and the baby, but was he serious or was it just friendship he was offering?

The great stone-flagged farm kitchen led out to the yard where geese roamed. There were ducks in a small pond and this led to the kitchen garden, where all kinds of vegetables were grown, and leading off from that an orchard, full of small trees, burgeoning now with pale green leaves and fleshy buds.

The orchard was walled, and in one wall was a high wooden gate. David opened this to allow Minnie through, and she found herself in a small rose garden, clipped back now but obviously a sight in summer.

'Would it be too cold to sit out here for a moment?' he asked. 'You can have my coat to sit on.'

'No, it's quite warm,' she said. 'What a lovely garden!'

'My uncle's pride and joy,' he said. 'I

only hope I shall be able to keep it going as he did.'

He turned to look at her.

'I'm afraid I'm rather a conventional chap,' he said. 'I suppose some would think me old-fashioned.' And Minnie smiled. 'But, well, it's the way I've been brought up, I suppose.'

At that moment, she felt she really wanted to hold him close.

He took her hand. 'I asked you out today because ... well, I wanted to say something to you. I shall quite understand if you say no so don't worry—but would you consider marrying me?'

Minnie gasped. Although she had wondered vaguely if he would ask, nevertheless the words came as a shock.

'David, you don't know much about me,' she warned.

'And you don't know me very well. I know we got off to a bad start but, well, I think we've made up for that, haven't we?'

She smiled at him, feeling quite weak.

'And there is India,' she said.

'I know all I need to know about India. One day, if you want, you can tell me all about it—but I'm not asking you to. I'm sure we could be happy together, although whether you would like such a country life, I'm not sure.'

'Oh, David.' And suddenly her eyes had misted with tears.

'Hey, steady on!' he said, putting his arms round her.

'Well, you are so nice,' she said, 'and so kind.'

'I'm no paragon of virtue.'

'And nor, I'm afraid, am I,' she said ruefully.

'Could you like me enough to marry me?' he asked. 'I mean, there's no hurry—take your time. Think about it.'

'I don't need to,' she said honestly. 'I like you an awful lot, and I think we could be happy together—if you can accept India?'

'No problem there,' he said. 'You mean, you will think about it?'

His eyes searched hers and presently he held her close, kissing her cheek, then her mouth—and she felt as if she had come home.

'Ah, David,' she said. 'It seems like a dream.'

He broke away, looking down into her eyes as though he couldn't drink in enough of her.

'I've some other news for you as well,' he said. 'Only, I must admit, I thought I would tell you when you accepted me—if you didn't accept me I might have had second thoughts.'

Minnie laughed. 'What? What news?' She could scarcely believe in her newfound happiness.

'Well ...' he said, kissing her again before they both stood up and began walking back to the house. 'I have decided to make the Butterfly Field a wildlife sanctuary.' Minnie felt a slight twinge of disappointment for her mother's sake, but it was only momentary.

'But,' he went on, 'I thought we could cut off a corner of land and build something small, like a Parish Hall, sufficient for the community's requirements. No need for it to be too large. We could call it the Mathieson Hall, in memory of my uncle and my mother.'

Minnie impulsively threw her arms around his neck. 'Oh, David! How wonderful!' she cried.

He seemed quite happy with this situation, and kissed her several times more.

'There should be no difficulty with the council over that request,' he said.

'It's the nicest idea I've ever heard,' she said, 'and my mother will be over the moon. It's the best present she could have had.'

'So, Araminta, I am formally proposing to you. What do you say?'

'Darling David, yes, yes, yes!' she said,

wondering if she was on her head or her heels.

There was great rejoicing in the Utox-Smythe household when they were given the news. An engagement party was held which everyone attended, even Graham, now back after three months in Australia.

Getting his father on his own, he said casually. 'By the way, Dad, guess who I met up with in Sydney?'

Sir John was not madly interested. 'Who?'

'Melissa Wilding,' he said, and saw his father start.

'Oh, yes?'

'Apparently she has a fabulous job and intends to stay there—' He didn't say he had taken her out there for that very purpose. Nor did he mention that she had ditched him shortly after their arrival there.

'Yes, I heard about it when she gave up the lease of the apartment. And now we must get back to the party.'

And that was all that was said on the matter.

At the beginning of April building was started on the Butterfly Field hall, and was well under way when one sunny day in July David came to call for Minnie in his car.

'Going to take you for a drive,' he said. 'Care to come?'

They drove for a short way, skirting The Mount, until they came across the Butterfly Field, now massed with wild flowers. David parked the car and they began to walk knee-deep in blossom.

'I wanted you to see this,' he said, 'which I don't suppose you ever have.' And there, to Minnie's amazement, were hundreds and hundreds of butterflies: Purple Emperors, White Admiral, Common Blue. David seemed to know all their names.

'Oh, David, how wonderful! It's almost unreal.'

'There, you see,' he said proudly, as they walked over the long grass amid the vetch and foxgloves, clover and willowherb. David seemed to know all about them too while the butterflies flitted from flower to flower.

'I never would have believed it,' Minnie said, enchanted by the scene.

'And always at the same time of year,' he said.

'No wonder your mother loved it.' She linked her arm in his.

'Next year we'll bring India,' he said.

'When is the hall due to be finished?'

'September, sometime.'

'Do you suppose we could have our wedding reception there—be the first to book the hall?' she asked.

He turned to her. 'What a wonderful idea! "Reception afterwards at the Mathieson Hall". I like that.'

'And doesn't it sound just right?' she said.

'Araminta, I love you,' he said, and held her close.

This Large Print Book for the Partially sighted, who cannot read normal print, is published under the auspices of

THE ULVERSCROFT FOUNDATION

THE ULVERSCROFT FOUNDATION

. . . we hope that you have enjoyed this Large Print Book. Please think for a moment about those people who have worse eyesight problems than you . . . and are unable to even read or enjoy Large Print, without great difficulty.

You can help them by sending a donation, large or small to:

**The Ulverscroft Foundation,
1, The Green, Bradgate Road,
Anstey, Leicestershire, LE7 7FU,
England.**
or request a copy of our brochure for more details.

The Foundation will use all your help to assist those people who are handicapped by various sight problems and need special attention.

Thank you very much for your help.

Other MAGNA General Fiction Titles In Large Print

FRANCES ANNE BOND
Return Of The Swallow

JUDY GARDINER
All On A Summer's Day

IRIS GOWER
The Sins Of Eden

HELEN MANSFIELD
Some Women Dream

ELISABETH McNEILL
The Shanghai Emerald

ELIZABETH MURPHY
To Give And To Take

JUDITH SAXTON
This Royal Breed